THE SAGA
OF
THE SOCIETY

BOOK 1

HIDDEN ENEMIES

STEVE REILLY

HIDDEN ENEMIES

Lands of
The North West

N

Freybor

Ptoraki

Allsvatur

Epli

Ingpor

Tjorvi

Sometime
Lake

Alveolar

Symrill

Bjotur

Konungssonur

Glimjandi

Moori

Numi

Ulffinnr

Orvar

Yrar

The Edge

Rainbow Forest

Thistledowne

Whitebridge

Greenacres

Arenia

Redhill

Greche

Three Oaks

CHAPTER 1

The lack of rain over the last three years had left the land looking parched. The trees had shed their leaves in order to conserve what little water they could glean from the dry soil and the yellow-green grass crackled underfoot when walked upon. Much of the bird and animal life had moved on in order to find more productive pickings.

In the midst of this dry country, where the Kings Road met the Northern Way, stands the small farming community of Thistledowne. This simple town existed as a resting place for weary travelers, the only reason the town had survived the drought for as long as it had. Thistledowne boasted a small inn, a blacksmith, a little church and, at its center, the now grassless village green. The people of Thistledowne lived in basic wooden houses topped with thatched roofs, working small farms on the land around the town. The biggest event that had ever happened in Thistledowne occurred in the previous spring when King Leopold and his entourage passed through on their way to more important places. The town had suffered through drought before knowing that the rains would come eventually, but if they did not come soon the growing season would be missed again, and next winter would be difficult.

One farm did not suffer as badly as the rest. This was the farm of Myrle Unwood, the local witch, and her only daughter, Camille. Myrle was gifted in the use of herbs, helping the villagers during times of ills or accidents, for which the townsfolk paid in food or services. Their farm was not like the others in the district. It did not have fields of corn or maize but instead remained in its natural state with small trees, shrubs and grasses. These provided Myrle with all that she needed to help and heal the townsfolk while a small vegetable garden behind the house provided for their own needs.

Camille walked slowly among the trees, her eyes searching the ground for the faint hint of red in the dark shadows that would indicate her quarry. The lack of rain made it harder to find the herbs she sought but she knew that she would find what she was after. She passed an old oak with roots deep enough to seek out the moisture it needed. A flash of red in the shadows caught her attention. Ducking under the low branches and creeping into the darkness, she found her quarry - a patch of nightweed. The little flowers were beginning to open as the darkness approached. She sat, placing her basket on the ground beside her, and gently ran her hand over the little patch of green. The small round leaves and tiny red flowers growing along the delicate stems hid the true value of the plant. Camille reached into her basket and took out a small digging tool to gently break up the ground. Carefully lifting a clod of earth, she ran her fingers through the softened ground till she found the swollen nodules on the plant's roots. Taking her time, she removed the nodules and placed them in the basket before delicately replanting the nightweed. She knew that many people just tore the plant from the earth and took what they wanted but she felt that the little plant was giving her its bounty and in return she was responsible for taking care of it. Her mother would grind up the nodules to extract the moisture they contained and then leave both out in the sun. The fluid would evaporate away leaving white crystals which she used to remove the pain of injuries, while the dried fiber of the nodules could be burnt, giving those that breathed the smoke a feeling of peace and calm.

When she had collected enough to satisfy her mother's needs she caressed the plants again with her fingertips in thanks before rising and taking her basket back out into the fading light. She decided to take the time to walk once more amongst the trees and enjoy the coming of the evening. She had done much thinking since her fourteenth birthday two weeks ago. She sat on a rock, watching the coming of the night sky. Sunset was her favorite time of day, when all was serene and the night birds became active. The night owl led the evening choir with other birds providing harmonies. The creaking of the crickets and the haunting tones of a far-off wolf added to the chorus of sound, all backed by the soft percussion of the rustling leaves. A full moon rested on the distant hills before beginning its dance across the darkening sky as the audience of stars took their places for the performance.

Nobody would ever describe her as pretty, least of all Camille herself, although the long black hair hanging down her back and tied with a simple leather thong was the one feature that provided any hint of beauty. Her face was marked with the scars of a long past pox, her nose was crooked and her chin too large. She wore plain black boots, good and solid for walking, and the dress her mother had given her for her birthday - plain black linen with long loose sleeves and a high square bodice. It hugged her small waist and fell to her ankles. There were no frills, no lace, nothing to decorate it except for the embroidered symbol stitched over her left breast in the shape of a gold shield over crossed gold swords. The shield was decorated with six colored bars diagonally across the center. Her mother had given her the dress along with the words that were etched into her thoughts. "This dress is you. When you understand the dress you will understand yourself and be the woman you were meant to be." She had asked her mother to tell her more but Myrle had refused to discuss the dress or the words since they were given. This was a puzzle that Camille must solve for herself. She did not know where life would lead her, she just felt something deep within her that told her she needed to solve the riddle. Every day since her birthday she had thought about those words but could get no closer to understanding them than when she had first heard them. A slight change in the direction of the breeze brought with it a hint of sound out of place in the evening chorus. As Camille turned to rise, she noticed the glow. It seemed to be coming from the town and moving along the road leading towards her home. The noise was rising with the glow, impinging on the peaceful evening. The glow was bright, too bright to be a villager coming to ask for her mother's aid; it was angry, threatening.

The beauty of the night was broken. She picked up the basket of nightweed bulbs and headed back down the track. The noise and glow continued to penetrate the sparse bush. She crested the final hill and saw the people gathered in the clearing at the front of her house. The crowd continued to grow as the tide of townsfolk flowed from their homes. They were waving torches and yelling. She kept herself hidden on the hill, crept forward to a small thicket overlooking her house and lay quietly watching. She could see her house clearly. The little mass of shrubs was barely large enough to hide her but they somehow offered security.

Her mother stood at the door with hands on her hips and a frown on her brow. Myrle's face was marked and twisted. Her yellow dress was cut plain and embroidered with patterns of green leaves over the bodice and around the sleeves and hem. Her long black hair with a streak of grey running from the left temple gave her face the appearance of ancient knowledge as well as strength of character. She appeared calm in front of the chanting crowd.

Camille could hear the shouts of "Witch," and , "It's all her fault". She was confused. The entire town knew that both she and her mother were witches. Her mother stood quietly in front of the mob. The noise grew as the crowd fueled its own courage with vicious words until Myrle raised both hands over her head, somehow quietening those gathered before her. Her mother's voice was clear.

"To what do I owe the pleasure of this visit from the good folk of Thistledowne?"

The silence persisted for a few moments until a lone voice called, "She's the witch. It must be her fault. She made the river dry up. She wants us all dead." The shouts began again. Myrle stood silent while the voices grew, then once more raised her hands commanding silence. The light of flickering candles from inside the house made Myrle appear to be glowing, adding to her appearance of power and control.

"Matt," her mother said, selecting one man in the front, "Do you really believe that I could or would attempt to bring you any harm? Wasn't it only last week that I gave you the herbs for your son's fever? How is he? And Jon, how is your leg after I set the break for you? Jobin? Bern? All of you I have helped in times of trouble. Do you believe that I would do this?"

Myrle stood silently looking as many in the crowd began to shuffle their feet and reconsider their actions. The hint of a smile showed on her mother's face as she looked at each man. Camille could see them waver. Myrle's confidence seemed to grow with each dropped head and each set of eyes that looked away.

Then the spell was broken. A rock thrown from the crowd caught her mother on the side of the head and she fell to the ground, stunned. The lone voice called again, "We must save the town. We must get rid of the witch." Other brave souls began to add to the calls. "Grab her, tie her up." One man cautiously approached the fallen woman, followed by another, then two more until the crowd had once more found its courage. Her mother was bound, gagged and dragged out to the open space in front of the house. The voice from the crowd was now bolder and Camille could see that it belonged to a worker from the neighboring farm who had arrived in town about two months ago. He looked to be in his early twenties, and she knew his name was Xavier, a despicable little man with ratty eyes and a long mane of dirty red hair. Xavier worked his way through the crowd and wherever he went the sounds of discontent became louder. It became obvious that something terrible was going to happen. She could see that others, friends of Xavier, were also fueling the crowd's courage. A call went up to search the house. Camille could hear the sounds of furniture being destroyed, breaking crockery and general destruction. Then she heard something that made her blood run cold. "She's not here," called an unknown voice and Camille realized that they could only be talking about her. She could not think why they would want to find her.

"Search the woods. Find her. She can't be far." Men ran off in all directions. Camille crouched deeper into her hiding place and hoped that the leaves and the darkness would keep her safe. The men swarmed around, searching every place while Camille huddled lower in the bushes. Then Xavier was standing right beside her. "Find her," demanded Xavier. "We can't let her get away." Camille was too scared to shake or even breathe.

It seemed an eternity but was probably more like an hour when the men finally gave up and began to gather back at the house. There Xavier and two other men had torn the pole from the front porch and driven it into the soft earth. Myrle was dragged to her feet and tied to the pole. Xavier worked the crowd into a frenzy, searching for someone to blame for all their woes. Myrle was the perfect scapegoat, trussed, gagged and unable to offer any resistance. The noise of the crowd grew dramatically with each passing minute. People who had been friends were acting as strangers. The whole situation was a nightmare. Scared and confused, Camille's isolated existence on the farm had left her unprepared. Her mind spun, trying to make sense of what was happening. She heard Xavier calling for timber and anything else that would burn and watched in horror as pieces were torn from the old walls. Two men brought her bed from the house, along with her mother's dresser. All of this was thrown around the feet of her helpless mother. Camille longed to run forward from her cover and call for the people to wake up.

Xavier walked to a nearby man where he took a torch and calmly threw it on the pile around the helpless Myrle. The flames sputtered, then slowly took hold to spread across the pile. The crowd was now silent as they watched the deadly scene unfold before them. The fire seemed to hold back as if savoring the moment before leaping forward to catch hold of Myrle's dress. Her death was not quick, but Myrle stood calmly in the pillar of flame staring down her attackers until the fire reached high to enjoy its meal. The crowd stood silent as the import of what had just occurred set in. The smell of burning flesh spread over the clearing. Another torch was thrown into the house and within minutes Camille's whole life was burning before her eyes.

She lay huddled beneath the bush and tried to think, but thoughts eluded her. She was wrapped in grief and lay her head down as silent tears streamed down through the valleys of her face.

CHAPTER 2

Camille awoke with a start, disoriented. The sun was well into its journey across a clear blue sky. Above her a single buzzard circled and the smell of smoke lingered in the still air. Memories began to fight their way through the fog of waking. She looked down upon the clearing now dominated by two large piles of ash. There was no sign of her mother, her house or the mob that had taken her life away. Her eyes rose toward the town unseen down the road. A hint of breeze passed over her, raising small puffs of ash in the clearing as if her mother were trying rise from the ground, and then the breeze took her away.

Fear submerged grief when she heard the sounds of men talking. Looking out through the leaves Camille could see three men and could hear another behind her. They were searching, prodding the clumps of bush with sticks, looking behind any rock or rise that could hide their quarry. One of the men was Xavier, his red mane shining in the morning light. As they passed, Camille heard part of their conversation.

"She's long gone," said one man to Xavier. He was a big man with powerful shoulders that held a balding head, shining in the light. He walked with a slight limp.

"I would expect so," said Xavier.

"Halfway to the next district, I reckon."

"Probably."

"Why're we wasting time here then?"

"Fire-oath, Thom, we can't leave her to come back and cause trouble for us now. We put too much time into stirring up the town to have her come back and ruin it. She must die. She is a witch and this land belongs to men who deserve it. The boss won't accept anything less."

"But she ain't here."

"Do you want me to send you to report back that we're not going to look any more because you think she's gone? Just keep looking."

The men moved out of earshot. They had not seen Camille wrapped in leaves, laying quietly. The words tumbled over each other in her head. So this is why her mother had died, so that someone could make claim to the farm, and she was to be hunted down like an animal so that she could not stop them. Waves of grief crashed over her throughout the day, unchecked tears blurring her vision and thoughts. Night again settled over the farm and Camille still lay huddled in the bush. She could not trust anyone around the town. At some point the sun had set without her noticing so she crept out from the bush and turned to leave. There was no need to pack or prepare for the journey - she had nothing to take. She turned her back on the two piles of ash and began to walk.

It did not take long before she had left the farm behind. The ploughed fields offered little to slow her progress but little protection from discovery. She stumbled through the night, unthinking and unseeing. The death of her mother had left her drained, but she knew that she had to keep walking. She didn't see the moon as it sailed across the clear night sky, nor the beauty of the stars. With morning approaching, her instincts drove her to seek shelter from searching eyes. She entered a small grove of trees nearby which offered protection. Thinking was too much for her. She slept through the day until, with the sun falling low in the western sky, she prepared to leave.

She stepped out of the trees to begin her night's walk but the beat of a startled bird flapping its way into the sky beside her made her jump. Its big black wings carried it into the air and when she turned at the sound she saw the riders on horseback coming over the low hill behind her. She quickly ran back to the little hiding place where she had slept and watched. As the riders grew closer Xavier's red hair became obvious and she could hear his words.

"I saw something move back in here. It could have been the girl. Don't let her get away."

Xavier had seen her! She didn't know what to do. There was not much cover, and she could not outrun them. They were going to find her. The men dismounted, leaving their horses at the edge of the trees. They formed a line and began to work their way slowly through the grove, checking everywhere as they passed. She huddled behind the little bush as the line of men approached. One of Xavier's men was only six feet in front of her. Discovery seemed certain when loud squealing and crashing further up the line distracted him. A large wild boar charged out of the bush and into one of the men. It knocked him down, ripping at the man's leg with its dirty yellow tusks before charging at the horses. The men ran to intercept it but the boar turned and disappeared out over the open land. Xavier ordered someone to see to the injured man and turned to look back into the trees.

"That must have been what I saw," he told them after some thought. "Get that leg bound and we'll move on."

Camille lay still until the men had disappeared over the next hill before emerging. She waited in the trees for the next hour, eating a meal of wild mulberries before resuming her trek. She was near the top of the hill where she had last seen the men when a raven landed in front of her. She stopped, taking in the beauty of the bird. Its feathers shone a deep blue black, a glistening darkness. The eyes that watched her were big and yellow. She stood transfixed by those eyes. They seemed to look into her. She felt that the bird was trying to warn her. She looked up the hill and decided that caution was preferable to discovery. A group of rocks at the top of the hill would provide cover and a view beyond. She approached as silently as she was able. The light was fading but she could see that Xavier had stopped his men and lined then across the land in front of her. He had obviously thought she had used the trees for shelter and would move again under the cover of dark. She turned back down the hill and began to circle them. Once she felt safely clear she set out as fast as she was able before morning would force her to take cover again.

Over the next days she travelled across open pasture with gentle rolling hills, dotted here and there with pockets of trees. She stayed away from the few roads that wandered aimlessly between the farms, climbing the occasional fence that attempted to bar her way. When the sun began to lighten the eastern sky each day, she found a comfortable hollow or bush and crawled in. Visions of her mother defiant in a tower of flame kept returning to her each night. She tried to understand why their friends had turned on them, but it made no sense. She would wake disoriented and confused with the sun low in the afternoon sky. Thornberry bushes or other plants and trees provided her with fruit when she needed it. Then, as the darkness began to claim the land, she continued her walk.

During this time, she saw Xavier and his men twice more. On each occasion she was able to hide and evade capture among some bulrushes that fought for survival beside a nearly dry creek and in a hollow that was once used to hold water for stock. Then they seemed to lose her, or she lost them, because she did not see them for weeks. There were fewer farms and roads. The low hills were now covered with bush and scrub and groves of dry trees were more common than wheat or barley.

One night as she trekked through thickening scrub, she discovered a rarely used narrow trail. A waning moon lit the way. She could see no movement in either direction. Though her instincts still told her to stay away from people, walking along the trail would be easier. Comfort overcame discretion. She stepped out and began to follow the trail. As she travelled north the hills became taller and the farms were left behind. She felt safer with each mile she travelled. She did not know or care how far she had travelled. Walking north was all that mattered.

As night threatened to settle over the land yet again Camille started her trek through a small, wooded vale. The moon was peeking over the distant hills when a movement broke the numbness of her mind. A raven stood perched on a low bough in front of her. It watched her with a steady gaze. Camille wondered if it could be the same bird. Time and movement were frozen as she watched the raven. Finally, the bird broke the spell when it raised its head and looked back over Camille's shoulder. It glanced quickly back at Camille before once again looking back down the road. It stood tall, spread its night-dark wings and with one brief squawk leapt from the branch and disappeared into the trees beside the road. Camille looked over her shoulder and, without understanding why, followed the raven into the trees.

Moments later she heard the sound of horses and watched as the group of riders approached, laughing and apparently in good spirits. One man however stood out from the group. He rode in the lead on a dappled grey stallion, his long mass of dirty red hair bouncing in harmony with the gait of the horse. They rode slowly by and disappeared down the road. Camille stood in the trees long after the riders had gone. The monotony had suddenly turned to fear and now the fear receded. Now there was relief. She wondered what drove these men to continue their chase. Movement once again distracted her as the silent black bird landed on a branch beside her. The yellow eyes again seemed to capture her before the raven leapt forward, turned and flew down the road. Camille knew the raven was telling her it was safe to go.

She continued to walk through the night. Something had changed within her during the trek. She was now aware of everything around her. The riders had again woken her to the dangers she faced, even this far from the place she had known as home. The countryside had changed considerably from the area around Thistledowne. The track wound through an area where the steep hills were littered with rocks and trees. Ahead of her a tall and unforgiving mountain range rose above the land. Even from this distance the peaks looked imposing. Her mother had spoken of these mountains at a time when she was a girl sitting in front of the warm winter fire. The thought of those times brought tears back to her eyes but she roughly wiped them on her sleeve. She remembered her mother telling her that people did not live in those mountains, but she could not recall her mother ever giving her a reason. This would be her goal. She would go into the mountains to hide and consider her future.

Each day brought her closer to the mountains. The days and nights were becoming cooler. The small roads and trails were left far behind and there had been no indications of habitation for many days. There had been no sign of Xavier and his men since they had ridden past her so long ago that she had felt it safe enough to begin walking during the day. Camille stood looking up at the white-topped peaks. The mountains grew out of the land, the steep rock faces disappearing into the clouds above. Around her the trees and plants were greener and the grasses looked healthier than the plants of Thistledowne had ever looked. Between her and the mountains stood a line of trees like none she had seen before or even dreamed possible. They stood tall with ample room to walk between the trunks but the canopy closed out the sky above. What made these woods different, as she looked beneath the leaves, were the trunks and branches. They were patterned with every colour imaginable. Many hues of red, green, blue and yellow laced each section of bark and the trees emitted a soft light, giving a magical glow to the air. She stepped beneath the canopy and the air became liquid. Each step felt like walking through deep mud. She forced herself to go on, concentrating on placing one foot in front of the other as her mind fought to overcome the beauty that threatened to engulf her. Inside her head a voice seemed to keep inviting "Join us."

Resisting with every step she pushed forward and finally reached the far edge of the woods, stepping out into the sun again. With the light, the suffocation of the trees left her and she sat on a rock to rest. The ground before her was littered with rocks of all sizes, harder to cross but insignificant compared to what faced her at the far edge. Stretching as far as she could see in either direction stood a sheer rock wall, its top about sixty feet above her. She could see no way past the barrier but had no desire to go back beneath the trees. She would need to work her way along the cliff until she could find a way into the mountains. Glancing at the sun hanging low in the west, she decided to wait until tomorrow before going on.

Next morning as she stood looking up at the barrier she noticed a bird high in the sky above her. It circled her for three or four turns, then drifted west along the wall on silent wings. She followed because it seemed right and by afternoon she started to notice changes in the face of the cliff. There were more cracks and fissures appearing, with small caves showing at various levels. With the afternoon drawing to an end a familiar shape appeared in the skies above her. The raven circled before flying ahead and returning. The dark bird continued to follow overhead for the next hour before finally alighting on a rock at the base of the cliff. It waited for Camille and only when she noticed the cave behind the rock did the bird spread its wings and, with one mighty thrust, launched itself back into the air.

The cave was tall enough for her to enter without crawling and extended back before angling to the right. It was about thirty feet deep; the floor was fairly level and a few loose rocks were scattered around the inner depths while enough light entered to make movement comfortable and safe. Camille chose an area among the stones as a bed for the night. As the darkness closed around her, she lay on the floor and wondered if the raven was telling her that this was her destination. It appeared to be a good place to stay for a while. She had crossed a small stream a short way back that would ensure a supply of fresh water and the colorful trees spreading from the base of the cliff would surely provide for her requirements if she could collect it without being overcome by the power of the shadows. She looked around the cave and thought it was worth considering.

Her eyes opened to find the sun brightening the entrance to her cave but it struck her that something was different. She lay still and allowed her eyes to roam the cave before settling on the entrance. Just outside the cave something sat on the rock where yesterday the raven had stood. She could not make out the silhouette so she lay still, hoping that whatever sat there was only resting and, if she gave it time, it would leave. But after some minutes the shape spoke with a voice that sounded like the deep rumble of distant thunder. "Can come out now. Wait for you." Camille lay still. It took a few moments before her sleepy brain realized that the rumbling noise was actually speech. Then the rumble came again. "I know you awake."

Camille watched. The shape had not moved so she climbed to her feet and edged towards the entrance. "I no hurt you," the voice said. Camille stepped out into the sun. Crouched on the rock was a massive creature. Its head was round and hairless with large eyes and an overly large mouth, filled with pointed teeth. The creature's body was much larger than any man's and it had long thick arms and short solid legs. Around its waist was tied some sort of animal hide that was hitched between its legs. The hide was obviously well used. But to Camille the overall appearance of the creature was blue, like it had just climbed out of a wine-maker's barrel.

"Welcome," said the creature.

"Thank you," replied Camille. They watched each other in silence for some moments before she continued. "I am Camille."

"I name Aiyu, son of Yent, son of Avgar, son of Goar."

"How did you know I was here?"

"Watch you. You walk along Edge yesterday. I see you. No see many humans come mountains."

"And what sort of creature are you?" she asked.

"No like be called creature. We people auchs."

"An auch?"

"Auchs live mountains many years."

"But the auchs are only a myth, tales that parents tell their children to make them go to bed."

"Do I look like myth?" he grinned. "Auchs no myth. Auchs proud and peaceful people. My family go back many generations. Aiyu son of Yent, son of Avgar, son of Goar, and go back Ngai the Brave."

"I am sorry but I cannot remember all of your family names."

"Friends just call Aiyu."

"How did you see me? Where were you?"

Aiyu simply pointed up.

"Up there?" asked Camille. "What were you doing?"

"Work on farm. Holdbori come speak."

"Holdbori?" asked Camille. This creature confused her. "Is Holdbori another auch?"

"Holdbori Great Spirit of skies. Come in black clothes. Land on tree. Tell me follow. Bring me to Edge. I see you come and watch. When you sleep, Holdbori tell I come wait for you wake."

Camille and Aiyu talked on through the early morning. She found it easy to speak to the big blue man. She told him of the attack on her home and the death of her mother. She spoke of her flight from the people of Thistledowne and she told him of the raven and how it had saved her from capture and death. "Holdbori protect you," Aiyu told her. The auch then sat and pondered for a few minutes.

"Come. It time go."

"Go where?" asked Camille.

"I take to farm and we talk Bhata."

"Who is Bhata?" she asked.

Aiyu's face lit up. "Bhata mate of Aiyu. She strong spirit talker, understand spirits. She tell us what Holdbori want. We go to farm. It no far."

Camille did not understand why she trusted this big creature but she agreed to go. Aiyu jumped off the rock and set off immediately along the cliff face. He was already well on his way before she reacted and followed him as he set a fast pace over the broken ground. The effort of keeping up prevented any further conversation. The fast pace was difficult. She was forced to stop and think of her route around or over rocks and fallen trees while Aiyu just seemed to step over the obstacles. Soon Camille was forced to stop and call to Aiyu. She explained that she could not walk through this broken ground and keep up; she did not have his strength or speed. After considering the situation for a moment Aiyu announced, "Carry you." In one flashing movement he leaned down and picked up Camille, slung her over his shoulder and started to walk again. With her head hanging over the back of Aiyu's shoulder and her legs bouncing on his chest she called to be put down but Aiyu took no notice. She punched him in the back with both fists while continuing to curse him loudly from her indignant position. Aiyu walked for some time, ignoring her screams and punches. They had travelled a good distance before Aiyu turned and walked into a small fissure in the cliff face. He placed her back on the ground and looked at her with a confused expression.

"What are you doing?" she yelled at him.

"Camille say she no walk. I strong so I carry," he explained.

"I just wanted you to slow down, you big oaf," she yelled.

Aiyu stood looking at the small human, not understanding her complaints. "No matter," he said. "We here."

Camille looked around at the dark rock wall. "Here? Where? I don't see any farm."

"No at farm," he replied. "This way to mountains. Walk easy from here." He turned and walked deeper into the fissure and in moments he was lost in shadows. She stood and waited, and shortly after he reappeared to ask, "Are you come?"

"I could not see you," she complained. "I do not know which way to go."

"You want Aiyu carry?" he asked but the expression on her face told him no. "I help," he said and held out his massive hand. Camille's hand was engulfed in his enormous yet gentle fist and with him guiding, she followed the auch into the darkness. The ravine cut deep into the cliff and as her eyes became accustomed to the dark Camille began to make out some of the shapes around her. They seemed to be climbing and the ground under her feet was reasonably clean of obstructions. The trail was about three feet wide, wide enough for a horse or an auch. To her right the rock rose in a vertical wall while on her left the ground was cracked deeper than she cared to think. She could not see the bottom but the sheer rock wall on the other side of the fissure stood about ten feet away. Ahead she could hear the roar of falling water. The two climbed further up the trail, around a bend and onto a rock platform. She stood transfixed by what she saw. They were standing inside a rock shaft stretching from sunlight to the depths of the land below. On the far side of the shaft water cascaded from the world above crashing and bouncing off the rock walls, disappearing into the darkness. Mist and spray shattered the light and sprinkled it over the walls where ferns and moss clung precariously to tiny footholds. Looking up, Camille could see a kaleidoscope of lights reflecting all the colors of the rainbow.

"It's beautiful," she said.

Aiyu allowed her only a moment to admire the sight before announcing, "Time to go." He walked to the far end of the platform. She just wanted to enjoy the beauty of this place. When Camille reluctantly followed, she saw a hidden cave in the rock face behind the falls. Aiyu walked into its mouth. The cave was a little taller than Aiyu, about nine feet, and about half as wide. It struck her that the cave was very square. She saw the hammered marks on the wall: this cave was man-made, or at least auch-made. It curved to the right in a shallow climb. After some time, she thought that they must have walked at least a full circle, yet still the cave curved upward while her legs burned and she fought for breath. When they finally emerged onto a lush green plain, stretching ahead of her were acres of verdant grassland interspersed with short healthy trees. A small river wound its way out of the valley ahead, cutting a path through the grasses before disappearing into an enormous sink hole about a hundred yards to her left. Below that must be the rock platform, she thought. She saw that this end of the cave was actually a simple stone structure erected to protect the entrance. It consisted of two great slabs of rock on edge while a third slab sat on top forming a roof which sloped from the opening height to ground level at the end furthest from her, fitting the walls so neatly that no joint was visible. The entire structure was covered with intricate carvings of plants and animals.

She turned to ask what the markings meant but Aiyu was striding across the grass and she was forced to run to catch up. They were headed straight towards the valley ahead, tracking closer to the river's edge as they walked. They had not gone far when Camille saw a lovely cottage nestled amid a grove of willows on the riverbank. She had not seen anything like it before. The home was built on a base of six sides with a steep thatched roof reaching to a central peak which was open and covered by its own roof, allowing a plume of delicate smoke to trail into the sky. The walls were a mixture of black stone and grey timber with open windows for ventilation and light. Shutters sat ready to fit over the openings in times of poor weather. The walls had been brought back under the roof line on the side facing the river, providing a comfortable veranda to sit and relax on the two large chairs it held. In one of these sprawled another large blue auch. "Bhata wait," Aiyu told her with a broad smile, showing his fierce-looking teeth. As they approached the cottage Camille saw a large six-sided shed hidden among the trees and the gardens spread out along the river. The gardens were packed with vegetables, some of which she recognized, many she had never seen before.

Bhata waited with hands on hips as they approached. To Camille she looked just like Aiyu with her bald head and solid body. She also wore an old hide wrapped around her middle and she gave off a similar aura of blue. The only difference Camille could see at first glance were the small tufts of hair growing from her ears and the leather lace hanging around her neck. A green stone carved in the shape of a tree hung on it. When they reached the steps Bhata held up one hand and pointed at Camille. "What this?" she asked in a grumbling roar.

"I come back," said Aiyu with a big grin.

"You come back? Bhaa," she spat. "You go find another stray. That what you do."

"Bhata, that no fair."

"You go work garden. I look up. You gone. You come back next day with stray. What no fair?"

"Bhata. Holdbori come. Tell me go to Edge. Tell me find her."

"Holdbori tell you? Bear-dung. How you know what Holdbori want? You no can talk to spirits."

"Please," pleaded Camille, "I do not want to cause trouble. I will go."

"Stay," growled Bhata. "No your fault. Men do anything get out work."

CHAPTER 3

Xavier crouched staring into the small campfire, deep in thought. They had tracked the girl for many weeks now without success, but his instincts told him that they were close. He had seen the signs of her passing. Now they had come upon an impassable cliff that stretched beyond sight in each direction. She could not have climbed it so she must be nearby. After that night in Thistledowne when the girl had escaped, he had not expected that he might need to return without news of her death and did not look forward to giving the boss a report of her escape. He took pride in being able to complete any job he was asked to do and he had not failed before. But he could not understand how a girl on foot, alone and without supplies could elude them.

The others sat around waiting for the evening meal to be cooked. They were good loyal men, proven fighters too. They would keep riding until he called for the chase to end. His second-in-command approached and crouched beside him. Jaimz was a man he would trust with his life. The man was the son of a sword-master, his best friend for the last five years.

"We'll find her soon," Jaimz promised.

"I hope so. It isn't helping either of our careers if one young girl can escape us so easily." Xavier sat silent for a few minutes before asking, "Why are we chasing her?"

"Because she is a witch."

"But she has done nothing wrong."

"Do you doubt the wisdom of the Council?"

"I am a loyal Society member but I can't help but wonder at the decision to hunt down all witches."

"It is not our job to wonder, only to obey."

"Of course I will obey, but have you never asked yourself what we are doing?"

"When I try to make sense of our orders and cannot, I tell myself that I do not have all the facts available to the Council."

"I suppose so."

"Why should it matter to you if the witches are all killed?"

Xavier thought about his reply. "It doesn't, but I would like to understand why we do these things."

"When you returned after your mother's death you were lost, and I took you to hear Piaz speak. He showed you the evil of the witches and what they were doing around the land. That was when you became a member and devoted yourself to our ideals. Why do you now doubt your choices?"

"I never told you about Redhill, my home town. This chase has me thinking about my childhood again. My father was a drunk, and used to beat me just because I was there. My mother tried her best to protect me. She would take me to see Jehane, the town witch, when I was badly hurt. Jehane would take the pain away and always had sweetcakes or such to comfort me. When I could bear it no more I left home to come to Whitebridge. I was twelve."

As the meal was being served, Xavier made up his mind. They had chased the girl long enough. He would search the area around here tomorrow and if they found no further sign of her in that time they would return, and he would be forced to report her escape. With his mind settled Xavier sat back waiting for the meal as the weight of frustration lifted from his shoulders.

Next morning as the early light brought the camp to life, the men broke their fast with cheese and dry biscuits before saddling the horses for another day's ride. He decided to search to the left for no other reason than his intuition. They set out along the cliff face searching for signs of her passing. Fallen rocks and rubble forced them to move away from the face into the strange trees that seemed to spread away before them. The meagre underbrush allowed Xavier and his men to move at a good pace. They had not ridden far when Jaimz came up to Xavier and pointed over to the rock face ahead of them without speaking. There was definitely movement along the base of the cliff, though from this distance Xavier found it difficult to make out.

"If that is our girl, you have earned yourself a bonus, Jaimz." said Xavier.

He ordered the men to follow while he and Jaimz went ahead to investigate. They rode quickly through the trees in order to outflank their quarry before dismounting and hitching the horses to a fallen branch. Taking care to remain hidden as they made their way through the rocky terrain, they worked their way towards the cliff to take up a position hidden among a group of larger rocks. From this observation point they could wait for the girl's approach. Xavier tried to estimate how long it would take her to get from where they had seen the movement to their current position. He thought they would be waiting a short while and was about to tell Jaimz to relax when something moved nearby, catching his attention. He was surprised when a beast stepped over a rock barely fifty paces away. The big blue animal seemed to lumber along, yet covered the ground at an amazing pace, carrying a bundle over its shoulder.

"What is that?" Jaimz whispered beside him.

Xavier didn't reply. He had seen that the load the creature carried was the girl they had been seeking for so long. She was screaming and yelling at the creature while beating at its back with her fists. As they watched, the creature turned and disappeared into a fissure in the cliff face.

"That, my friend, was an auch," Xavier finally answered. He had read stories of such animals.

Jaimz looked to where the creature had disappeared. "What do we do now?" he asked.

Xavier just sat and looked at the dark hole that had swallowed the auch and the girl. When neither reappeared after some minutes Xavier told Jaimz to return and fetch the other men. "Leave the horses and men in the trees," he ordered, "and then come back here with Thom."

Jaimz rejoined him shortly and Thom followed him into the rocks. He left them watching the entrance while he returned to the others and ordered them to set up camp. He suspected that they would be here overnight so he organized shifts of lookouts. Two men would keep the opening under surveillance at all times while he planned their next move, though he didn't like the idea of following the beast into the dark. They kept their vigil for the rest of the day but there was no sign of the auch or the girl. As night fell, Xavier began to believe that the girl had to be dead. He could find no other reason for her not emerging from the fissure. Even so he had the men prepare for their watches throughout the night. They would wait until the auch left its den and then check for the girl's body.

The next day, the men were restless. None had seen an auch before and few had believed in their existence. They sat in silence, away from each other, and all interaction was strained. If he ordered it they would fight any man but the thought of fighting an auch made them edgy. The stories of their childhoods haunted them. Discontent grew and when Harry and Jack bumped each other with part of Jack's meal ending up on the ground, the fight broke out. Jack swung a bony fist landing it squarely on Harry's jaw who retaliated by picking up the smaller man and throwing him across the camp. Jack rolled to his feet and both men faced each other in fighter's crouches before coming together with fists flying. Xavier let the fight continue, seeing it as a way to relieve some of the tension, but when Harry drew his sword he called for them to stop. Discipline hadn't deserted them yet and both men stepped back. The time had come to do something before he lost control of them completely. He told them that if there was no sign of the auch by morning he was going into the fissure to find it and the girl. He asked which of them would like the honor of going with him.

Both men stood silent until Jaimz spoke out. "I will go."

Xavier ordered the men to break camp and prepare to travel while they were gone. "If we do not return by noon, you are to leave and take a report of all that has happened here directly to the boss," he told them. The men all moved back to their places and settled quietly to eat and wait.

He went to sit with Jaimz. "You didn't need to do that," he said.

"If you go after that beast you will need a good sword to stand beside you."

"Harry or Jack would have stood with me."

"But they are not trained by my father in the skills of a sword-master. Besides, if we have to run, I'm faster." Xavier chuckled.

The early morning half-light invaded the camp as Jaimz and Xavier checked their weapons before moving up to the observation post. "No sense in waiting any longer," said Jaimz, nervousness showing in his voice. "Let's get this over with." Xavier moved toward the dark opening, with Jaimz carrying the torches that they had prepared the night before. At the entrance they paused long enough to strike flint to stone and light the first torch before entering the darkness. It took only moments for their eyes to become accustomed to the torch light and together they worked their way deeper into the fissure. There seemed to be no hollows or dark corners that could hide the auch so they cautiously continued up the trail with their swords drawn. Although they knew that time was passing the two men hidden in the darkness had no concept of how long their walk up the trail was taking. Time seemed suspended. They continued walking, surrounded by the glow of the torch until the brightening of daylight ahead and the roar of falling water hammered at their senses. Turning the next bend, they found themselves on a wide ledge cut into the side of a vertical shaft. Water fell from above.

"There have been no other passages," Xavier thought aloud. "The auch must have come this way. Where has it gone?"

"Maybe down there," said Jaimz, looking over the edge of the platform into the depths.

"I don't think so. There must be another passage," said Xavier. "Look around." It did not take them long to find the cave hidden behind the waterfall. Xavier entered; Jaimz took a deep breath before following. As they walked up the spiraling tunnel Xavier sheathed his sword and began to stride. He was becoming certain that this was a passage and not the lair of the creature. When they emerged from the tunnel and found themselves on the lush land above the wall they stopped and stared. The mountains stood over them. A river poured from the valley before them, snaking its way across the narrow plain before disappearing down the sinkhole.

Jaimz sat on a nearby rock. "Where now?" he asked.

"The auch could have gone anywhere," said Xavier. "But do you realise what we have found?" Jaimz looked up at him questioningly. "We have found a path to the mountains and proof that the auchs still live here. The boss will be very pleased with this knowledge. Come on. Let's go back and join the others."

Noon was rapidly approaching when the two men emerged from the fissure. The lookouts were relieved to see them. "Did you find them?" one asked.

"We found…" started Jaimz before Xavier cut him off.

"Let's go and join the men." His look told Jaimz not to say any more.

"Let's go and join the men." His look told Jaimz not to say any more.

When they returned to the camp, everything was packed and the horses stood saddled and ready. "Mount up," he ordered. "We are going to Whitebridge."

CHAPTER 4

"Bhata, this Camille," Aiyu told his mate. "She come long way. People kill mother. Chase her."

Bhata waved her huge arm toward the door. "Come eat." She turned and led Camille into the cottage. It was a well-kept home with a stove to one side and a large table in the middle. A heavy ladder beside the door led up to a loft and she guessed that the sleeping area was up there. This is a doll's house in reverse, she thought. Everything is too big. "Sit," Bhata commanded, waving her to the table. Camille was forced to climb like a toddler to get onto the chair while Bhata moved to a covered pot hanging over the kitchen fire and served up three bowls of food. She placed one in front of Camille. "Eat," she ordered. It contained what appeared to be a vegetable stew. Delicious aromas caused her stomach to rumble. The hot and spicy flavor bit her tongue and she wolfed down the meal, suddenly realizing how hungry she was. She had nearly finished her second bowl when two young auchs catapulted into the room. Aiyu barked at them to slow down but they had come to a halt as soon as they saw the human.

"Camille, this Agort, son of Aiyu, son of Yent, son of Avgar," he said indicating the first of the children, "and this Paulk, daughter of Bhata, daughter of Mizq, daughter of Draal. Agort, Paulk, this Camille. Now sit eat." Bhata filled two more bowls while they took their seats.

"Where from?" ventured Agort.

"From lowland," Aiyu told the children. Agort and Paulk exchanged glances. They were not permitted to go to the lowland. They had been told that it was a place of danger and strange beings. Now one of them sat at their table. Aiyu's stare warned the children as Bhata asked Camille to tell her story. All four remained silent as Camille remembered that night so long ago and her flight across the country while being chased the entire way. Bhata seemed to take special interest when she told of the raven and how its appearance had saved her from the hunters. When she had finished her tale, Bhata questioned her on everything she could remember of the raven, about the time and nature of its appearance and its every action. Finally, Bhata sat back and pronounced with a smile, "Holdbori protect you. Holdbori like you so Bhata like you."

Now that both her meal and her story were completed Camille excused herself and went out to the porch to enjoy the end of the day. She was joined by Aiyu and Bhata after the children were put to their beds. The stars seemed particularly bright in the clear sky and the sounds of the night helped to put Camille at ease. As they sat there enjoying the stillness of the evening Aiyu asked his mate what she had made of Camille's story and the appearances of Holdbori but Bhata was forced to admit that she did not know the potent of the signs. "No able read meaning now. Wait and message come clear," Bhata told them. "I fix bed in kitchen near stove. Camille sleep there. Aiyu and I sleep now." With that they both rose and went inside, leaving Camille to enjoy a few more minutes of peace under the night sky.

When Camille awoke the next morning, the cottage was quiet. The sun streamed through the kitchen window to play on the air in the room. A plate of sliced fruit sat on the table. She picked up a piece of green melon and ate it while looking out the window. She ate some more of the fruit before leaving the house and making her way toward the vegetable plot where Aiyu and Bhata were working in the garden. Before she had walked a dozen paces she heard squeals and the cracking of bushes. Fearing a pack of wild boar charging out of the trees beside her she was on the point of running when she saw Agort and Paulk racing towards her, and coming to a skidding halt. "Come play?" Agort asked. Camille looked across to where Aiyu and Bhata were working before laughing and agreeing. They took her by the hands and ran towards the trees and it took all her effort not to be dragged over the ground by her enthusiastic new friends.

No sooner were they in the trees than Paulk called "Wrestle" before leaping on her brother's back and driving him to the ground. Agort rolled and grabbed his sister, throwing her as far as he could but Paulk jumped to her feet and called to Camille "Come on. Wrestle" before diving and taking Agort's leg out from under him. Still holding the leg she braced herself and swung, throwing Agort up against a tree with a crunching thud. He bounced back to his feet, shaking his head.

"What is matter?" he called to Camille.

"You're too good for me," she laughed. "I don't know how to wrestle."

"Not know how to wrestle?" Paulk asked. She stopped and thought. "What we play then?"

Camille thought back to her childhood with her mother. "I've never really played," she said. "There was only ever my mother and me."

"No wrestle?" asked an astonished Agort. "You play dodge or slapstick?"

"I don't know what dodge or slapstick is," confessed Camille.

"Play slapstick," decided Paulk. "It easy. We show you how." With that she began to look around under the trees till she found a piece of branch about half her height in length. As she picked it up Agort attacked with a bough of his own. His blow was aimed at Paulk's ribs but Paulk anticipated the attack and raised her stick in a solid two-handed block before she spun it in a wide arc towards Agort's head. The mock battle went on with solid attacks being deflected on both sides until Paulk swung a low attack at Agort's legs. His defensive thrust drove down but at the last moment Paulk twisted her wrists and brought her attack straight up. Agort was taken by surprise and the blow took him across the side of the head. They both immediately stepped back.

"You win today," conceded Agort, shaking his head. He turned to Camille and invited her to play but she told him that he was too good and would hurt her. "I no hurt you. Come, I teach," he promised. Agort allowed her to get used to swinging the stick in attack while simply blocking the blows and showed her how to defend and switch her point of attack. After half an hour of being slapped, hit and thumped she called a halt and told them that they could continue without her. She told them she was going to talk with their parents, feeling lucky that she was getting away with only a few bruises.

Agort stood for a moment before yelling "Wrestle" and slamming into Paulk. Camille started to walk back to the garden with the sounds of crashing bodies behind her, but once she was clear of the children she turned away from the cottage. Finding a quiet bend in the river she removed her boots and walked into the cold water, took off her dress and rinsed it as best she could, then scrubbed her body with handfuls of grey sand. The water was icy but after weeks of walking and hiding it felt luxurious to sit and soak in the river, better than any hot bath with scented soap. Feeling cleaner she crawled out onto the bank and lay down to dry in the sun.

She woke later, surprised that she had dozed off, checked her dress to see if it had dried, slipped it over her head and started back. When she reached the cottage she found Aiyu sitting on the porch with Bhata. They were enjoying a cool drink of minted water. Camille smiled and joined them. She had not felt so comfortable for many weeks. They chatted for a time before

Aiyu broached the subject of her plight and asked if she wished to stay with them for a while. He told her that there was plenty of space and food and that they would be happy if she were to live with them until Holdbori made his wishes known. She was about to thank them and take up their offer when a raven swooped over the roof and banked, landing on the handrail beside her. All three were stunned into silence. The bird stood looking at Camille. It almost seemed as if the bird were trying to decide if this girl was worth the effort. Having made up its mind, it broke the spell by raising its head and looking towards the mountains, turning back to look back and forth between Aiyu and Camille. It looked back to the mountains again before spreading its midnight-black wings and taking flight in a line directly towards the valley. "Holdbori speak," Bhata declared. "Message now clear. Holdbori want Aiyu take Camille into mountains. Go see Obiri."

"What is Obiri?" asked Camille.

"Obiri very wise," stated Bhata. "Obiri elder of Aiyu clan." Camille began to object. "Holdbori say, go," repeated Bhata. She clapped her hands. "Go, Aiyu. Get ready. No time wait." Aiyu went into the cottage and prepared for the trip while Camille sat dazed by the speed of events over the last few minutes. Just as she had begun to believe she had found peace and a place to stay, she was being swept up again in events seemingly beyond her control, beginning yet another journey.

By midday they were ready to go. "Night very cold in mountains," Aiyu said. "Take this." and passed her a rolled pelt to carry on her back. They set off, following the riverbank towards the mountains, and by nightfall they had entered the valley. The mountains climbed on either side in steep vertical walls as if hanging from the sky, at the bottom the walls blended into the valley floor in a sweeping arc of rock and loose stones. Small trees and pockets of bush found footholds in the rocky slopes while the lush green lands of the high plains narrowed to a strip of green along the valley floor.

Aiyu called a halt to their march and began to prepare for the night. From the sack he carried over his shoulder he pulled fruits and raw vegetables and a large pelt. They ate their meagre meal before Aiyu wrapped himself in his pelt and lay down to sleep. Camille copied him, only then realizing how tired she was. She fell into a deep sleep on the rocky ground in moments. Next morning Aiyu woke her before light had entered the valley. Sunrise found them well on their way again.

By the fourth day the valley had climbed higher and grown wider as if spreading itself over the mountains. They had left the trees behind, the bushes became fewer, until even the grasses gave up their battle with the rocky ground. The wind blew constantly in its attempt to stop intruders by cutting them to pieces. Pockets of white began to appear in shaded hollows. "Snow," Aiyu informed her, picking up a handful. Camille was shivering too much to appreciate her first sight of this strange powder. Aiyu took the sleeping pelt from her back and wrapped it over her shoulders. He showed her how to tie part of it up to form a hood. Camille realized that they had reached the top of the valley. They were walking on an uneven field of black rock scattered with pockets of white and blue. The white she now knew to be snow and the blue patches were hollows filled with water reflecting the clear sky. Ahead lay a field of white glaring in the morning sun. Camille hoped that they would not be going there. The cold had long since numbed her senses but she felt that travelling over the white plain would make the previous hours seem warm. He led her over the land, weaving between the water and snow before stopping at the top of another cliff.

Far below her another river wound its way along the valley floor, coming from somewhere up in the snow and weaving its way down to where it flowed into a deep green lake. Aiyu pointed to a smudge on the valley floor beside the lake. "Konungssonur," he told her. "Clan city of Aiyu. Obiri live Konungssonur." Camille tried to make out the details of the smudge without avail. Even though the air was crisp and clear, the city was too far away.

"Path close. Come," said Aiyu. He had only gone a dozen paces when he stepped off the cliff. Before she had time to scream, his fall was stopped. He called for her to approach and she saw that he stood on a narrow ledge about six feet below the top. She stood trembling, not knowing if from fear or the cold. Surely he did not expect her to climb down the cliff face. "Come. Aiyu help," he said. Before she could think, he reached across and picked her up, setting her down beside him on the ledge. "Come," he said and began walking along the narrow shelf. He stopped when he realized that she was not following. "It safe to walk," he encouraged. Camille looked down over the side of the ledge to the ground far below. "No look, just walk," Aiyu told her. "Or you want Aiyu to carry?" he asked. Camille thought of lying over Aiyu's shoulder and looking down to the ground so far below. "No," she decided. "I'll walk."

She started slowly along the ledge, hugging the cliff face as she went. When she reached Aiyu he nodded and continued along the trail. It struck her that they were moving away from Konungssonur and that she could no longer see the lake. At the same time the trail had been dropping away from the cliff top as they walked. After about fifteen minutes Aiyu stopped. "What's wrong?" she asked.

"No wrong. Time to change trail," he replied, stepping off the edge. This time he disappeared fully from sight. Camille froze. "Come."

She stepped closer to the edge and looked down. Aiyu stood on another ledge about ten feet below her.

"I can't get down there," she told him.

"Jump. I catch you," he encouraged.

She looked to the valley far below and shook her head. Aiyu reminded her that she had no choice. He could not come back up so she must come down to get off the mountain. She knew that the longer she waited, the harder it would be to step off the ledge so she shut her eyes and stepped out into the air. Aiyu caught her in gentle hands and set her down beside him. "Good," he said before walking off along the ledge, reversing direction back towards Konungssonur. The trail was barely wide enough for Aiyu to stand on and below was nothing until the rocks at the bottom of the valley. She shut her eyes and, with an effort, tried to control the twisting knots inside her. She finally opened her eyes and with a deep intake of breath, she began to walk. Aiyu nodded. Trail by trail they zigzagged their way to the bottom of the cliff until finally they walked out onto the rocky screed slope. Camille looked out across the valley, then up at the cliff standing so tall above her. Her stomach turned at the thought of what she had just done. "Is this the only way to Konungssonur?" she asked, finding it difficult to pronounce the city's name.

"No," replied Aiyu. "This is fastest way."

She spun on the big auch. "Do you mean that we could have come to Konungssonur without climbing down that?" she demanded pointing up at the rock wall.

"Yes," he answered "but it take two days more walk. Holdbori tell hurry. Say walk this way." Camille stood silent looking at him, trying to understand. "Damned auch," she mumbled, finding that she could not be mad at the big man that had done so much to help her. They set up camp for the night on the floor of the valley. She felt much better now that she was no longer shivering. Next morning after a breakfast of fruit and honey, they set out along the river towards the lake. The trees and scrub soon gave way to fields of crops, but something about the scene appeared wrong to her. She was used to the farms being fenced and fields dedicated to one crop. Here she could see no fences and the fields were randomly planted with crops of all types. Tracks seemed to meander aimlessly through a diversity of vegetables and fruit. There were a number of auchs working the fields and as they passed each of them stopped to watch the pair. They had walked for some time before Camille realized there was something else she had not seen. "Where are the farmhouses?" she asked.

"No houses," Aiyu answered, without breaking stride.

"Then where do the farmers live?" she asked.

"Live Konungssonur," he told her. "Everyone live Konungssonur."

"But why not live close to the fields?" she persisted.

Aiyu spoke to her as if explaining the obvious to a small child. "Auchs live in mountains," he told her. "No much land so no waste. No cover up good ground. Put house on rocky ground. No waste." She kept her eyes on Aiyu as he led her through the maze of crops. When they reached the outskirts of the city, a smile split Aiyu's face in half and his arms spread wide to embrace the buildings as he announced, "Konungssonur."

Camille was amazed by what she saw. There were more buildings here than she could have ever imagined in one place: wooden structures with any number of sides and roofs of shingle, thatch or large wooden slabs, and some buildings that had no regular shape to either walls or roof. There seemed to be no order to their placement, as if some great being had thrown them out. The only things she could see that they had in common were the large doors and oversized shuttered windows. What Camille found most extraordinary was that they all stood on poles driven into the ground. The buildings before her were about ten feet above her and seemed to be interconnected by a maze of galleries and walkways. As she stared Aiyu laughed at her. "Welcome to clan home of Aiyu," he said.

"It's beautiful."

"Come meet Obiri," he invited as he walked to a nearby ramp leading up to the galleries.

They started to weave their way between the buildings. The galleries seemed very stable until she remembered they were built for auchs. They twisted left and right, crossing narrow bridges and wide boardwalks that lacked order, similar to the buildings and fields. Aiyu led her, always sure in the directions he took. Soon Camille was totally lost. They were passing an area of larger buildings with no windows when Camille called to Aiyu, "How do you know which way to go?"

"I just know," he answered.

"But how?" she asked again.

Aiyu stopped and thought. "I just know," he said with a shrug of his enormous shoulders.

He was about to start when Camille pleaded, "Wait. I need a rest."

Aiyu looked at her. "You want Aiyu carry?" he asked.

"No, I just need a moment." To give herself more time she asked, "Why don't these buildings have windows?"

"They store food," he said. "Auchs store for longnights. No can work on farms in longnights. Snow cover all farms." Her memories of the snow made her shiver. She asked him why the city was built on poles. His simple response of "snow" still left her confused. By now she had caught her breath and allowed him to lead her further into the city. About twenty minutes later Aiyu stopped in front of a door to a small home. To Camille it appeared no different to any of the other doors they had passed.

"This home of Obiri," he announced as his fist rattled the massive timber door. Camille heard movement inside before the door opened to reveal an auch of obvious years. He was much larger than Aiyu but the folds of loose blue skin hanging from his body suggested that he had been even larger in his prime years. One eye was clouded over and he walked with the aid of a solid cane. The blue of his skin was mottled with patches of white.

A broad smile lit the old auch's face. "Aiyu," he said. "Welcome home."

Aiyu smiled back. "Good see Obiri again".

CHAPTER 5

The small fire burning in the iron hearth cast flickering shadows on the walls of the room. Obiri sat in a large, padded chair and considered what he had been told by Camille. He was not surprised. He had known that humans could be dangerous and cruel from the histories passed down through generations and more recent stories he had heard had convinced him of their truth. The story of the auch's fight for freedom was still told around the fires during longnights, though Obiri feared that many did not believe the tales these days. This was the reason that auchs had isolated themselves from humans for the last seven centuries. "I very sad for you," he told Camille. "I not know your mother but meet you. Hear truth in your story. Make Obiri sad."

Camille thanked Obiri but told him the time of grieving had passed. "For now I need to rest and stay away from the men who hunt me," she told him. "In time I would like to see those responsible brought before the king for justice."

Obiri poured fresh glasses of minted water for his guests while he considered what he would do next. "I no think auchs able help seek justice. Auchs no do this," he finally told her. "Many years auchs stay away from humans. No put people at risk for you get revenge. But Camille stay Konungssonur, be safe."

Aiyu spoke up. "Lowlanders chase Camille. Holdbori bring her to auchs. He protect her. Holdbori tell Aiyu help her. Auchs should help."

Obiri looked at him and Aiyu squirmed under the gaze. "I no say Auchs not help Camille," he told Aiyu. "I say auchs stay away from humans." He turned to Camille and smiled. "You stay at Konungssonur. There more like you live here."

"More like me?" she asked.

"Yes, four come last four seasons," Obiri explained. Camille's head spun with the news - four others driven from their homes and finding their way here! From what she had overheard she had believed that hers was an isolated case driven by greed.

"Something happen in lowlands," Aiyu said. "Auchs do nothing, more come. Auchs be found. We can no hide now. World begin change. Time for auchs change too."

Obiri ignored the comments and instead asked Aiyu how Bhata and the children were managing and if they were still enjoying their time on the farm. While they chatted, Obiri considered Aiyu's comments about Holdbori and what the spirits wanted. Aiyu was in the middle of a question about friends in the city when Obiri interrupted and asked him to open the door. The conversation had barely started again when a young auch appeared in the opening.

"Obiri need something?" he asked.

"Yes, Urak. Find Kallu, tell I need her call Torkeen. Next bring Alayna here." Urak left, closing the door behind him.

"Who are Kallu and Torkeen?" Camille asked.

Aiyu answered her. "Kallu next clan elder. Obiri teach her lore of auch people. Torkeen no auch. Torkeen meeting of clan elders. One elder speak for one clan. Important decisions affect all auchs need more elders talk. Torkeen speak for all Sysla. Now must wait for elders gather and talk."

Obiri told her, "I no think auchs can help but hear Aiyu words. I speak at Torkeen and say this. You will speak too, and Aiyu. Then Torkeen decide."

"I understand and thank you," she told Obiri. "I will not ask that auchs put themselves at risk for me and I do not seek revenge. I know there will come a time when these men will be forced to stand to account for their actions."

The door opened to reveal Urak. "Kallu organize messengers to leave in morning. Alayna here," he said stepping aside to allow a woman to enter. She was tall and thin with long grey hair flowing down her back. She wore a long-sleeved red velvet dress with a high collar, drawn at the waist and falling to the floor. The top was patterned with yellow jagged flashes. Her drawn face was clear of any marks and Camille, guessing her age to be nearly seventy, thought that she had once been a beautiful woman. Alayna's eyes widened when she saw Camille though she said nothing.

"Alayna, this Camille. She will stay Konungssonur. See she comfortable," Obiri asked of her.

"Of course," she said, turning to Camille. "Follow me." Camille rose and thanked Obiri before following Alayna and Urak out of the room.

As they walked, Alayna said to Camille, "Girl, I have many questions but there are three others who would hear your story as well." Urak led them over a series of galleries before stopping in front of a door carved with the image of a crescent moon. Alayna told Camille that the auchs had made the symbol on the door in the hope of assisting her and the others in finding their own rooms. "We know when we are here," she admitted, "but we still have no idea of how to get here." She opened the door and entered followed by Camille. The furniture in the house was smaller than she had seen in Aiyu and Obiri's homes, more suitable for people of her size, which she found comforting. The front of the room held a plain table and chairs with a cooking fire set up at one end. The back of the room was divided into curtained cubicles.

"Is that you, Alayna?" a voice called from behind the curtains.

"Yes," Alayna replied, "and I am not alone."

An olive-skinned face wrapped in blonde curls appeared through the curtains. "Well, I'll be a flea's backside," it said before disappearing. Moments later a woman joined them still buttoning up the yellow dress she had obviously rushed to put on. It was decorated with a similar pattern to the dress her mother had worn. "Who is this, then?" she asked.

"Girl, this uncouth woman is Marie. She joined us last year. I have been here for three years. Marie, this is Camille. I know no more than that Obiri has asked us to care for her. Now, where are the others?" Alayna asked.

"They should be back soon. They have gone to collect supplies," Marie told her.

"Then we will wait for them. Marie, make us some tea. Come and sit down, Camille. There will be more than enough time for your story when the others return." Camille asked them where they get their supplies.

"The auchs treat us well and see to our needs," Marie told her.

45

Alayna went on, "We only need to go out and tell the first auch we see that we need food and they take us to the storehouses and give us what we want."

"What do they want in return?" Camille asked.

Alayna said that in the three years she had been in the city the auchs had asked for nothing. She explained that the auchs were a very communal society. "Everything is there for the whole community. It seems that they need the close contact with each other that their society creates," she said. "Each auch only takes what he or she needs and if anything needs to be done, whoever is able does the work. It sounds strange but it works. We offer our services but they tell us that others are more suited to do what is needed. Konungssonur is essentially a farming community and the auchs are bigger, stronger and faster. They are far more able to do the work, but we help where we can. This leaves us with much free time."

Marie served the tea and Camille raised the cup to her lips. It had a sour citrus flavor but was quite refreshing. Something nagged at her about Alayna's statement. "But what of Aiyu and his family?" she asked. "If auchs need the closeness of the community then why have they isolated themselves from it?"

"As far as I can tell," Alayna said, "Aiyu and others like him have volunteered for this isolation as their work for the community. Their stories say that many generations ago an auch known as Ngai the Great led them away from humans to hide in the mountains and for all these generations the auchs have lived with the fear that they will be discovered. Families agree to live above the great cliff they call the Edge and watch for any possible intrusion by humans. I do not know why, but their distrust of lowlanders, as they call us, is a major factor of their lives. Some families may last there for five or six seasons but most only stay for one or two. When they can no longer tolerate the isolation, another volunteers to replace them." Before she could ask any more questions Camille heard voices outside. The door opened to reveal two more women with arms full of vegetables who were thanking someone out of sight. They shut the door, stopping when they saw Camille. "For pity's sake close your mouths and come in," Alayna snapped at them. She turned to Camille. "These are the other two of our little group, Lysandra and Yvonne." Each of the women smiled as they were introduced. "This is Camille. Now put those down and get yourselves some tea so she can tell us her story. We have waited long enough for you to get back."

While they poured the tea Camille watched them. Lysandra was a hard-looking woman with short black hair. Her dark blue dress was decorated with a light blue lace frill at the neck, cuffs and hem. Yvonne was much prettier, with long red hair falling over her shoulders. She wore a green blouse and pants with calf-high boots. The blouse was embroidered with the insignia of a tree on the left breast. When they sat, Camille began to tell her story while the women prepared the vegetables that Lysandra and Yvonne had brought back. They questioned her as she spoke and offered opinions throughout the tale. They offered sympathy at the news of the death of her mother and were surprised at her ability to outdistance and elude the hunters. With numerous interruptions the meal was cooked and eaten before Camille finished with her arrival at Konungssonur and her meeting with Obiri. Her mind was taken back to her mother again because meeting these women raised the problem of her mother's words. She asked a question of her own. "My mother wore a similar dress to yours," she said to Marie. "Are you also gifted with healing?"

"I am," Marie answered simply.

"When our powers begin to mature at about your age, someone with the knowledge provides us with the clothing that tells others of these powers," Alayna told her. "Each of us has different skills and our clothes are representative of these."

Camille looked at the women sitting around the table. "Can you tell me what my dress means?" she asked.

Alayna's face saddened. "That I cannot do, child," she said. "If I were to tell you what your powers were, it would restrict your mind to my vision of your abilities. None of us know the extent of another's powers. You must discover your own path and not restrict yourself to the limitations of other's expectations. But I can tell you that your powers are becoming obvious to you because you have been given the dress. You must look to yourself and see what is there."

Camille knew that, as with her mother, there would be no further discussion on the subject. "Well, can you tell me what your skills are?" she asked.

"All in good time, child," Alayna told her. "Now it is time to rest. Tomorrow I will show you Konungssonur. For now you will sleep in Lysandra's bed. She will share with Yvonne." Camille protested that she would not put anyone out. "Don't be concerned," said Alayna. "She spends most nights in there anyway. I'm sure neither of them will object." Yvonne and Lysandra both dropped their heads and laughed when each noticed the other.

True to her word, on the next morning Alayna took Camille walking around the city. She found it bigger than anything she had ever seen or could have imagined, but everything looked the same and she was soon lost. At one point she looked down from the galleries to see that they were above the lake and she could see fish feeding on the weeds and shellfish living on the city's pylons. At other times they walked above rocks and stones. "How are you finding your way around?" Camille asked. Alayna told her that she had no idea where they were but that she recognized some of the buildings.

"Don't worry," she said. "The auchs will see us home."

#

Time passed slowly for Camille. Life in Konungssonur was uneventful. It seemed to her that the other women spent their lives preparing meals and eating them, or drinking tea. She was becoming restless after being idle for five days. It gave her time to think but thinking only brought back memories that she wanted to forget. She decided that the time had come for her to do something so she rose early on the next day, left the rooms and walked to the nearest junction of galleries where she looked to see if there were any markings to indicate where each led. There were none that she could see so she walked to the next junction. Still she could see nothing to indicate where she was or where the galleries led. She backtracked and returned to the rooms.

When the others had risen she asked them, "How do the auchs find their way around the city?" Their answers were all similar. The auchs will tell you they just know and they are unwilling or unable to explain it further. "I will find out how," she promised. Marie's smile was one usually reserved for small children declaring they can achieve the impossible, and the indulging looks of the other women only helped to make her more determined. She rose and stamped out of the rooms, slamming the door behind her. Standing on the gallery, she wondered what she would do now. She had not stood there long when an Auch appeared and asked her if he could be of help. "Can you tell me if Aiyu is still in the city?" she asked him. The auch didn't answer immediately but looked around the galleries. Another auch quickly approached and she asked her the same question.

"Yes. Aiyu still in Konungssonur," she replied.

"I am Camille, a friend of Aiyu. Can you please take me to him?"

"I am Feeta. I take you to home of Aiyu," the female auch said and turned to leave. Camille turned to thank the first auch but he was disappearing along another gallery, so she hastened to catch up to her guide. They had not gone far when Feeta knocked on another plain wooden door. When it opened and Aiyu saw Camille, he smiled a big toothy grin.

She accepted his invitation to come in and have some minted water while they chatted and thanked Feeta for her assistance. She quickly turned the conversation to the subject of navigating the city. "When I was coming here," she said, "the first auch I spoke to did not know if you had left the city. Then another was able to assist. From that I assume that auchs do not talk to each other with their minds." She waited for his reaction.

"Auchs no able talk with minds," Aiyu agreed.

"So how do you find your way around the city?" she asked.

"I just know," he told her with a shrug.

"I know that you just know, but how?" she pressed.

Aiyu tried to explain. "I want go somewhere. I know I am here. I just go."

Camille tried to think of another way to ask her question. "How do you know where your house is? Stop. I know. You just know." She thought through her question and rephrased it. "If you want to go and see Obiri, how do you know how to get there?"

Aiyu considered his reply. "I am here. I know where Obiri live. I just go."

Camille was becoming frustrated with his answers, or lack of them. "But if I wanted to go and see Obiri," she asked, "how would I get there?"

Aiyu's face lit up as he answered, "I take you."

"You will not take me," she snapped back. Aiyu looked at her in confusion. She tried again. "If I wanted to go and see Obiri without help from any auchs, how would I get there?"

Aiyu tried to understand what he was being asked. Finally he said, "We here. Obiri live two cells closer lake, three cells closer high mountains."

"Cells?" she asked.

"Not know how to say," he told her. "Some houses in cells, some houses no cell."

Suddenly the right question came to Camille. "Is there a pattern to the houses in the city?" Aiyu told her that there was and she was happy. The pattern might not be obvious but, now that she knew that there was one, she knew that she could find it.

.

CHAPTER 6

The day was coming to an end as Xavier and his men crested the hill. The road ahead led down to the Anura River and Whitebridge. The city walls skirted the far bank of the river before turning to surround the city. From their horses they could see the King's palace rising out of the parklands at the city's center. Homes, shops and other businesses were squeezed into the space between the parks and the walls. The city had long ago outgrown itself and small villages had sprouted in pockets outside the city proper. However, there were no villages occupying any land on this side of the river. Just to the left of the city from where they stood were the docks where the city's lifeblood of supplies were collected, taxed and sorted before being sent in through the south gate. The road trailed down the hill to the massive white stone bridge that had given the city its name before entering the east gate. The bridge appeared to be cut from a single piece of rock and was wide enough to take twenty horses abreast. It had spanned the river since before memory and, while some believed it to be an odd natural phenomenon, others attest that it is an artefact of an earlier more magical time.

Xavier spared the bridge no thought. His concern was getting into the city before sundown. He nudged his horse and set off down the hill at a fast walk and ,s they approached the bridge, Xavier raised his eyes to take in the great walls of stone standing as tall as five men and broken only by the watchtowers set at every one hundred paces. The open gate was wide enough for his entire squad to enter abreast if they so desired and tall enough for a horseman to enter with lance held aloft.

Xavier knew that the gates would be closed and locked at sundown, remaining closed until sunrise. The men rode across the massive bridge into the shadows that took them under the city walls, which were about thirty feet deep at the gates. Above the far end of the tunnel stood a heavy iron portcullis and between it and the gate arrow slits were positioned higher than a mounted horseman's head. Overhead the stone roof contained a number of holes, too small for a man to get through but large enough for defenders above to pour boiling oil onto any attacker that had managed to breach the massive metal-reinforced oak gates. Xavier thought, not for the first time, that he would not like to be laying siege to this city.

They passed under the portcullis into a city bathed in late afternoon light. A wide avenue bordered by ancient oaks led directly from the gate to the king's palace and he knew that similar avenues from the city's other three gates also ended there. They ignored the avenue and instead turned aside along a familiar road into the working area of the city. This road was lined with business houses offering all sorts of conveniences to the traveler. The buildings were generally clean with signs above open doors displaying the services that a person could find within. Amongst the numerous taverns and stables stood shops offering everything from cloth to weapons, meals to saddles. The blacksmith stood sweating in front of his forge with hammer in hand, shaping what appeared to be a dagger.

Xavier stopped his men in front of a large well-kept building of two stories with recently white-washed timber walls and large, clean windows. A plaque over the door proclaimed it to be the White Star Inn. He instructed the men to take the horses and see that they were stabled and fed while he arranged for rooms. The tavern was dark and noisy with groups of drinking men talking or playing games of chance. Tables were scattered around the floor while at the back of the room were small private booths, each containing a table and bench seating. Serving girls wandered among the tables carrying mugs of ale and goblets of mead or wine. A heavy table on one side of the room was laden with casks of wine and barrels of ale.

A large man stood at the table with his back to the door as Xavier entered. His arms were thicker than Xavier's legs and his bald head seemed to sink into his huge round body. A clean blue apron covered well-made clothes as he drew a mug of ale from one of the barrels.

Xavier walked through the tables till he stood behind the big man. "Still watering down the ale, you old thief?'

The man turned with fire in his eyes before his face split into a huge grin. "Welcome back, old friend," he said. "It's been a long time."

"Too long," Xavier replied shaking the extended hand. "It's good to see you again, Marcus."

Marcus looked back up the room. "You alone?" he asked.

"My men are seeing to the horses. It's been a long ride," Xavier told him.

"You'll be needing rooms then." Xavier nodded. "How many?"

"Six rooms would be comfortable if you have them," said Xavier. "It's been a while since we were comfortable."

Marcus signalled one of the serving girls over and told her to prepare six rooms while he poured two ales. "Come and sit," he said, "and give me the news of the world."

With tankards in hand they moved to one of the private booths to talk and a big-muscled man ensured their privacy. Xavier lifted and swallowed half the ale in one swig before answering, "The world moves on."

They swapped polite conversation until their tankards stood empty between them. "It feels good to be back in the city again. There is no life in the villages. They all remind me of Redhill, and I have no intention of ever returning there."

"You have spoken of Redhill before. Is it really that bad?"

"It is my past. My destiny is in the future, and here is where my future waits. I love Whitebridge with its people and politics, and I need to be close to the heart of our group."

Marcus leaned close before asking in a whispered voice, "What do you need at this time?"

"I need to talk to the boss," Xavier told him.

"I can set up a meeting but it won't be for about a week or so. He's busy," Marcus said.

"This is too important," Xavier told him. "He will not want to wait to hear this news."

The innkeeper's eyebrows rose as he looked at his friend. "And you will not tell me what this is about? That is probably wise, though no word would pass my lips. I'll see what I can do," he said. With that he stood and went back to the serving table.

Xavier looked at where his men sat. Having seen to the horses they had entered while the two talked and had left them to their privacy. Xavier rose and joined them while Marcus had his girls bring them all fresh tankards and plates of spicy rabbit stew. Although he had issued his orders on approaching the city Xavier reminded them once again that they were to say nothing regarding the events of Thistledowne or their time since. Though he trusted his men to obey, he also knew the effects of ale in loosening a man's tongue. Xavier did not see Marcus leave or talk to anyone but when the meals were finished a serving girl approached and passed him a note. It told him only to be alone in his room at noon on the next day. He slipped the note in his pocket and ordered another round of drinks. Marcus looked over and gave him a nod and for the rest of the evening the men enjoyed the atmosphere of the tavern. The sounds and smells of the city began to relax him.

Next morning Xavier took the opportunity to lie in his bed late. When he finally rose and went down to the tavern for his morning meal his men were waiting. They had already eaten so he told them to go out and enjoy the free time, but that he wanted them back in the tavern before midday where they were to wait for him. Xavier took the time to enjoy a bowl of hot porridge laced with honey. When he finished his meal he went back to his room and waited. He was sitting on his bed cleaning his sword as the sun reached its peak when he heard a knock at the door. "Come," he called and looked up as the door quickly opened and shut. When he saw the man who had entered, he dropped his sword and rose to take the man's extended hand. "Lipstadt," he said. "It's good to see you again."

"Welcome back, Leader," Lipstadt replied. "What news do you have that is so important that I must put aside my duties to hear it?"

Xavier proceeded to provide details of all that had occurred since the chase for the girl had begun. Lipstadt listened in silence then questioned Xavier for more details of the auch and the entrance to the high country until he was satisfied that he had the full story. He sat and thought for some minutes before he raised his head and said, "You have done well. Wait at the inn for further orders." He went on to give Xavier more instructions before rising and walking to open the door where he paused. "We will meet again soon," he said and then he was gone.

Xavier waited a few minutes before going down to the tavern to join his men. Marcus approached and asked if all was well. "Service is excellent as always," Xavier assured him. Marcus gave a quick nod and left them to talk. "We will be staying at the inn for a few days," he told the men. "We will meet here each morning and evening for further orders but otherwise the time is yours." Most of the men would search out the gambling rooms for some fun while others would find different ways to spend their money. Jaimz was the last to leave and he asked Xavier to join him. "You go and enjoy yourself," Xavier told him. "I have many things to think about." Jaimz waited a moment before leaving in a hurry to catch up with the last of the men. Marcus joined Xavier later and the two old friends chatted much of the day away. Although he trusted the big innkeeper he made no mention of the events at Thistledowne or the auch.

In the late afternoon he left the tavern and took a walk around the streets nearby. He had been away from the city for more than a year and missed the bustle and the pleasures it provided. While he walked his mind wandered back to the days before his departure and his orders to take his men and find work in the little villages in the north. His men never knew who their instructions had come from but they were loyal to him and the cause. As usual the mission had been delicate and required careful orchestration. He still did not fully understand the meaning of the orders but he was a soldier and did his duty with pride. Like every other member he believed in the superiority of mankind, just as he knew that the Council only issued its instructions with this in mind. He did not have the full picture but still he wondered why he had been instructed to incite the people to rise against anyone with powers. He did not understand it, but if his dream was to succeed he must be seen to be loyal. It would be much easier if the Council simply ordered them to kill the witches. The Council, too, obviously had a greater plan in motion and, even though he couldn't see the importance of having the people turn against the witches, he knew that he had the skills to do this work well. Since the day he had first heard Piaz speak he understood the power of words and their use in influencing people. His world changed when he discovered his ability to unite people in a cause. The witch of Thistledowne was a perfect example. The townsfolk had respected her and considered her one of their own but they had turned on her with his intervention and later were too embarrassed to even talk about what they had done. Words, he thought, could be more powerful than an army.

By the fifth day after their arrival in Whitebridge the men were showing signs of restlessness. Unlike Xavier most of them could take only so much of city living. They had quenched their appetites for city life and spent their money at the gambling houses. Now they found themselves with nothing to do and no money to do it with. Xavier sat in his room oiling his saddle again when a knock at the door stopped him. He put the saddle aside and rested his hand on the hilt of his sword as he called for the person to enter. One of Marcus' serving girls slipped into the room. He had seen her before but given her no attention. She was dressed in a black skirt and white blouse, the uniform of the inn. Her dark hair hung down either side of an innocent-looking but not-too-pretty face. "Leader Xavier," she said while touching her right fist to her left shoulder. "I have been requested to take you to a meeting.

Would you come with me, please?"

Xavier hesitated. He had expected Lipstadt to come and give him his instructions, as he had before, but the girl gave the correct signal and so he buckled his sword belt and asked her to lead on. The girl took him down the servant's stairs at the back of the building. As they approached the bottom she held up her hand for him to wait. The stairs flowed onto a hallway leading towards the tavern room with two doorways on one side, the second of which led to the kitchen, from the sounds within, and where Marcus stood guard. She quickly led Xavier down the remaining stairs, slipped through the closed door, down another flight of stairs and into the cellar, weaving her way among the barrels, leading Xavier to the far wall. Opening a trap door hidden in the floor and taking a torch from the wall, she signaled Xavier to go down the ladder. She followed, shutting the trap door behind her. Without a word the girl set out along a tunnel. As they walked, they passed the entrances to other tunnels and at each intersection a plaque set in the floor indicated directions with glyphs, only some of which made sense to him. Xavier had not known of the existence of this maze beneath the city, but the girl clearly showed she was accustomed to traveling in these tunnels and it did not take long to reach their destination. She stopped at another ladder and set the torch in a bracket on the wall before climbing up through another trap door into a small room. Two armed guards sheathed their swords when they saw the girl and opened a plain timber door set in one wall. Xavier walked through and the girl followed, closing the door behind them.

The room he found himself in was comfortably furnished and lined with timber but there were no windows, and the only door was the one they had entered through. Torches hung on the wall, giving off a warm glow, and vents in the ceiling allowed the smoke to escape. The room held a table inlaid with a four-pointed star and six large, padded chairs, three of which were occupied by well-dressed men. A large black flag bearing a single four-pointed white star hung on one wall. Xavier recognized only Lipstadt. His jaw dropped when the girl stepped past him and took one of the spare seats.

"Welcome," said Lipstadt. "Please take a seat." Xavier did as he was instructed although he was not sure why he was here. When the boss had not come to his room, he thought that he was being taken to see the man and receive further instructions. Lipstadt smiled at his confusion. "Don't be alarmed, Leader. Allow me to introduce some friends," he said. "We, along with one other who is not available, make up the Council of The Society. Their names are unimportant at this time." He laughed at the expression that crossed Xavier's face. Very few people knew the names of the councilors and even less had ever seen them in their role. Xavier only knew that they had great influence within the city where more than a quarter of the common folk were members. He suspected that each of these people had different responsibilities. He knew The Society was structured so that each member only knew the person directly above them in the organization. Secrecy was the key to The Society's survival until they were strong enough to declare themselves to the seven kingdoms.

Lipstadt continued. "I believe that now you are wondering why we have brought you to this meeting." He waited a moment before asking, "Can you suggest a reason for this unusual circumstance?"

Xavier looked at each of the council members before answering. "You have discussed my report and its implications," he told them confidently. "You wish to hear my story for yourselves because it requires a change in the direction of your plans or may require work by someone with certain abilities or particular knowledge that you do not wish to make known at this time. You think I may be the person you seek but each of you wished to make your own decision."

The Council members looked at each other. Lipstadt laughed. "I told you he was a good man," he said. "You are correct in your assessment," he told Xavier. "Your sighting of the auch and the discovery of a route beyond the Great Wall have given us much to consider. While this news forces us to reconsider the Grand Design, it also provides us with a great opportunity. Our members are spread over the seven kingdoms, but our strength has always been here in the Kingdom of Arenia. King Leopold's reign has allowed us to consolidate and build our resources and we now have the chance to advance our plans but, as you suggested, we need someone with particular knowledge and the commitment to ensure that we succeed."

"And you believe I may be that person?" stated Xavier.

"Yes. We have watched you for some years. You have impressed us with your ability to achieve the required results and your commitment to the cause," said one of the seated men. "But we have another task for you. You must take your men north again and return with proof of the auch attacks on the unprotected human communities there. You will bring this proof straight to the king and plead for his aid." Xavier looked at the four faces in the room. He understood what was required of him, and it both frightened and excited him. The unknown man spoke again. "The king will be strongly advised that he must ride forth and defend the northern borders from invasion by the auchs. He will decide that he should request aid from the dwarves. When the dwarves are sent into battle against the auchs, our purposes will be served, no matter what the outcome."

"But what if the king does not react as expected."

The serving girl answered him. "All is not as it seems. Our friend Lord

Lipstadt will see that Leopold makes the right decisions."

"Lord Lipstadt?" he asked looking to the man who had given him his orders these last years.

The girl smiled and spoke again. "Leader Xavier, let me introduce Lipstadt, Lord of Whitebridge and senior advisor to King Leopold of Arenia." Xavier looked at the man he knew as the organizer of operations with new eyes.

"What do you make of our plans?" asked Lipstadt.

"A bold plan," said Xavier, "but one with great possibilities."

Lipstadt looked at each of the Council members and each gave a single nod to his unasked question. "This meeting is over," he said. "We are all busy people and have many things to attend to. Have a productive trip, Leader."

They rose and filed out the door before disappearing into the tunnels. The serving girl turned to Xavier. "Time to go," she said. "For convenience, you can call me Beth." Xavier followed her back through the tunnels to the inn, his mind a storm of thoughts.

At the base of the ladder Xavier stopped and turned to Beth. "Councilor?" he asked.

"Yes," she told him, "but beyond this point I am just a serving girl. It allows me to observe without being seen." She smiled and climbed the ladder.

That evening Xavier told his men to prepare to ride on the next morning.

"Where are we going?" asked Thom.

"Back to the mountains," he told them with a grin..

CHAPTER 7

Aiyu leaned against the wooden rail on the outskirts of the city. Before them the surface of the deep green lake was undisturbed and reflected the mountains beyond. The sky was clear and the air crisp while below him small fish darted in and out around the pylons looking for food, trying not to be seen by larger fish. "This one of Bhata favorite places," he said to Camille who stood quietly beside him. "When she first come here, we spend many times watch world from this place."

"I can see why," she said. "It is so beautiful. There is nothing to compare it to where I come from."

"No where she come from too." Camille looked at him in surprise. She had assumed that Bhata's home town would also be in the mountains. "Ptoraki past mountains across Sometimes Lake. It sit on edge of world. It is beautiful place and when I there I sit and watch water like Bhata watch mountains. Be just different."

Camille looked out from the gallery and wondered if Thistledowne ever had anything that could grab at a person's heart as this place took hers. "When did you meet Bhata?" she asked.

"Many seasons back. Elders choose her for my mating. On fourteenth year father take me to Ptoraki. I meet Bhata for first time, stay next season. After mating ceremony we return, begin to make home."

"Why did you decide to come back here?" she asked. This time it was Aiyu's turn to show surprise. "I mean," said Camille, "you could have stayed and lived in Ptoraki." She had trouble saying the name.

"It not way things be," Aiyu explained. "After mating ceremony woman always move to live in clan of mate. Just wrong to live in clan of woman." They settled back again to enjoy the scenery. Something moved beneath the surface of the lake, breaking the smooth image of the reflected mountains. Aiyu glanced down to the water but paid the hidden fish no attention. Instead, he spoke again. "Next season I take Agort to Randvar to meet mate."

Images of Agort teaching her to play slapstick and wrestling with his sister flashed through Camille's mind. "He is too young," she said.

"It his time. Elders choose Qark to be mate many years back. Say she be good with him. He stay one season, learn to know each other. Be mated after longnights. Return here to begin life."

"But he doesn't even know her."

"No need. Elders decide it be right. It is way of things in Sysla."

"In the Sysla? I've heard that word before. What is a Sysla?" Camille asked.

Aiyu tried to explain, "Konungssonur is Sysla and nine more Sysla."

"So a Sysla is a city?"

Aiyu shook his head. "No. Sysla is area." He tried to think of a comparison. "Like country but no king. Sysla have many cities. All city guided by elder.

Important matters happen affect all auchs, then elders meet. One elder selected to lead others until he die, then new elder leads. Obiri lead Konungssonur."

"Now I am really confused," said Camille. "You told me that this city is called Konungssonur but now it is not. Konungssonur is a country that is not a country. Next you'll be telling me that you are an auch who is not an auch."

Aiyu laughed. "It no hard. Sysla name is Konungssonur and Obiri lead Konungssonur. While he lead, this city also Konungssonur, but when die this city go back to old name, Ulffinnr. Simple. Then all auchs know which city lead Sysla. Until time come for new leader we live in Konungssonur." They sat quietly enjoying the peace as the sun slowly crawled down the western sky while Camille tried to make sense of what she had just been told. Aiyu's words cut through her thoughts.

"Could be right."

"And what might I be right about?" asked Camille.

"You say Aiyu is auch who is no auch."

"How do you mean?"

"Auchs love live in city. Need others, no be away from people. Most auchs no can move to farm at Edge. I love be at farm or mountains. Bhata too. That maybe why we mated. As child I love leave city, go explore valleys. Sometimes no come back many days. I think that why this place special to both of us."

"I feel the same. I appreciate all that you have done for me but I would rather be alone in the trees or out on the open plains. I love the open sky and the animals."

They sat together in silence for some time until the cold air caused Camille to shiver. Aiyu offered to take her back to the warmth of the rooms. As they rose, Camille gave one last look over the lake before turning to follow Aiyu across the maze of galleries. Just as they were approaching the rooms a loud roar cracked the air. Aiyu spun as a mass of blue hit him, knocking him to the ground. Both auchs came quickly to their feet and faced each other before breaking into grumbling laughter. Aiyu flung his arms around the other auch and lifted him clear of the ground. "Good see Battok," he said. When they stepped back from each other Aiyu introduced him. "Camille, this Battok. We run around galleries, grow up together, or I did. I no think Battok ever grow up." Battok gave her a big tooth grin. "Battok, this Camille. Her mother killed by her people. Holdbori protect her, bring to us."

With a deep bow Battok said, "Honor to meet one Holdbori choose."

"I am not chosen. I am just a girl who was in need of help," Camille told him.

"She no yet discover path," said Aiyu. The two auchs exchanged glances that seemed to Camille as if an entire conversation had just taken place about her.

"Come," said Battok. "Others wait see you. I sure they want meet Camille too."

Aiyu looked at Camille with an "I'm sorry" expression on his face and she laughed. "I would love to meet your friends," she said. Battok roared his delight and set out at a brisk pace over the galleries. As she rushed to keep up she could see that Aiyu and Battok were of similar size but where Aiyu appeared quiet and thoughtful, Battok was the opposite. His face seemed to be split into a permanent grin while his left eye sagged, pulled down by a scar on his cheek. He was loud and his deep rumbling voice gave the impression that he was always laughing.

"Is Zon with others?" Aiyu called.

"She wait with others."

"That answer why such hurry," Aiyu gibed, then explained to Camille, "Zon is Battok mate. They no bear be apart." He laughed at Battok's pained expression.

"It just she much better be around than you," he said.

Aiyu laughed again. "Battok and Zon always in hurry. Both like have fun. Careful or end up in one of their jokes." Battok was about to reply but Aiyu cut him off. "Hurry. No want keep Zon wait, or need find way to apologize." Battok waited only a moment without answer before walking on. Aiyu laughed and followed. Fortunately for Camille they had not gone far when Battok opened a door and stood aside to allow them to enter. Though the room was quite large inside, it seemed crowded. She guessed that all of Aiyu's friends had gathered to see him again. Space was made for the three of them and Aiyu was buried in hugs and mock tackles. Camille was introduced to Aiyu's childhood friends. The room was loud with laughter and friendship. When Camille tried to find a corner to sit out of the way Zon came and drew her back into the group. She was bigger than Battok with a face that was relaxed and comforting. Her eyes sparkled and she had a tuft of blue hair on her chin. Her skin was a little lighter in color and shone with a warm glow.

Battok controlled the conversation with his stories and jokes.

"Camille must hear time Aiyu and Hirith had half city searching them. If caught they be hung by feet from tree full day." He doubled over in laughter at the thought.

"Remember well. Also remember you disconnect ramp to farms. Run to hills, We follow, keep you safe. But you leave, come back. Make sure we get blame."

"Great joke. When you found, no one believe either able pull such good prank. I get blame in end."

The stories continued. It seemed that everyone in the room had some tale to tell about the havoc caused around the city. The other member of this childhood gang sat quietly at the end of the table beside his mate. As the biggest auch in the room, Hirith's entire bulk shouted strength and control. Ethru, his mate, was almost as big. Camille tried to think of what made these two different from the others in the room. She decided that neither of them said much, but when they did, everyone stopped and listened. Hirith was more than liked by his friends, he was respected. The last of the day faded into night and the night crawled on. The lateness caught up with Camille. When she began to doze in her chair, Aiyu called an end to the gathering, wishing them all well as he picked up the girl, cradling her in his enormous arms, and took her home. Camille opened her eyes long enough to say, "I like your friends, Aiyu," before rolling over, sound asleep..

CHAPTER 8

It had taken weeks of effort, marking intersections with pieces of charcoal, and Camille had been totally lost on many occasions, but eventually the pattern of the city began to reveal itself. With some simple directions she could now find her own way from point to point most of the time. "We are very impressed with the way you have learnt the secret of Konungssonur," Alayna told her once she had poured herself a cup of dandelion tea and joined them. "I have been living here much longer, and it is only by looking at the map you are making that I begin to understand the shape of the city. I still cannot see any pattern in what you draw." Camille explained that she needed something to occupy her time and mind and that any of them could have done it if they needed to. Alayna looked at the other women before answering. "Maybe, but none of us had the drive to do so. And even if we did, the pattern of Konungssonur is very complex. I don't think that any of us could have seen that it existed."

"Neither did I," admitted Camille, "but I knew that auchs could find their way around with ease. I kept asking Aiyu questions until he eventually told me that the city was laid down on a pattern. Once I knew that one existed, I just had to figure it out."

Alayna took a sip of tea and looked closely at Camille. "Have you thought any more on your abilities?" she asked. Camille realized that she had not. She had devoted herself to mapping the city, and all other problems had taken second place. "That is as I thought," Alayna said. "Your mother gave you your dress to initiate your learning. Unless you start the process, your powers will die within you and you will not reach your potential. Once the powers start to show themselves, they must be developed or lost. The power will grow as it is used. The only limits to our powers are those we place on ourselves."

Camille complained that she had no idea of what her powers were. "So how can I develop and use them?" she asked.

Alayna sat back in her chair. "You have already begun the process and you need to continue this. We recognized this when you first told us your story. You have been distracted by mapping the city and the time has come when we must intervene. It is time to stop this work. We have decided that we must help as best we can before you throw away your destiny. The time has now come to explain our powers. Long ago, in the memory of the world the magic was strong, far stronger than any of us could imagine. At that time all people held abilities, men and women. But over the centuries, the magic has left the world and the abilities left the people. Only a few now live who can grasp what remains of the magic and these cling to what they have. No talent may be permitted to be forgotten."

Marie took up the discussion. "You recognized my dress because it is similar to your mothers. I have not met your mother but by knowing that she wore the yellow I know the direction her powers took her, if not her ability."

Alayna continued, "The powers of witches can be divided into five abilities. Most witches are limited to one of these. Your mother and Marie have the ability to see into the body and know what is to be done to make things right with it. Most refer to this as healing and through time the healers have taken to wearing yellow as a sign of their calling."

Lysandra spoke next. "Then there are those that wear the green. We refer to ourselves as forestals. We are able to communicate with the life of the land. We can hear the voices of the animals and birds. Some have the ability to understand the plants and trees, some are even able to influence the life of the forest in small ways. I wish that I were powerful enough to hear the trees," she finished with a wistful tone in her voice.

"There are not many witches among the auchs," said Marie, "but the few that exist are mainly forestals."

Something occurred to Camille. "Bhata wears a green stone around her neck carved in the shape of a tree. It is said that she speaks with the spirits and receives instruction from Holdbori. Is she a forestal?"

"Yes. It is the way of the auchs to believe that the spirits are their ancestors who have moved on, speaking through the creatures of the land, but it is only a connection with the mind of these animals that they hear," explained Alayna. "The other three groups are all known as elementals. These witches have strong ties to one of the three earth elements: fire, air or water. Depending on their strength they are able to influence these in different ways. I wear red to show my ties to fire and Yvonne's blue ties her to water."

Camille looked around the table at the women watching her. "Then my abilities must be in the element of air."

"No. That is an example of why we must allow you to develop your own abilities and not have them influenced by our words. We must be careful not to taint your learning. It is a logical conclusion, but it is not correct. You will have to think further on this."

"But my dress is black and that is the only ability remaining," complained Camille.

"Elementals with their abilities tied to air generally wear clothes of purple hues," said Yvonne. Camille had been told there were only five abilities, yet she was not tied to any of these. Her confusion showed clearly on her face.

"Don't worry child," said Alayna. "You have shown that you have the strength and ability to solve this problem as you did with the city map. Look to your dress and look inside yourself. You know the answer but you must look before you can see. Now we can say no more, but I have faith in you." Alayna changed the subject to more general matters and Camille knew that she would get no more from them. She sat quietly while the others chatted and thought about what she had been told. But the answers would not come. That night she removed her dress and hung it on the hook beside her bed before retiring. She lay awake in the half-light contemplating what she had been told. Alayna had implied that her abilities had already shown themselves, but when? Her mind took her back to the night her mother died and her flight to safety. There was something about the story that she needed to remember or understand. She fell asleep with scraps of memory bouncing around in her head. Dawn had come and morning had long settled on the mountains when her mind yelled at her to wake. Her eyes snapped open to see the dress hanging before her eyes. The dress is the key, her mind repeated over and over. She quickly rose and grabbed the object of her thoughts, throwing it over her shoulders as she threw the curtain aside. The four women sat eating breakfast and she joined them, excited by her new-found knowledge. "Will you tell me anything more about my abilities?" All four shook their heads in reply. "Then if I tell you my thoughts, will you tell me if I am correct?"

Alayna looked to the others before answering, "We will do what we can."

Camille went on with her thoughts. "My mother was a yellow and I think she was strong in her abilities. You told me that yellows could see inside a person and know what needs to be done. I think they can also see the possibilities or what could be within a witch. Is this correct?", she asked Marie, who nodded in reply. My mother gave me a black dress. My thought is that she saw in me more than one ability. Am I right?"

Finally, Alayna answered her. "Yes. The black is reserved for those with abilities beyond one field. You have proven again your skill at solving problems when you set your mind to them."

"But the emblem is still a problem," said Camille. "I cannot understand the meaning of the shield or the swords and then there are the six colors. Do these represent my abilities? And why are there six colors if there are only five abilities?"

"Patience, child," Alayna assured her. "You may be correct, but things are not always as they seem. I cannot advise you on this or I may distract you from the real truth. I can only suggest that time will reveal its secrets. You have proven your abilities with problems. When the time is right, the meaning will be clear. I will say no more. Just remember, you must not limit yourself to the thinking of others or to your own doubts."

"But the sixth bar, the orange bar, what is it?" pleaded Camille.

The women shared glances. Alayna said, "We will tell you one last thing and no more. There was once a sixth ability. It is a long-forgotten art and in truth I do not know of anyone who can remember even the nature of it. None have shown anything other than the five abilities for many centuries. Ask no more."

#

Camille walked around Konungssonur to think. She walked to the edge of the city. In front of her lay the fields of crops with auchs tending to them. A nearby ramp led down to the ground, and she felt herself drawn out into the farms. It was comforting in some way to walk among the plants. She had gone only a short distance before she found a rock to sit on. Closing her eyes, she tried to reach out over the fields and immediately felt she was being watched. The feeling was not strong but was familiar as it floated at the edge of her perception. She focused her mind and asked the presence to show itself but nothing happened. Concentrating even harder she sent a message of safety. A squirrel slowly approached from under the leaves of a broadfruit plant. It came to her feet, and she attempted asking what it had been doing. In a strange way she seemed to understand that it had been collecting seeds and pods and storing them for when the cold white came.

The sound of someone approaching interrupted them. The squirrel quickly returned to its hiding place under the leaves before an auch appeared along the track carrying a basket of mixed fruits. Camille sat for a few moments and thought about what she had just done. She knew that she had somehow communicated with the squirrel. When she rose to return to the city, her head spun and she fell to her knees. Nausea flooded through her. She sank slowly to the ground waiting for the feeling to pass. When the surges of illness eased, she climbed carefully to her feet and stood for a few moments before starting back. Each step was an effort and brought fresh waves of giddiness. Another auch appeared and, seeing her difficulty, picked her up, cradling her in his enormous arms as he carried her back to her rooms. She was too overcome with illness to be embarrassed at being carried.

Seeing Camille prone in the arms of the auch, Alayna ushered him in to lay her on her bed. Lysandra fetched some water and a mug while Marie knelt beside the bed to check on her. Camille was beginning to feel better but she submitted to the examination. After satisfying herself that nothing serious was wrong, Alayna asked her what had happened. She told them about finding the squirrel and somehow communicating with it but explained that thought it was more a transfer of feelings rather than a crude conversation. "You have overexerted yourself," Alayna told her. "Your powers will grow with time and use. Learn them but do not try to rush them." Each day Camille went to the fields to test herself. Soon the squirrel came to expect her visits and showed itself when she called.

CHAPTER 9

As the women sat around the table preparing lunch some days later there was a knock at the door. Marie opened it to find Urak waiting. "Obiri ask Camille come Torkeen now," he asked. He led Camille towards the center of the city, an area she had not explored much. Urak brought her to a large timber wall with two wide double doors held open by young auchs. They entered and Camille found herself in a massive amphitheater. Tiers of seating surrounded the room. She stood beside a raised area between the doors. Hanging on the wall above the stage was a gold chain and medallion inlaid with a white star. A few auchs sat on the bench seats to watch the proceedings. Obiri sat with Aiyu and three others at a large table on the stage. He invited Camille to join them as the Torkeen was about to begin. "This Torkeen ready. All who need talk, all who need listen, now here. Obiri of Konungssonur call this Torkeen to hear words of Camille of lowlands. Aiyu of Konungssonur ask talk too on events affect Camille and auch nation. Torkeen welcome elders of southern cities. Is honor to hear wisdom Asiron of Orvar, Veetan of Numi, Yuntak of Nott. Four elders speak for Sysla. All who hear our words honor them as will of auch nation."

Each of the elders responded, "Is honor speak for all auchs at this Torkeen."

Obiri smiled at Camille. "Now Torkeen begin. All words we hear will be true. Auchs will no hear false words. All agree?" Camille assured everyone present that everything she would say would be the truth. "Then begin. Tell story," said Obiri. While Camille once again related the events at Thistledowne and her escape to the mountains she studied each of the elders. Asiron was a huge man, even by auch standards, yet despite his size he looked feeble. His face drooped and his hands shook while resting on the table. Even so Camille saw that his eyes were clear and focused. Yuntak listened intently as the story was told. He looked younger than the others and appeared uncomfortable with his position. On the other hand, Veetan seemed not to be listening as she sat shelling peas with nimble fingers.

When she had finished her story she added, "I arrived here by accident or luck. The auchs have been kind and protected me and for this I am grateful. I would like to see those responsible for my mother's death brought before the king's justice but I wish no harm on the auchs. I understand and accept your desire to remain hidden from humans and I accept any decisions you make. Thank you for listening to me."

Veetan looked up from her peas. "Your story terrible. But why Holdbori choose bring you Konungssonur? What he want us do? Sometimes his wish clear, other time shroud his will in smoke. Auchs must have clear air to understand but smoke gather around you like flies on spoiled food. I think Holdbori no want us know wishes yet. Sorry for mother. Sorry you must tell again."

Obiri spoke again. "Aiyu now speak to Torkeen on this matter."

Aiyu sat forward in his chair. "I thank elders for let me talk. Holdbori come, tell me go to Edge. I see Camille walk at bottom. Holdbori tell, go bring to Konungssonur. All know Holdbori protect and guide her to us. Five spirit talkers now come from lowlands, find way Konungssonur last four years. Humans fear spirit talkers. Wonder how many no reach

Konungssonur. How many die. Believe Holdbori want auchs act. Time come auchs no more hide. I no want see auchs fight against humans but ask, do humans want fight auchs? Auchs live in peace many generations. I no think humans want fight auchs. I think humans forget auchs. But humans attack spirit talkers. If humans no want spirit talkers live with them, auchs offer they live in auch cities. There no many spirit talkers in auch nation. Auchs can offer help for any want live with us."

"Auchs hide for good reason," said Asiron. He pointed back over his shoulder. "Every city hold symbol of freedom. It remind people of suffer at hands of humans. Auchs will no risk freedom."

The comments took Camille by surprise. She looked up again at the medallion hanging on the wall. The round black stone hanging on the heavy gold chain highlighted the white four-pointed star on its face. She wondered how the auchs had suffered when people didn't know they even existed. She determined to ask Aiyu at a later time. "Lowlanders chase spirit talkers, find auchs. Auchs no more able hide. Ngai teach peace but also teach auchs sometimes need fight. I ask elders look what happen in last years. Change come to lowlands. I think auchs be involved. Auchs have no choice. We must prepare," said Aiyu.

Veetan spoke sternly. "Elders know change happen in world. This reason Torkeen now gather. Camille story not new. Others live in Konungssonur. More live in other cities. We finish listen now. Elders go think, we make decision. Then tell all. Now Aiyu return to family. I sure he be away too long."

"More items elders wish to discuss. We talk on this problem about lowlanders over next days. Many things we must consider," said Asiron.

Camille followed Aiyu out of the meeting room and together they walked along the twisted galleries in silence, each unscrambling their own thoughts, until they found themselves once again overlooking the lake and mountains.

"What will you do now?" Camille asked.

"Elders tell Aiyu go back family. I go."

There was a hint of disappointment in her voice as she answered, "Good. Bhata acts tough but it is obvious that you love each other, and I am sure that she misses you. I appreciate the help both of you have given but my problems are now in the hands of the elders. We must accept their decision. I hope to see both of you again soon, and the children. But I won't climb that damn cliff again," she said with a laugh. Aiyu told her that he would be leaving as soon as he could get his things together. She threw her arms wide and gave him a big hug though tears threatened to pour from her, she would not have him see her cry. Ashamed of her own weakness she pushed herself back and changed the subject. "In the Torkeen you said Ngai saved the auchs from the humans. Is he the same auch you can trace your name back to?"

"Same auch."

"But how could he save your people from us if we have never heard of auchs in our histories?"

"Not know that."

"Then how did he save your people?"

"Elders are keepers of wisdom. Ask Obiri."

Camille was disappointed with his answer. "Obiri is busy with the other elders. He will not have time for my questions."

Aiyu's eyes lit up as an idea came to him. "We ask Kallu. She learn wisdom of Obiri." They rushed back through the maze of galleries. When they found Kallu and explained what they wanted she was only too happy to tell the tale.

"In time long ago auchs work farms in land past end of world. Humans take auchs, put in cages with other people called wraith. Humans make cages walk on water, bring to this land to fight but auchs and wraith no want fight. Wraith try leave but humans attack. Wraith fight humans. Humans begin kill auchs, Darkward fight to save auchs. Darkward remembered by auchs because he die to save Ngai. Then Ngai call auchs to fight. Many humans die, others run away. Ngai lead auchs into mountains to hide from humans."

"And what happened to the wraith?" asked Camille.

"Wraith leave. No see again but always remember."

In the days following Aiyu's departure life went back to normal. She continued to make her trips out of the city to talk with her squirrel and her skills were improving. At one stage she tried to find other animals but only received brief glimpses of awareness. It seemed that distance made contact more difficult, but she remembered Alayna's advice and did not take distance to be a limitation but rather something that she could improve upon.

#

The table was a hive of conversation as the five witches ate breakfast. Zon rushed in without knocking. "Marie, come please. Battok be injured."

Marie rose immediately. "I'll come with you," Camille told her. "I may be of use." Zon rushed them through the city towards the lake. The problem was obvious when they arrived - a piece of the walkway was missing. Battok lay on the oyster-encrusted rocks below, not moving. A piece of the broken gallery protruded from his leg and he was bleeding from lacerations over his body.

"We need to get down there. Bring a ladder," demanded Marie. They waited agonizing minutes until the ladder arrived, then rushed to get down to the rocks below where they knelt beside the unconscious Battok and quickly examined his injuries. His skin had faded from its natural blue to a dull grey and his body seemed to be painted in blood. Zon appeared beside them, frantic with concern for her mate. Marie was forced to have her taken away while they examined the injured auch. Marie thought out loud, "The cuts are bad but not life-threatening, and the timber through the leg can be fixed, but there must be something else. Any auch can take this type of punishment without too many problems."

"Can you not look into him to see what is wrong?" asked Camille.

"I will try but I am not sure that I have the power for this." Marie began to focus her mind on Battok. Camille thought of what her mother would do and she too began to look for the auch's injuries. The timber in his leg would cause no concern, though Battok would probably walk with a limp for some time, so she continued to scan up through his body. Everything seemed fine until she reached his head and saw a fracture in the skull with blood pooling beneath, putting pressure on the auch's brain. "Marie, you can see this, can't you?" she thought.

Marie sat up and looked at Camille with wide eyes. "What did you do?" she asked.

"Nothing," defended Camille. "I just saw the problem and hoped you saw it also."

Marie continued to look strangely at her while calling for a sharp knife. Then she said to Camille, "Show me again."

Camille again scanned the injured auch's head and found the blood. "Here," she thought and watched intently as Marie made the incision in Battok's head. Blood pooled from the cut. Marie asked if the pressure was easing, and Camille watched as the mass of blood above the brain diminished. "It is," she said. Marie had the watching auchs prepare a litter to carry the injured Battok to a safe place while she and Camille began stitching the lacerations and removing the timber from his leg. After they had done all they could, Camille asked some auchs to carry him back to his rooms and lay him on his bed. When they were at Battok's rooms, Marie told Zon that all they could do now was to wait and that they would return later to check on him, but Camille showed no intention of leaving. She dragged a chair across the room and sat beside the bed, across from Zon.

"It going to be great joke," Zon whispered after they had sat for a while.

"A joke? What joke?"

"Battok have idea. He always have best jokes. We going blame Aiyu. Be remembered as best joke of year. Now he lie here, afraid he no live."

Camille scanned Battok's head again. "He will live, he is already beginning to heal, but he will be sore for days to come. What joke were you planning?"

Zon gave a little laugh. "We prepare all night. Disconnect galleries, hang on rope so swing when walk on. Be good see faces of people try cross. We begin lower last one, but it caught. Battok climb under to fix. I pull from top. He nearly fix problem when whole gallery swing and fall. It knock Battok, he fall after. I try call to him but he no move."

For the rest of the day the two women sat beside the bed as Camille regularly monitored his condition. Even though Camille said that he was doing fine, Zon remained worried until Battok gave a groan and opened his eyes for a moment. Camille again looked into his body, searching for signs of burning blood. The cuts and the wound in his leg were clean and his brain appeared to have suffered no serious damage. Pleased with his condition, she told Zon he was healing well and to watch him and inform her if there were any changes. She stretched and walked to the door. She needed some rest. Outside she asked a passing auch if he could guide her to her rooms. When she entered the other four women were sitting in wait for her arrival.

"Sit down," commanded Alayna. "Yvonne, get her some tea." Camille wanted to rest but did not have the energy to argue. She joined them at the table

"What happened?" Alayna demanded.

"Battok was injured and we tried to help him," she answered.

"Not the auch," Alayna dismissed. "I want to know how you grabbed Marie's mind and dragged it to the injury."

Camille's eyes widened. "I did what?" she asked.

Alayna studied her for a moment. "You really don't know what you have done, do you?"

Marie told her, "I was looking at his leg when you grabbed my mind and dragged it up to look at his head. Then when we looked again you took control of my hand and guided it to the exact place needed to relieve the pressure in his skull. I have not heard of anything like this."

She stared at Marie without understanding. None of it made any sense to her. She slumped in the chair and only then did the women realize how tired she must be. They put her to bed but next morning the women were ready to continue their questions. She could not give them any answers and the best she was able to offer was a promise to think about it.

After a quick breakfast she went back to check on Battok. Her scan showed that his head was improving, and his cuts were clear of burning. She asked if there was any nightweed available, but no one had heard of the herb so she asked instead that a broth be prepared with pumpkin, thornbush and thistle flowers. It would have to suffice. Over the next few days, she kept a regular check on Battok and was happy with his improvement. At the same time she considered what had occurred on the rocks below the city. She had acted on instinct and could not remember what she had done.

#

Urak's knock stirred Camille from an afternoon nap. "Is everything all right? Is Battok worse?"

"No," said Urak, "Battok well. Torkeen return. Obiri ask you come."

She followed him back to the meeting room where the elders were sitting at the central table. About thirty auchs sat in small groups on the benches watching the proceedings.

Obiri did not waste time. "Elders talk problem in lowlands. Make decision, ask here so all hear. We try answer questions if you have them."

Veetan spoke next. "Decision of Torkeen is first concern, must be safety of auch nation. Elders no put people at risk. History tell auchs of Ngai the Brave and Darkward the Wraith. Lead people to fight against humans but only when no choice. We peaceful people. Elders only wish auchs stay in peace."

Asiron continued. "Elders hear of efforts save Battok after injury. We grateful. We offer freedom of Sysla. You all live and travel anywhere but no able to help in any way with people of lowlands. That need us make auchs known to lowlanders. Put people in danger. This is our decision."

Camille had been expecting this decision and deep within her she was somehow pleased with the outcome. "I thank you for your decision and your explanation. I would not ask that your people be put at risk on my behalf. In the short time I have been in Konungssonur I have come to think of it as my home and I will honor and keep the decision of the Torkeen." She was relieved that she had thought to ask Alayna as to how she should respond.

"Torkeen ended," announced Obiri. As they rose to leave with Obiri thanking the other elders for their time and wisdom, Urak burst into the meeting room.

"Aiyu return to city. He come to Torkeen," he told them in a rush of words. The elders looked to each other and took their seats again, waiting patiently. Aiyu approached the table.

Obiri spoke in a stern voice. "Why you return? We tell you decision."

"Bhata dead," he told them flatly. "Bhata and children all dead. They be murdered by lowlanders." Camille was shocked. She had not known them for long but they had been good to her.

"Speak," said Yuntak. "What happen?"

"I return farm after leave Konungssonur. Lowlanders be there. I see tracks. They hang Bhata, Agort and Paulk in trees by feet, cut bellies open, leave them die. I follow tracks. They return lowlands through tunnel. Must see me bring Camille up and follow. They cut off Bhata's head and take with them." He sank to the floor and buried his face in his hands.

Camille rushed from her chair and threw her arms around the big man's neck. "I am so sorry," she told him. "They died because of me, because you are kind and wanted to help me." For the first time in weeks sobs of grief wracked her body.

"This change much," said Veetan.

Obiri looked at the auchs gathered in the seats before them. His eyes settled on a young auch sitting near the front and called him up to the table. The young man seemed shaken. "Hirith, I know you are friend of Aiyu. He need you help," Obiri told him. "Find people, go Aiyu farm. See what need do for family. Set guards at tunnel watch if lowlanders return. Must no let them back on high country. Destroy tunnel if lowlanders come. Go quick. When guards organized, return report what you find." He looked to the other elders. "We talk again."

CHAPTER 10

King Leopold stood looking out the window of his private apartment as the lone rider approached the palace. The man rode from the east gate on a horse that was clearly well cared for, and sat his saddle as if he was comfortable in it. But something did not appear as it should with what he saw. His page approached with a morning glass of chilled juice which he swallowed without moving. As the boy turned to leave, Leopold stopped him. "Willian, look out there and tell me what you see."

The boy stepped to the window. "The city is waking, there are more people than usual walking about and smoke is beginning to rise from cooking fires."

"Look again and do not play the fool now. I want you to tell me what you really see."

"A man rides towards the palace dressed as a farmer, but he is not a farmer."

"Why?"

"His horse and saddle give him away and he does not ride like a farmer."

"Thank you, Willian. That is all."

The king watched as the man continued up the avenue to the palace gate. The rider was out of place in farmer's garb. He reached the palace gate and was stopped by the guards. His long red hair flowed over his shoulders, glowing in the early sunlight. Leopold watched as the man dismounted and grabbed a bag tied to the saddle. His horse was led away to the small yard beside the gate while another guard led the man into the palace. He walked with confidence, his eyes straight ahead, unlike any other farmer who had come to the castle seeking aid. Leopold walked to the door, his page scurrying to open it for him. He walked down the old stone stairs, along a corridor decorated with wall hangings and tiled in a blue and white pattern, to the private door that gave him access to the throne room. He told the page to wait outside. His throne was carved from a single ancient oak and decorated with the symbols of Arenia. Its high back carried the image of a shining sun rising over the land while the top of the throne was a series of spikes as the sun's rays extended into the sky. The yellow cushion sat between two carved horses at full gallop with their heads stretched forward so that when he sat he could rest his arms on the horse's backs. The throne rested on a small dais tiled in green stone. The entire effect was very imposing. Leopold thought that it suited him.

His advisors were in the room and bowed as he approached. They waited till he took his seat before taking their places on either side of the throne. "I believe you have both heard what this man told the city guards?" he asked them. He had told them of an attack on a small town and they had detained him while word was sent to the palace. Now he was here. Leopold looked around the room to satisfy himself that all was ready. Six of his private guard stood before the throne and others were in their positions in the stone alcoves around the room. He had asked that no other members of the court be present for this meeting. Custom allowed that all petitions to the king be open to the court, but he wanted to meet this man in private and the unusual request might start tongues wagging. He could give no reason other than his suspicions that this meeting was not going to go well. With all in place he nodded to the guards, and they opened the large metal-studded doors. The man walked nervously towards the king, his eyes flickering over the guards until he dropped to his knee in front of the throne.

"Look at me," Leopold ordered. The man clasped the sack he carried to his chest and slowly raised his head. The King studied him. He dressed like a farmer, now showing the timidity that would be expected, but his clear, strong eyes showed no sign of nervousness. Leopold decided that he would not trust anything this man had to say.

"You have asked for audience with the crown. What is your name and what do you ask?"

"My name is Xavier and I come from a small village called Thistledowne, my King. I have come on behalf of the people of my town to ask for your protection."

"Thistledowne? I recall that name from somewhere." The king glanced quickly at his advisors.

The man to his left spoke. "We passed through the town on your travels last year, my liege."

"Ah, yes, thank you, Lord Darveed. I wonder why a small town like

Thistledowne would require my protection."

"My town has been attacked, my King. We fought but we are only farmers and have no weapons. Many of the town's people died in the raid."

"How did you fight without weapons?" Leopold asked.

"We have pitchforks and scythes but these were no match for our attackers."

"And who were these attackers?" pressed the King.

"They were auchs come down from the mountains. Fortunately for Thistledowne, there were not many, but we fear that more will come."

He did not believe the man's story but a raid by the auchs was something he could challenge. He looked at the men on either side of him. "You are my advisors. What should I do with this man and his strange tale?"

Lord Darveed was quick to answer. "Throw him out. He is obviously a liar. Either that or throw him in the dungeon until he tells us his true reason for being here."

The king watched Xavier. The man did not flinch or cringe at the prospect of internment. Without looking away, Leopold asked, "And you, Lord Lipstadt, what is your advice?"

"I would offer the same advice as Lord Darveed," he said. The King saw Xavier's eyes widen briefly with this reply. After a moment's pause Lord Lipstadt continued. "Of course, if this man can provide proof of his story, we would need to consider his request."

Leopold spoke to Xavier. "Well, can you provide any proof of your story that will stop me having you dragged out of here and thrown in the dungeons for lying to your king?"

Xavier held the sack out before him as he spoke. "Although we are only farmers, we were able to kill one of the attackers. The brave man who did this died defending Thistledowne but with his death he speared his attacker with a pitchfork." Xavier emptied the bag as he spoke. The auch's head fell to the floor with a thump and rolled to the base of the throne, staring up at the King with lifeless eyes.

Leopold was unnerved by the big blue head at his feet. He called one of the guards to remove it from his sight. Then he spoke to Xavier again. "You will remain in Whitebridge while I think on this matter."

"I will have someone take him to an inn. There we will know where to find him," said Lord Lipstadt. When the king agreed he told a guard to take him to the White Star. Leopold rose to go to his apartment, telling his advisors he wanted time to think before he would talk to them. From his window he watched as Xavier was led back down the avenue. The inconsistencies of the man unsettled his mind. Suddenly he knew - Xavier sat his horse like a soldier. But why would a soldier pretend to be a farmer, and if he was not one of his soldiers, who held his loyalties?

He called his page and asked him to fetch the captain of the guard. "Tell him to bring the item from the throne room, and see it is hidden," he instructed. After that, he was to find Lord Darveed and have him come. "But Lord Lipstadt is not to know of these instructions," he told the young boy. The page ran off to do as he was asked. Leopold sat waiting. Shortly both men entered and sat at the King's invitation. The page turned to leave when the King called him back. "Lord Darveed, Captain Lachlan, this is Willian whose father is Richard, from the estate of Gibbons." Both men nodded to the page, wondering where the King was leading. "His father is a loyal man. I would trust him with my life as I trust Willian. What we are about to discuss may not be passed to anyone, but Willian has proven useful in learning of things in the palace that others would not know. He can go where you or I cannot, and he will not betray my trust. Now sit with us." Willian was surprised but did as he was told. Leopold then turned to his captain. "Lachlan, no word of what happened in the throne room must get out."

"The guards have already been warned."

"Thank you. Now what do the two of you make of our farmer?"

Darveed looked around as if expecting to see Lord Lipstadt. He answered, "There is something strange about the man but the proof he brings lends strength to his story."

"And what about you, Lachlan?" the king asked.

"I would not trust him. He is not what he makes himself out to be. I do not know who he is or what he wants," Lachlan told him.

Leopold warned them, "I have more serious concerns than the lies of a petitioner. From that window I can observe those coming and going on the east avenue. I watched this Xavier approach and saw that he does not ride his horse like a farmer, and his horse is too well trained for a farm animal. I am glad that you share my unease. I believe this man to be a soldier."

"A soldier? Who would he be working for?" asked Darveed.

"He is not of the King's guard, and I doubt that he is of the Arenian army but I will check," said Lachlan. "However, he does appear to be an Arenian, or maybe Grechan."

"There is more," Leopold told them. "Did you watch his face when he spoke? His eyes were cold and calculating. When you suggested he be thrown in the dungeons, there was no reaction. He had expected it. But when Lipstadt made the same suggestion, his eyes showed surprise. That is when I suspected that our friend Xavier and Lord Lipstadt knew each other before our meeting and that this request was a staged event."

The others were clearly disturbed by the king's statement. "Why? What is their purpose?" asked Darveed.

"That is what we four will discover," Leopold told them. "Now you see why I require secrecy. Lachlan, show Willian what is in the sack."

Willian's eyes widened. "What is that?" he asked.

"That is the head of an auch," Leopold told him. "This is another secret that has been kept through time. The Kings of Arenia have long known who lives beyond our borders to the north. They fear contact with us and put great effort into their privacy."

"But how could this be kept secret for so long?" asked Lachlan.

"There is a natural barrier stopping passage to the north. The auchs live beyond this in the mountains. All the kings of Arenia have met with their elders on occasion to confirm our commitment to keeping their secret."

"You have met with them?" asked Darveed with surprise in his voice.

"Yes, last year when we journeyed through the northern districts. Do you recall the time I went riding alone and returned the following day? You all showed such concern that I was safe. I had met with their elders and renewed our vow of peace. They are so paranoid about being seen by humans that I cannot believe the auchs attacked this town so soon after our meeting."

"We could send a small number of guards to the town to confirm the story. They could ride fast and return with the truth. Others could be sent to the White Star Inn to observe this Xavier," suggested Lachlan.

"You will dispatch two trusted men to Thistledowne. They are to leave in secret, so have a squad sent out with spare horses. When they return there will be two less men, and horses. If any spies are watching, they may not think to count the men. They are to ride hard and return with the truth as fast as possible," Leopold commanded. "Send another two men to the inn to watch this Xavier, but they are not to wear their uniforms."

"The soldiers will be recognized for what they are, even without their uniforms," said Willian, "Just as you saw through Xavier."

Leopold saw the logic in the page's statement. "You know the staff. Is there someone who would not be out of place at an inn but whom we can trust?" Willian suggested Ben from the stables.

"Good. I will give you some coins to take to him. Tell him that he is to go to the White Star and watch the visitor with long red hair. He must not be noticed. Have him report back tonight with everything Xavier does and everyone he talks with. He will be paid well for his service. We will end this now. I do not want Lord Lipstadt to become suspicious. I expect you to keep your eyes open. There is more going on than we have seen yet and I want to know who is behind this. Willian, find Lord Lipstadt and ask him to come to my quarters."

#

King Leopold looked up briefly from the papers on his desk when the knock sounded on his door. He signaled Willian to open it and went back to his work as Lord Lipstadt entered. "Thank you for coming, Lord Lipstadt. Please sit down. Page, fetch us some wine." Leopold continued reading while Lipstadt fidgeted in his chair. He pushed the papers aside when Willian returned and began filling the goblets.

"I must admit that I was taken by surprise today when this Xavier emptied the sack in front of the throne. What do you make of this man?"

Lord Lipstadt sat back and sipped his wine before speaking. "I, too, had my doubts about the man until he showed us his proof." He glanced across to the page but the King indicated that he should continue. "How did he come by the head if the town was not attacked? Without the head I would find it difficult to believe. But he has brought us proof of his truth. For this reason I would consider the man reliable."

"You ask a good question, where did the head come from? I can think of no other obvious answer than a raid on his little town. Until that moment the stories of auchs roaming the world were just tales from vivid imaginations. My problem is that I do not know how to act on this news."

"Our first priority must be the safety of our people. We cannot stand by and allow anyone to attack our towns, auch or otherwise."

"Of course I must protect my people, but I have many questions. Where did these auchs come from? Why have they not been known before this? Will they attack again, and where? We need more information and a plan."

"We must send soldiers north to search out these animals and destroy them."

Leopold sat back as if in thought, watching his advisor as he asked, "Do you think that this Xavier might be able to provide further information?"

"He told us of the attack on Thistledowne and that they came from the north. I doubt there is much more that a farmer would be able to see or understand."

"I agree," said Leopold. "A farmer would not understand the strategies of battle but he may have seen things that he does not appreciate as important. If we could hear his story again in detail, we may be able to understand what happened and be better able to make the right decisions." He took a sip of his wine. "I will have Darveed meet us in the palace gardens tomorrow morning. I want you both to consider any questions we need to ask this Xavier. The captain of the guard should also be there to give a soldier's perspective. When we are ready, I will send for this Xavier, and we will listen to his story again and ask our questions." Leopold dismissed his advisor with a wave of his hand. He did not look up as Lipstadt left the room.

That evening when the palace was quiet, he donned a dark hooded cloak and left his apartment with Willian. They went to the servant's quarters and descended the narrow stairway to the kitchen. The cooking fires had been banked and the room cleaned, waiting for the morning's work. All was quiet as they crossed the floor and left by the back door. More stairs led to the palace vegetable garden where Ben was waiting on a seat. He dropped to his knee as soon as he saw the king approaching. "Rise," said Leopold. Ben stood with head bowed. Leopold went on, "Did you find the man we are interested in?"

"He were there," replied Ben.

"Good. Tell me all that he did," commanded Leopold.

"When I got to the inn, he were sittin' at a table in the back. He was talkin' to the innkeeper an' he did not move from the table until he went upstairs."

"Who else did he talk to?" asked Leopold.

"He spoke for a while with one of the servin' girls but mostly he just sat there. The innkeeper spoke to him a few times. His name is Marcus. I tried to get close enough to listen but a large man that works for Marcus made certain that no one got close."

"Willian said that you were a good man. You have done well. Do you know the name of the serving girl?"

"She were the one known as Beth."

Leopold gave him two silver pieces for his effort. "Remember," he said, "no one must hear of this. Tomorrow, I want you to go to the inn in the morning and see that the man is still there, and check Marcus and the girl too. Stay only a short while. I do not want anyone to be suspicious. When you leave, go down the road towards the east avenue. A man will be waiting who will walk beside you and greet you by name. You will give him assurance that all are inside." Ben nodded and the king left with Willian trailing behind him.

When they reached the kitchen, he sent his page to find Lachlan. A short time later the three were sitting in large, padded chairs in front of the hearth of his apartment. "I want you to send a squad of armed men ready to move in on the inn," he told Lachlan. "They must not be seen. Have one man wait on the road down the street tomorrow. When Ben comes out, he will greet him as a friend. Ben will tell him if Xavier, Marcus and the girl are inside. If any of them leave, they are to be followed. We must know where they are at all times."

"I will send them immediately," Lachlan assured him.

"Lipstadt expects to see you at the meeting tomorrow, but you will not be there. I want you to be with your men. Willian will wait nearby. If I ask for fruit to be brought it will be a message for him to get word to you that all three are to be arrested. They must not escape to warn whoever is behind this."

"It will be done," Lachlan promised.

Next morning Leopold sat on a bench in the garden waiting for the others. He wore his formal robe which he used to hide the sword strapped around his waist. Lachlan arrived and informed the King that all was ready before departing to join his men. When the others arrived, the king said, "We are here to discuss this man, Xavier, and his story. I have spoken with Captain Lachlan and decided he can provide no value to our discussions. The fewer who know of what we decide, the better for now. If he is present when we speak with Xavier, it may be intimidating, and we risk not gaining the information we need. Have you both thought of questions for this Xavier?" They assured him they had thought of nothing else. "Then how should we proceed?" he asked.

Lord Darveed spoke first. "We should not rush into a war against an enemy that we do not know."

Lord Lipstadt cut him off. "But they attacked us. We cannot allow any race to attack us without punishment."

"I did not say that we should do nothing," Darveed said. "If we send in the army the only outcome can be war. More of our people will die, perhaps many more, because we do not know the strength of the auch forces. It is madness and this raid may be only a trap to draw out our forces."

"Then what would you advise?" sneered Lipstadt.

"We should send an envoy north with the protection of a small guard. We should try to speak with these auchs and see if we can come to a peaceful understanding."

Lipstadt cut him off again. "How can we have a peaceful understanding with these creatures? They are no more than animals."

"How can you be certain that there can be no peace? What would you have us do?" Darveed demanded.

"We must send the army north to protect our people. We must go to war. I agree that we do not know our enemy's strength, and because of this, I would recommend sending envoys east. Arravale will be of no aid but we should approach the dwarves. We could explain the situation and call on them to assist us in our time of need."

King Leopold held up his hand for silence. "Something needs to be done. I like the suggestion of calling on our allies for help if needed, but why the dwarves and not the other kingdoms of man?" Lipstadt opened his mouth to reply but Leopold's raised hand cut him off. "I will soon send word to have Xavier brought to the palace to hear his story again. But before I send my people to war, I want to ask you all again, does this story carry with it the truth and can we trust this man?"

Lord Darveed spoke. "I do not trust him. His story is clearly false. He should be arrested and locked in the cells until the full truth is discovered."

Lipstadt turned to the king. "Would you arrest a loyal citizen for bringing word that his village was attacked?"

"No, I wouldn't. But is he a loyal citizen?"

Lord Darveed spoke before Lipstadt had time to reply. "There is something not right about this Xavier. He has his evidence and his story but I find it difficult to believe. There is something in the man's eyes that I find does not fit."

Lipstadt cut him off. "If my opinion counts for anything, I believe Xavier to be an honest and loyal citizen of Arenia. He leads his men here to ask for help - and we are talking of arresting him? It is our responsibility to protect the people. If that means war, then I for one am willing to accept that responsibility."

Leopold called for calm and signaled Willian to fetch cold fruit and drinks. "I agree with Lord Lipstadt regarding his main assessment of our situation. I think I have no choice but to prepare my people for war." Lipstadt relaxed and smiled at his success. "We will need to speak with Captain Lachlan about what he needs to have the army ready for a war with an unknown enemy of unknown strength. Lord Darveed, can you prepare the envoys? I will write letters for them to take to our allies. Lord Lipstadt, you will be at the heart of our preparations." Lipstadt's smile spread across his face. "I have another question that only you can help me with. How can you be certain that the auchs are no more than animals, as you put it? And Xavier came into the gate alone, making no mention of others. How do you know that he has men with him and that he is their leader?"

The smile quickly left Lipstadt's face. "He must have said something." Leopold shook his head and Lipstadt realized that they were accusing him. He began to rise but Leopold's sword was faster. It slid from its sheath and rested against Lipstadt's throat before he was fully standing. Guards appeared and took him by the arms.

"Why? Who are you loyal to?" demanded Leopold in a deep threatening voice as he looked his former advisor in the eye. Lipstadt made no reply. "Throw him in the cells and place extra guards," he ordered. "We will question him when we have the others. He is to speak with no one." The guards departed, dragging Lipstadt with them.

Willian returned and reported that word had been sent to Captain Lachlan. "These men that Lipstadt spoke of must be nearby. They are probably somewhere in the city. Send some soldiers to find them." The king sat impatiently waiting for news of the arrest of Xavier and the others.

CHAPTER 11

Before Beth had the chance to warn Xavier, soldiers began pushing through the door of the inn, shouting at the patrons to remain seated while they searched. Thinking quickly, she gave a signal to a man playing dice at a table on the side. Jumping to his feet, he yelled, "Cheat. You dare to try that in here!" With that he leaped across the table, sending dice and money flying as he grabbed the accused man and threw him into the nearest soldier. The pair crashed to the ground. Someone attempted to help but others objected. The first man moved fast, coming to his feet and crashing into more soldiers as he rose. The impact knocked more men to the ground. One soldier swung his sword and knocked the first man unconscious with its hilt, but the action only seemed to infuriate the patrons who charged the soldiers.

Xavier grabbed his sword but Beth grabbed his arm and called for him to follow. A quick look told him that the soldiers would quickly win the scuffle. He followed Beth into the corridor and the cellar door. He could hear more soldiers coming in the back. The trapdoor was almost closed when the cellar door burst open. He dropped down the ladder, almost landing on Beth, and stood ready.

Nothing happened and the tension in his muscles was easing when the trapdoor was thrown open and two soldiers looked down on the couple. The first jumped, rolling to his feet behind Xavier, while the other began to descend the ladder, leading with his sword. With one behind him, Xavier was forced to retreat down the tunnel. The two soldiers approached shoulder to shoulder. When Jaimz had taught him swordcraft he had emphasized one phrase: do what your enemy is not expecting. So he attacked with a furious flurry of blade swinging. The soldiers held their ground. The sounds of clashing metal echoed down the tunnel. Xavier threw himself to the ground and rolled, swinging at one man's legs but the man was fast and moved to avoid the attack, almost taking Xavier's arm as he did. Falling back, Xavier tripped and almost fell. One of his attackers took the opportunity to close. But Xavier had planned the move and dropped to one knee, bringing his sword up in a quick thrust that entered the soldier's belly and travelled up beneath his ribs. The man's sword fell from his lifeless hand as his momentum carried him forward onto Xavier, trapping the sword in his body.

The second soldier saw his chance and closed before Xavier could free himself or his sword. However, as he raised his arm to deliver the killing blow, his face froze in shock and disbelief. He fell to the ground with the haft of a knife showing from the middle of his back.

Beth approached, removed the knife and cleaned it on the soldier's tabard. "Are you going to lie there all day? Get up and check that no more soldiers are coming, and get that door closed." Xavier did as he was instructed. When he joined Beth again she had dragged the bodies aside. "I'll get someone to clean up this mess later."

She led him through the tunnels. As they walked she explained the warning she received only moments before the raid, that the soldiers had planned to arrest him, but she had no idea what had gone wrong. At one of the many ladders to the city above, he waited while she climbed up to gather news. It was not long before she was back, telling him that they would wait here while those above discovered what the king was doing. He placed his sword across his legs, glad that he was able to have that at least, his saddle sat on his bed at the inn with his change of clothes, and his horse was in a stable. He hated the thought of losing the big stallion; he was strong and reliable, able to hold steady in any situation.

When the trapdoor above them opened, Xavier came to his feet, sword in hand, but it was one of the councilors who climbed down to join them. "What news?" Beth asked.

"The soldiers raided the inn and brought everyone into the street. When they could not find Xavier they searched the rooms. They arrested Marcus, all the staff and one of the patrons and took them all back to the palace when they left, but no one knows why. They were also asking about you," he said, looking at Beth.

"Why would they want Marcus or me?" Beth mused.

"They were watching me," Xavier said. "They are investigating everyone I spoke with."

"But what has made them suspicious? Did they give any sign when they spoke with you?"

"None that I could see." Xavier explained what had occurred during the meeting with the king. The king had not given anything away but had watched him with narrowed eyes, even when talking with his advisors.

Someone was approaching fast. Xavier's sword was in his hand and Beth rose from her place on the floor. A young girl ran around a corner. Her fist came quickly to her shoulder and Beth signaled her to come forward.

"What is your rush, girl?" asked Beth.

"I bring news from the palace. Lord Lipstadt has been arrested for treason and has been locked in the cells with a double guard."

The shock was clear on the faces of all three. "Now we know what went wrong. Lipstadt has made a mistake and put us all in danger. Is there any way we can get him out?" asked Beth.

"I don't think so. The captain of the guard has selected the men to watch over him," the girl told them.

"Then I am afraid Lord Lipstadt is lost," said Beth. She looked to the other councilor. "He cannot be allowed to talk any more than he has," she said.

"If you wish, he will say nothing," promised the girl. "I work in the kitchens and will deliver his meals. This next meal can be his last."

Beth thanked her, telling her to return to the tunnels after the meal was delivered and they would see her out of the city. Otherwise, she would come under suspicion when Lipstadt died. "I will take Xavier out of the city and then return to see what is happening. It would be a shame if I had to leave also," Beth said. "When the girl returns, make sure she cannot talk." As the man climbed the ladder again, Beth set off through the tunnels with Xavier following. After many twists and turns they came upon a section of tunnel cut through solid rock. Beth told Xavier that they were passing through the foundations of the city walls. "This is where I leave you," she said. She took a spare torch from its place on the wall. "Stay on this passage to the end and you will come out north of the city. Follow the river north to a farm with a star over the barn door. It is owned by a man called Nate. He will send word for your men to join you. Stay at the farm and I will get word to you about our next move." She wished him well before walking back down the tunnel.

Xavier walked into the distant darkness. The tunnel ran in a fairly straight line away from the city. As he walked Xavier began to think of what could have gone wrong. He could see no fault in his performance and so he was left with two possibilities. Either Lipstadt had made a mistake, possible but unlikely in a man who had risen to his position, or the King already knew about the auchs and did not believe that they would attack the town. The more he thought about it, the more he became certain that the second option was the correct one but this led to the question of why the king would keep this knowledge to himself. He certainly hadn't told his advisors because The Society would have acted differently if Lord Lipstadt had known.

The tunnel started to climb and shortly light began to show ahead of him. It became easier to see so he extinguished the torch. At the end of the tunnel a ladder led to daylight above and soon he was standing at the mouth of a cave overlooking the land back towards the city. The cave entrance was hidden by blackberry bushes. Xavier received a few scratches as he left to make his way towards the river. The going was easy and a little over three hours later he was approaching the small farmhouse nestled among the river willows. A man stood in front of the house casually leaning on a pitchfork. Xavier touched his fist to his shoulder as he approached. A smile crossed the man's face as he returned the gesture, walking forward and holding out his hand in welcome greeting.

"I am looking for a farmer called Nate," said Xavier.

"You've found him. Welcome to my home."

"Beth sends her greetings," Xavier told him. He followed Nate into the house and briefly told him of his sudden but necessary departure from Whitebridge and his instructions to wait for further orders. "I need to get word to my men and have them meet me here," he said.

"My son, Jake, has gone to the city for supplies. I will send him for your men when he returns," Nate offered.

"They are on the other side of the river," Xavier said, "and they will not be able to come through the city at present."

"Don't worry. You were able to get out of the city without alerting the guards. Do you think that a bridge is the only way to cross a river?".

CHAPTER 12

Aiyu sat alone in his room while the elders discussed the attack on his family. He ignored the knocking at the door. Thoughts of his family filled his mind as he sat in the dark, images of them hanging from the tree filling his every hour. He tried to ignore the knocking when it started again but the door opened, and Camille entered. She sat beside him without talking, waiting, knowing that when Aiyu was ready he would speak. "I love her from first meeting," he finally said. "Elders decided our mating when we small. Then we meet, know elders pick well." He went silent again.

She let him sit quietly for a few minutes before she asked, "Tell me about Bhata."

The auch's eyes searched back through the years. "When I come of age my father take me to Ptoraki. It beautiful place. She live there with family." He stopped and looked at her. "Someone must tell family," he said. Camille promised that she would go to Obiri and have him send a message. Aiyu again lapsed into silence. He looked up later and saw Camille sitting quietly and stared as if only just realizing she was there. "Why they do this?" he asked eventually. When she told him that she did not know, he said, "Must be ones that kill you mother and chase you. What they want?" She put her

106

hand on his, unable to give him an answer and he put his head down on the table. Camille waited while he sobbed silently. When he finally looked up again, he told her of Bhata's family and their courtship. "We mated, move back Konungssonur. Difficult time for Bhata. Ptoraki large peaceful city, much beauty. Konungssonur small. Mountains make many hardship. Houses in Ptoraki larger, fields vast and fertile." He turned his head to look better at her. "Bhata mother is spirit talker."

"It sounds like a lovely place," she said. "Maybe you could show it to me sometime."

"I know Bhata find difficult but she no complain," he continued. "We return Konungssonur, she make home. Agort born this house, Paulk too. They grow up running around city."

"Why did you move out to the Edge?" Camille asked. She could sense he needed to talk.

"Work in fields one day. Holdbori come down, speak to Bhata. Tell her important events come soon, must be there make sure happen. I think Holdbori send us find you."

"Me?" she asked. "How can I be important?"

"Bhata say you very strong. Holdbori want you safe in our people."

Camille pleaded with him. "Please don't make me responsible for the attack. If I had known, I would have given myself up to them long before I met you."

"You no responsible. Holdbori demand you come. It no you choice." Again, he dropped into silent thought for some minutes before saying, "Agort no meet Qark now. Need tell her family."

"I am sure that someone will take her the news."

"Who do this must be punished," he said. "Elders must see this."

Camille squeezed his hand. "The elders will do the right thing," she assured him.

Aiyu sat for a moment before asking, "You go to Obiri, ask him send message to Bhata family. Need rest now. Talk later."

Camille watched him for a moment before telling him that she would do as he wished. "Take care of yourself," she said as she left.

He waited long enough for her to be out of sight before rising, taking his pack and leaving. He knew what he had to do. He left the city and began making his way through the fields. His route was the fastest he knew and he did not rest. In just two days he was approaching the farm. But as fast as he was, Hirith and the others had the start and travelled just as fast. They had cut down the bodies and buried them in simple graves behind the farm before he arrived. Aiyu went to the graves and crouched in silent bond with his wife and children. After he had taken the time to be alone with them, Hirith approached.

"Thank you take care of them," he said.

"Honor mine. They good people," Hirith told him. "I very sorry for what happen."

"I need find out why this happen. I need go lowlands, see if they follow me here. I must know if they die because I make mistake."

Hirith considered the request before replying. "I go with you but this no happen because of you. You no make mistake."

The two friends walked to the stone entrance where a pair of auchs stood guard. Hirith told them that they were going to the lowlands and would return soon. Together they walked down through the tunnel and fissure and out onto the lowlands. It did not take them long to find the remains of the camp where Xavier and his men had waited. Their tracks and passage through the forest was clear and they followed the trail of the horses for about an hour until they passed out from under the canopy of the forest and into the sunshine. Hirith suggested they return to the highlands. "You go back," said Aiyu. "I find men who do this."

"What you do then?" asked Hirith.

"They must pay for what they do to family."

"Come back. Let elders do this," suggested Hirith.

"Elders do nothing. Elders say they protect people. I understand but I need do this."

"You risk all auch nation if you seen," Hirith told him.

"Lowlanders already find auchs. Kill for no reason. They take Bhata head. That for proof of auchs. Maybe I no able catch but if I catch then auchs stay secret. I save auch nation, get justice for Bhata same time."

Hirith thought for a moment before stating, "I come too. We do this together. Kill humans, fight world, fight memories too." Aiyu stood looking at Hirith. They had been friends for many years but it had not occurred to him that others would join him in the search for his family's killers. "But must have plan," Hirith said. "We no risk humans attack people because our mistakes."

"What suggest?" Aiyu asked.

"We go back farm, tell others we find trail of humans. We talk what we do when we find. We get supplies, send word elders. When all done we begin quest."

"No need supplies. I get from land. You go back, send message to elders. I find Bhata killers." Without another word he turned and began to run, hoping that Hirith would leave him but his friend ran silently at his side. The open country was no barrier and they ran through the day and night without break. Only when the sun lit the following morning did they stop in a small grove and look for food. Berries and leaves were all they could find but while they ate, Hirith spoke. "Lowlanders far ahead. Must go fast if catch."

"I go fast."

"I come too. But if too far ahead, we no stop they tell about passage."

Aiyu looked at his friend. "Lowlanders kill Bhata. Must catch."

"But I think too late. Lowlanders be ready. Kill Aiyu, Hirith too. Bhata want Aiyu die or Bhata want Aiyu save people?"

Aiyu ate in silence and for the first time thought of what he was doing besides tracking and killing those who murdered his family. He knew they were long gone and probably back in the cities of man by this time. Although he would gladly follow until he found the men, even if it meant his own death, he understood the danger he was putting his people in and the conflicting emotions suddenly became too much for him to bear. He fell to the ground as tears of grief and frustration flooded from his eyes.

In his release Aiyu heard Bhata speak to him. He knew it was his mate, for only she would say the things he heard.

Bhaa. Aiyu fool. Find more excuse get out work.

"No try get out work. Try find men who kill you."

Bhaa. Time Aiyu go home. No chase lowlanders. Wait for lowlanders come back mountains. Then time come kill.

"No can wait."

Bhaa. You chase so Hirith chase. People need Hirith, but Hirith no go home while Aiyu hunt lowlanders.

After further racking sobs, he grew calm. He told Hirith he was returning to the mountains and began the walk back to the fissure. He did not speak but rather thought of the possible outcomes of his actions, and he was ashamed. For all her gruff talk, Bhata was the kindest person he had ever met and as much as it pained him he must allow the elders to act. But he also knew her belief in Holdbori.

As they exited onto the upper platform Aiyu turned to Hirith. "I no go back lowlands. Bhata no want this. I return Konungssonur, then go Ptoraki, talk with Bhata family. Bhata mother listen Holdbori tell what I must do. It is what Bhata want me do. You are good friend." Hirith did not speak. He just smiled and reached out to clasp Aiyu's hand in a firm grasp before setting out over the grassland towards the farm while Aiyu turned towards the valley and began the trip back to Konungssonur.

CHAPTER 13

Marcus sat in the hard wooden chair and looked around him. The room was small with few fixtures though it was not uncomfortable. Apart from the chair he sat in, there was a small table against the wall that held an empty wash bowl. Nothing decorated the walls and he could see nothing out of the small window except the blue sky. King Leopold and Captain Lachlan stood over him.

"Tell us again," said Leopold, "when did you first meet this Xavier?"

"I first met him when your guards brought him to stay at the inn, my king."

"You were seen speaking with him in confidence. What did you talk about?"

"I was only curious. It is not often that the king's men bring a person to stay at the inn. I only wished to know who he was and what he was there for. He had obviously come from a distant place and I have lived my whole life on that one street in this city. I wished to know how it felt to travel the world, for as you can see, I would not sit a horse well, and if I did it would not last long beneath me."

"And where is Beth, your serving girl?" asked Lachlan.

"That I do not know. She was working this morning and only when the soldiers entered and gathered us together did I notice she was not with us. Be assured I will dock her wages if she is malingering when she should be working."

Once outside the room, Leopold asked Lachlan what he made of the man.

"I do not know. He appears honest and friendly, and his story has merit, but he could have learned the skill of convincing lies while operating the inn. I am convinced I saw Xavier at the inn when we entered but the fight distracted me and when I looked back, he had gone. He was not at the inn when we searched, and he was not seen leaving."

"Do you think the fight was staged to allow his escape?"

"I don't think so. If that were the case, then all the patrons would need to know him and know that we were looking to arrest him. I think the fight was just a coincidence."

"I am not so certain. Have you found the two guards who disappeared?"

"We have been searching but there is no sign of them."

Leopold considered the turn of events that had conspired against him. He was not as confident as Lachlan that the inn was not a key to recent events. After a moment he called Willian to him. "This is a situation where a page may be better able to find out what we want," he thought aloud. "Let him sit for a while and then take in some fruit and wine," he told the young boy. "Be friendly and let him talk. See if he lets anything slip and then come to my apartment and report to me. Lachlan, come with me and let the boy show us what he is capable of."

#

Beth left the butcher's shop, casually walking towards the inn. She expected to be stopped at any moment and was surprised when she reached the door and entered without hindrance. Two of the king's soldiers sat at a nearby table. They rose as soon as they saw her, grabbed her arms and walked her back out into the street. She had expected their intervention and offered no resistance as they set her on a horse and started toward the palace. When Beth tried to ask where she was being taken, they refused to answer. Arriving at the palace gates, Beth was led inside to a small room where she was left alone. Guards stood outside the door, but they too refused to talk. The door finally opened, allowing King Leopold and Lachlan to enter.

"Where is Xavier?" demanded the King immediately.

"Why ask me?" she asked.

Ignoring the question Leopold continued, "When did you last see him?"

"This morning," she told him. She thought it interesting that the king would be the one to conduct the questioning.

"Tell me what happened."

"He was alone in the city and had been flirting with me. There were not many at the inn so we slipped out the back door and went off to have some fun. When I left him to return to work he said he was going for a walk around the city. I've not seen him since."

"And where did you go?"

"We went to my home."

"Why did you not go to one of the rooms at the inn?" Leopold continued, while Lachlan stood silently against the wall.

"That would have been too obvious and Marcus would demand a cut from my takings. I didn't want him to know."

"You left this man in your home?" Lachlan asked.

"No, we left the house and he went for his walk while I came back to the inn."

"How did you get out without being seen by my guards?" Leopold demanded.

"I don't know. You will need to ask your guards that question. I did not know anyone was watching. We simply left by the back door and walked through the stables."

"And where was Marcus?"

"He was checking and cleaning the tables before the crowd started to build after lunch."

"Marcus spent much time yesterday talking with Xavier. What did they discuss?" Leopold asked.

"I don't know, but I can guess. Marcus talks with all the strangers who stay at the inn. He is curious about the world and likes to know what has been happening. Information can be profitable to the right people."

Leopold told her to wait, and he left the room with Lachlan. "The story matches that of Marcus in most respects, the differences seem to be only points of view. There may be something more to this inn and these two but we have no evidence of their treason," said Lachlan.

"We must learn more of what has been going on. I think these two are involved and would be happy to throw them in the cells, but I want the people behind this plot. I am sure these two are not the leaders of this scheme. Let's go to my apartment and wait to see if Willian was able to get anything more out of Marcus."

Leopold was talking to Lachlan and Darveed when Willian entered. Although nothing had been admitted the page believed that Marcus and Xavier knew each other already. "I may be wrong," he said, "but he made mention of events from months ago, though he did not say what these were."

"One thing is certain," said Leopold. "There are events occurring in my kingdom that I need to know more about. We will hold them for now while we determine what they know."

"Are you sure we should not lock them up now? There is something going on and we cannot afford to risk Arenia," said Darveed.

"I think we can make some preparations," said the King. "What do we know?"

"We know that Xavier was not a farmer, and we know that he does not fight for Arenia," said Lachlan.

"And we know that whoever he is loyal to wants you to move your troops to the north," said Willian. "That would weaken your defenses in the city should anyone try to lay siege to it."

"True," said Leopold. "But I don't think the city is the target of this plot unless it is an uprising of disloyal members of the court. The city is too well fortified to be taken easily, even with only a small guard to defend it. They could hold until the army returned to defeat anyone who tried."

"So there are three possibilities," said Willian. "Either the people of Whitebridge are plotting to overthrow you, this is a plot by Greche or Arravale, or this is an uprising of the court. I don't think it is an uprising."

"Why do you say that?" asked the King.

"It is too obvious and makes an ideal diversion should the plot be discovered. The problem is that it would require many people in the palace who oppose your rule. Plots and comments would have been heard in the corridors, and I have heard nothing. Also, they would need armed support which would mean that Lachlan or someone near him would have been approached. Since the captain has said nothing, he either has not been contacted or has joined the plot, and I think his loyalty is unquestioned. So no one has approached him and he has not heard of any other approaches in the guard."

"Our young page shows great insight and understanding. Thank you, Willian."

Lachlan considered the alternatives. "So we are facing an intended invasion by forces from Greche or Arravale. What would be their purpose and how do they think they could win such an attack?"

"I do not think we need to consider Arravale," said Willian.

"I agree," said Leopold. "They are a nomadic people who place little importance on borders. They will not fight, even in defense of their lives, and have never been known to enter another kingdom. Arravale is not behind this."

"That leaves Greche," said Darveed.

"It is the only possible answer," said Leopold. "If our forces were committed to the north and we were to attack the auchs as Lord Lipstadt wished, then we would be trapped in a battle with them while the forces of King Woldemar crossed our borders and took the kingdom without hindrance. I doubt that even Whitebridge would hold if they knew our armies were unable to return in time."

"So what do we do now?" asked Darveed.

"We fall for their trap," suggested Willian. Leopold looked quizzically at his page. "Xavier and Lord Lipstadt will not be the only ones working for Greche. Others will be watching and reporting back with news of what is happening here. Marcus and Beth may be spies, and we don't know how many others there are. If they are innocent and you release them then you have done the right thing. If they are spies and you release them then we may be able to use them by letting them hear false information."

The King looked at his page with a newfound respect. "Where did you gain such skill in politics?" he asked.

"My father's land is close to the border of Greche," he said. "He taught me to be skillful with words and actions since I could first walk but I assure you of my loyalty and that of my father. These skills are only used to allow the forces of Greche to feel comfortable with our presence. Should they be needed, my father's troops will be the first to join the battle in defense of Arenia."

"Can we gather enough troops?" asked Lord Darveed.

"We could be ready to leave in five days," said Lachlan, "but if King Woldemar has spies in the city, then word will be sent of our preparations."

Lord Darveed said, "They want us to march north to attack the auchs and will accept the preparations. But if we turn south they will send urgent word to Greche. I hope we have the time then to prepare our defenses."

"Then why turn south?" asked Willian.

"What are you thinking?"

"If we leave by the east gate and turn north to follow the Kings Road, they will think we are still falling for their trap. Word will be sent of our march on the auchs. Once we are well out of sight we could turn and circle the city until we reach the South Road. We may even reach my father's estate before word of our movements reach Greche."

"An excellent idea," said the King, "but you will not be coming." The young boy was crestfallen. He had hoped to prove his value in battle, and to see his family again. "I will lead the army south and Lachlan will command the troops. I will hold him responsible for my personal protection. Lord Darveed, I will leave you in charge of the city, but you will not be alone. You will have the help of my new personal aide. Willian has shown that he is both intelligent and wise beyond his years. He will continue is duties as page until I select a new boy. Willian, you will offer your advice when called for and assist Lord Darveed while I am away. I want you to remain in the city and help by keeping your eyes and ears open, making sure that we are not wrong, leaving ourselves open for an overthrow by our own people. Can you do this for me?"

"Yes, sire," Willian promised.

"One last thing," said the King. "Lachlan, I want some of your men to go and get drunk."

"What?"

The King grinned. "I want them at a tavern near the White Star Inn, and I want them to think that we are going north. They must not know the real plans. Drunken men let information slip. Let's make sure the information that slips is that which we want our enemies to know."

#

Leopold stood looking out of his window towards the east gate in the distance while the army filled the avenue and overflowed into the nearby parklands. More than a thousand men waited, ready to follow him into battle. He checked the tall looking glass in the corner of his room again and was satisfied with what he saw. His red riding britches and shirt, both embroidered in fine gold thread, fitted him well and his black thigh length boots with gleaming gold buckles shone with the efforts of his servant's polishing. A black coat was also trimmed in gold and his hat with its broad black brim and gold feather on top finished the outfit. Yes, he thought, he looked very much like a king ready to strut before the court. When Willian opened the door, he rested his hand on the boy's shoulder. "Take care of my kingdom till I return," he said before going down the stairs and out into the courtyard where a stable boy stood holding his horse. The broad-shouldered black stallion had been carefully brushed and carried a dark saddle inlaid with gold over the blanket of gold and red.

"Let's go," said the king. The army wheeled and set out north along the King's Road. "This should impress Woldemar's spies," said Leopold, and Lachlan agreed. It had taken much work to ensure that their departure was convincing. After six miles they set up camp for the night. With guards carefully placed to ensure no one approached his tent, Leopold offered a glass of wine to each of the ten commanders while he explained that they would set out east on the next day and turn south when he felt it right to do so. His commanders were confused. Leopold explained they were on their way to stop an invasion by Greche and that Woldemar had spies in the city but he did not know how many. He told them of the ruse that they had embarked upon. "I want you all to be aware when we move tomorrow. There may be spies in the ranks and, if so, they will try to fall behind or disappear into the countryside so that they may race to warn Woldemar of our approach. This cannot happen. We must surprise Woldemar at a place of our own choosing."

CHAPTER 14

Obiri slouched in his big chair in front of the fireplace. The room was hot and stuffy. Camille would have liked the door open but the old auch asked her to close it and sit with him. "Elders want speak with Aiyu. Messengers no can find him."

"Do you wish me to look for him?" she asked innocently.

"I think Camille know where Aiyu go," Obiri told her.

"He did not tell me his intentions."

"He no tell but Camille know what he plan. He go to lowlands seek revenge family. True?"

"I believe that could have been his intent," she agreed.

"When you last see him?"

"Five days ago, in his home."

"He travel quick," Obiri mused. "We no be able catch. I inform elders." He sank back in his chair. Seeing the resignation and sorrow in Obiri's face Camille regretted not coming to him and telling him earlier. "I have a message from Aiyu. He asked that a message be sent to inform Bhata's family of the attack." When Obiri nodded Camille rose and left.

She decided not to return home where Alayna and the others would be waiting to question her about Obiri's call. Instead, she walked to the edge of the city and took the ramp down to the farmlands. She had been practicing reaching out to her squirrel most days and her skills were improving. When she called, he appeared almost immediately and came to take the seeds she had collected on the way. After a few minutes with her squirrel, she allowed her mind to roam. Practice made the task simpler, and she could sense a few more small animals and the farm workers. She did not know when or how but something new changed within her and her mind broke free of her body. She floated higher and drifted with the winds. She sensed rather than saw the auchs and other animals around the city and as she looked, she felt more and more as her mind spread over the land. She sensed the animals in the mountain valleys as they rested or searched for food and the fear of others as they tried to hide from them. As she floated over the land absorbed in her new-found freedom, more animals came to her awareness, and then she felt the birds. She felt their joy at the freedom they knew as they soared or flittered above the ground. The feeling was intoxicating as she let herself soar higher and further. Then she felt a presence on the edge of her mind that seemed familiar. She wanted to be closer and her mind lurched, catching her unaware, but she recovered quickly. She floated in front of the presence, trying to decide what had attracted her to it. Cautiously she reached forward and touched the other mind. At that moment she felt the presence of Aiyu, knew his grief and feelings, and she knew without knowing how she knew that he was returning home. She searched for other clues and a vision appeared of the valley where Aiyu had led her on the first days of their trek into the mountains. She pulled back and the image broke. As it faded, it struck her that Aiyu was over twenty miles away.

She sat on the rock trying to understand what she had just done before rushing back to the city. Stopping the first auch she saw she asked, "Please send word to Obiri that Aiyu is returning to the city and will arrive in a few days," There was no sign of the nausea that followed a strong session although she could feel the fatigue coming on. She wanted to lie down but as she entered the other women saw her and began to fuss over her. By now they recognized the symptoms of her overwork.

Alayna took control. "Lysandra, sit her down here. Yvonne, get her some tea. What have you done now." The tea was refreshing, and she had found in recent days that her recovery was becoming easier. The others sat patiently waiting for her.

"Aiyu is returning," she told them.

"Was there a messenger?" asked Maria.

"No," said Camille and she looked directly into Alayna's face. "I saw him."

"Where?" asked Alayna.

"In the valley near the farm," she told them.

"Then how did you…?," began Maria but Alayna held up her hand to cut her off.

"What happened?" she asked.

"I don't know," she admitted. "I was practicing letting my mind seek out the animals in the farmlands when I seemed to break free and go beyond my body in some way. I felt the world as I have not known before. I sensed something familiar and so I focused on it. When I touched it, I saw it was Aiyu. I felt his feelings and saw what he was seeing. I recognized the waterfall in the valley we took when he brought me here. I can't explain how I know, but he is returning."

"Did he know you were there?" asked Alayna.

"I don't think so and I don't understand how I knew it was him. I think I could just sense he was there," she said, trying to convince herself that what she saw had been real.

"No matter. We can ask Aiyu if he sensed you when he returns. In the meantime, your powers continue to amaze."

The door opened to reveal Kyra, one of Obiri's messengers, who told them that the elders wished to see them all in the great hall. They followed Kyra through the city. Camille was surprised to see the hall was full. Not only were all the seats taken but auchs were sitting in the aisle steps while others stood around the wall. On the dais sat Obiri, Asiron, Veetan and Yuntak with their aides, attendants and messengers standing ready behind them. Sitting at the table with his head bowed was another human. He was an old man, stooped at the shoulders. He had long grey hair and a scruffy beard that showed from beneath his hood. His brown cloak was patched and frayed and loose at every seam and his face showed the markings of time, but little else showed beneath the drawn hood.

"Torkeen thank all who come," said Obiri. When the five witches had taken their places Obiri went on. "Torkeen welcome Pouliquen, wizard of land. Pouliquen wisdom known in all Sysla."

"I am pleased to be in Konungssonur and be offered the privilege of attending," said Pouliquen.

"We begin," continued Obiri. "All hear of attack on our people by lowlanders. Elders pleased Aiyu return too. Our decision easier now he come back. We decide all passage to lowlands be destroyed. Auchs no want war, we hide more until humans forget auchs again. Then Auchs live peace. This decision of Torkeen. All here witness, bound by decision."

As the decision was being announced Pouliquen raised his head to look directly at the witches for the first time. When he saw Camille, his eyes momentarily betrayed his surprise. He studied her for a few seconds before speaking. "Elders of the auch nation, I beg a favor."

Obiri, who was about to formally close the Torkeen, stopped and looked at Pouliquen. "What do you ask?" he said.

"I understand the choice of the elders and I applaud their wisdom. A war with the humans will bring many deaths to the auch nation as well as the humans but I request that this decision of the Torkeen be delayed," said Pouliquen.

"Why does Pouliquen ask this?"

The wizard stood and faced the elders. "I believe that I may hold a key that will alter your decision. I only ask for the time to check my facts and the chance to present them privately to the elders. The elders have long prided themselves on hearing all facts and making wise decisions. I would not ask this if I did not feel the importance of my knowledge."

Obiri looked to the other elders and asked, "What time do you ask?"

"I only ask for one day," Pouliquen told them.

One by one the elders nodded. Obiri announced, "Torkeen will wait, hear words of Pouliquen. Then we make decision." To the wizard he added, "We curious to hear information so important."

"Thank you," answered Pouliquen. To the women he asked, "Could I walk with you?"

"Yes, of course," said Alayna. When they were all sitting together in their rooms he asked Camille, "You are new to the city. Where are you from?"

"I grew up in Arenia near the village of Thistledowne," she told him.

"How long have you been in Konungssonur?"

"Not long. I came here only a few weeks ago after my mother's farm was attacked by the local townsfolk."

"I was in Thistledowne many years ago," he mused. "In my memory it remains a beautiful place, and I recall it as a very friendly town. Why did they rise up against your mother?"

"I don't know," Camille answered quietly. "There was no warning that I could see. They just came one night, burnt our farm down and killed my mother. I only survived because I was out in the trees." She fought her tears with effort and taking a deep breath and went on. "They were saying she needed to die because she was a witch, but that makes no sense. The town had always known about us and there had been no trouble before this. They seemed to have been under the spell of a man named Xavier. They were not thinking, only doing as he told them."

"I have heard this tale across much of Arenia and I don't know what drives them. What was your mother's name?"

"She was known as Myrle Unwood," she said. "Why do you ask?"

He ignored the question and turned to the others. "Have any of you heard of the prophesies of Afi?" Their blank faces showed him they had not.

"What are you talking about?"

"Who is Afi?"

"What prophesies?"

Pouliquen ignored their questions that came from all directions. "I was drawn here by the powers of the world because something of importance is about to occur. Now I must go and contemplate what the omens are saying. I will speak with you again before the Torkeen returns." Without another word he rose and left.

CHAPTER 15

Nate stood at the stove stirring a rich rabbit stew while Xavier and his men helped out by splitting a store of wood for the cooking fire. Xavier signaled the men back into the barn at the sight of an approaching man. Nate saw the rider through the kitchen window and took the axe from Xavier, leaning on the improvised weapon. The man walked his horse up to the farm and greeted Nate while touching his fist to his shoulder. "I bring a message from Beth for Xavier," he said.

Nate turned towards the house, telling the man to follow. Inside Xavier sat in silence, waiting for the visitor to speak. "Beth asks that you return the way you left tomorrow morning. When you get into the city someone will meet you. They will look after you from there."

Xavier pushed for more information, but the man knew no more than he was told and the message gave nothing away. If he returned to the city tomorrow, he could be walking to his own death if the Council thought the recent setbacks were of his doing. But he may also have been called to receive his next instructions. There was no question in his mind. He would go to the meeting tomorrow. He needed to tell the Council of his suspicions.

Xavier rose early next morning and began his journey back to Whitebridge with some trepidation. He rode a borrowed horse and was soon at the rise overlooking the city. After releasing the horse to find its own way back to the farm he climbed to the blackberry thicket and forced his way into the cave entrance. There he lit the torch he had left behind and set out along the tunnel towards the city. His concerns of a trap still sat heavy on his shoulders but his confidence in himself and his ability to control any situation kept the feelings at bay. As he passed through the foundations of the city wall a young man stepped out of the tunnel ahead.

"Leader Xavier?" he asked touching his fist to his shoulder.

"I am Xavier."

"Follow me, please," he said, leading Xavier back through the labyrinth beneath the city. A short time later he stopped at a ladder. "I will wait here in case you need me. They wait for you up there." Only after he opened it did Xavier know it was the same door that Beth had brought him through to previously. She sat waiting in one of the large chairs and chatted with the other members of the Council. She greeted him with a warm smile and introduced the others in the room. Jozef was a tall man with dark sunken eyes and unkempt hair but his coat, once of good quality, now showed its age. Next to him sat Grarm, a tall man with broad shoulders and a hard face. Luke was the youngest of the three, about ten years older than Xavier, but he appeared both keen and intelligent. He was the type of man that would fit into his squad, he thought. Arwen sat a little apart from the others. He had not been at the previous meeting and Xavier thought he looked to be a strong man, not physically but in strength of character. He was well dressed in a brown jacket with yellow blouse and brown pants, his mouth a straight line across his face while his eyes remained unmoving as they surveyed Xavier.

He was the first to speak. "So this is Leader Xavier about whom I have heard such glowing reports." He studied Xavier as if trying to see the man he was from his appearance. "Beth speaks highly of you," he said. Xavier smiled his thanks. "As you know we form the Council of The Society. It is our responsibility to guide our members and control the direction of all that The Society does."

Jozef asked, "Leader, of all your men, who is the best to lead in your absence?"

"In my absence?" asked Xavier.

"Yes."

"That would be Jaimz. He is intelligent and reliable and has the respect of the others. But where will I be going?" They ignored his question.

"We have looked at your achievements," said Arwen. "You have proven yourself very capable. Finding that passage to the north was very conducive in putting your name forward. More importantly, finding the auchs and bringing back evidence of their existence was well done. Unfortunately, Lord Lipstadt did not handle his side of the task as well and he has been lost to us. I doubt that we will be able to get someone that close to the king again for some time. That will make your job more difficult, but his loss has not been without benefit. The king gathers his army and makes ready to travel north to defend Arenia from invasion. Our plans did not succeed as we wished, for it appears the dwarves will not be involved at present, but we will have the satisfaction of finally destroying the auchs."

"That is good news," Xavier said before he realized he had spoken. "I am sorry. I did not mean to interrupt."

Arwen went on. "As you know, we are concerned only with the purity of the human race and to ensure that we remain the dominant species of the world. To do this we must be sure that the human race is not compromised in any way. Your task has been to find and eliminate the witches who have spread themselves throughout the land. The traits that these women show are definitely not human in origin and we have concluded that they must be the product of interbreeding with another race, probably the elves."

"But why the complex plot? Why not just kill them?"

"That would be easier, but our charter guides us. It tells us we must teach our people that they must be alert to the dangers of all the lesser races, and that includes the half-breeds. We must lead the people to rise against all threats if we are to ensure that our race remains pure." When he stopped, a silence fell over the room. "As you know the Council has recently suffered the loss of one of its members. We will not quickly replace Lord Lipstadt's role as advisor to the king. He also had the responsibility for the operations of the various squads across the land. The position is vital, and the Council believes we have found a capable replacement. From this day you will take command of the operations of the Society's forces and Jaimz will take the position of Leader of your squad. You will arrange for Jaimz to be informed of our decision and after the meeting Beth will see that you are taken to Lipstadt's office in the tunnels and given his books to study. They hold details of all The Society's squads and their achievements and abilities. You will coordinate all that the Council wishes the squads to do. This is a position of great responsibility and is not given lightly, so we must also give you the authority necessary for the task. You are to take Lord Lipstadt's position on the Council and the responsibility of The Society is now also in your hands. Welcome, Councilor Xavier.".

CHAPTER 16

Rarbin took his bow and quiver from its place beside the door. His horse stood saddled and ready beside the water trough.

"I will be back tomorrow," he said to his wife Emma, "and I will bring back some rabbits for you to cook. If I am lucky we might also get a nice boar."

"Only if it falls on your arrow," laughed Emma.

Although she only joked, the comment hurt Rarbin who had not been able to find much game this season. He decided then and there that he would not hunt the usual woods and turned towards the hill country to the north. It took him further away but if he was able to return with good meat it would be worth the ride. He travelled most of the day but the pace was slow: his horse was old, having given him a lifetime of service on the farm, and deserved an easier time in its final years. As he approached the line of small trees at the base of the hills he was rewarded with the sight of a startled deer racing back into cover. He had not expected such a prize to be out in open ground and cursed himself for his clumsy approach. He walked the horse more slowly toward the trees and dismounted, taking his bow and arrows before tethering the horse on a long lead. When he moved into the shadows he waited, allowing his eyes to adjust to the low light, then worked his way forward, following the path of the deer. Although he searched for some time he could find no further sign of his quarry. Cursing himself, he worked his way up the hill in the hope of finding a place where he could see over the trees. As they gave way to bush further up the hill he glanced up, instinctively coming to a halt. Higher up the hill Rarbin saw a large goat standing on a projecting rock, looking like a king in a long white coat watching over its realm.

Without moving a muscle Rarbin's eyes crawled over the ground until he saw a small gully running down the hill that could provide cover for his approach. He dropped back into the trees and worked his way across until he was able to begin the climb. He could not see the goat from the gully, but at least the goat could not see him either. Climbing carefully so as not to dislodge any stones or make any noise, he worked his way up the hill to a point he thought would give him a good shot. Taking a deep breath, he raised his head slowly and looked over the rocky edge. The goat still stood looking out over the valley. He dropped back into cover and knocked an arrow to his bow before inching himself up again. He must have made a noise because the goat turned its head to look directly at him although it still stood its ground. Rarbin did not move, hoping not to startle the animal, and it turned its head back to the valley. In that moment he raised his bow and released an arrow in one quick movement, watching the arrow fly as he reached for another. The first struck the goat in the neck, travelling forward into its head. He was elated at the perfect shot and watched as the animal slumped to the ground, dead.

Feeling the excitement of the hunt burning through his body, Rarbin raced to his prize. He was thinking of what he would say to Emma. They would eat well in the weeks to come. He knelt and pulled the arrow from the carcass, cleaning it before returning it to his quiver. He drew his knife and butchered the animal, saving the heart, liver and kidneys in a bag. With the animal prepared, he stood and collected his gear before hoisting the goat onto his shoulder to carry back to the horse.

As he turned he saw the cloud of dust in the distance. He stopped and looked more closely. From his position on the hill he could see up the valley and out onto the plains beyond. It only took a moment for him to understand the meaning of the dust. An army traveled over the plains and from the size of the dust cloud he was seeing a very large army.

Running down the hill as best he could with the goat bouncing on his shoulder, he reached his horse, threw the carcass over the front of the saddle, untied the tether, mounted and kicked the horse into a run in what seemed one movement. He pushed the old horse as hard as he dared to arrive back at the farm in the dark. Without taking the time to dismount, he called Emma from her bed while tossing the goat to the ground.

"There is danger approaching. I must ride to town and give warning. Store the meat and be ready to leave when I return. If you see any signs of people approaching from the north, don't wait. Do you understand?"

He did not wait for her reply, trusting her to do what she should, and kicked the horse into motion again. Riding hard, he made good ground and by sunrise entered the town of Three Oaks. He rode up the main street, calling at the top of his voice for the mayor. People flowed out of their homes to see who was causing a ruckus so early in the day. Rarbin kept up his calls for the mayor until a large well-dressed man stepped in front of him. "Good morning, Rarbin. What is it that you must rouse the whole town to find me?"

"You must send word to King Woldemar. The army of Arenia marches on Greche. I have seen it."

The mayor was momentarily stunned by the news. "What are you talking about?" he asked.

"I was hunting in the hills and I saw the dust out on the plains. A large army approaches, thousands of soldiers. They will be coming through the hills in a few days. King Woldemar must be warned."

"Are you sure?"

"Yes. There is no time for delay. I am going back to the farm to get Emma and we will come back to Three Oaks. But this town is in danger and the King must send the army to protect us and the kingdom."

The mayor immediately called for two men to ride to the capital to warn the king and two others to ride to the hills and bring back word of the Arenian army's progress. Rarbin turned and rode out of the town without another word. He hoped Emma would believe him as easily.

#

Six armed men rode across the meadows not far outside the grand city of Winesprings. It had been a quiet month and King Woldemar had become bored with sitting in his palace, listening to the whining of storekeepers and businessmen who felt that they had been wronged in some way. He had called his personal guard and had the horses readied on a whim, a whim that had been occurring more frequently in recent times. The petty complaints could wait because he was going to take some time to relax. One of his sons could take some time out from chasing chambermaids to adjudicate on his behalf. He was an old man and the grey hair on his head had long since given way to baldness. He was still fit and very capable with a sword, but age had eaten away at his patience. More and more he found himself ignoring his responsibilities in favor of riding in the countryside. One day soon he would step down from his position and then his sons would have to step up to their responsibilities. He turned to the guards.

"We'll go east till we reach the road before we return. Now let's see how well I can still ride." Without another word he kicked his horse into a gallop across the field. The guards appeared to be taken by surprise and Woldemar was twenty paces clear before any of them reacted. They ran their horses hard, but the king held his place at the lead. By the time they reached the road and stopped, the horses were gulping for air and King Woldemar was laughing with pleasure. "I may be old," he said, "but I have not lost any of my skills on a horse." The guards agreed. They knew better than to outride the King in a horse race, as long as they were close enough to offer their protection if needed. "You will have to make some time to teach your guards how to ride, sire," said one guard in their little ritual. The King knew that his guards allowed him to win, and he appreciated their compassion for an aging man.

"Sire," one man called with alarm in his voice. The guards swung their horses in a circle around the king and drew their swords in readiness as two riders galloped hard towards them. "Halt," he called, when the riders were about thirty paces away. "Who are you, and why do you treat your horses so badly?"

"We come from the town of Three Oaks in the north with urgent news for the king."

"What news?"

"Our mayor has said we must tell the king. Can you take us to him?"

Woldemar nudged his horse forward and the guards fell in beside him. "I am King Woldemar," he told them. "What news do you bring?"

The two men bowed their heads.

"Arenia is invading. Their army has been seen moving south across the plains towards the hills that border Greche. They will cross into our lands within days."

"When did you see them?" asked the king.

"We did not see them, my liege. A farmer from near our town saw them while hunting in the hills. He said they are coming straight towards our town."

"What is this farmer's name? Is he reliable?"

"His name is Rarbin, a solid and trustworthy man. He brought the news to our town and the mayor sent us here with the warning. He also sent men to check on the Arenian's movements. He would not have done so if he did not trust the word of Rarbin."

The king made his mind up quickly. "Ride with us to the palace," he told the men. "I wish to hear more of this farmer as well as the lay of the land in the area. Come, men, our ride is over."

When the small group arrived back at the palace the king called for his sons, advisors and captains to join him while his servants had maps of Greche and Arenia brought and spread out on the tables.

"Gentlemen, these two loyal men are from the town of Three Oaks near our northern border, and they bring with them some very disturbing news. It seems that King Leopold is planning to invade Greche."

Disbelief and outrage filled the room until the King waved for silence.

"I have spoken with these men, and I cannot ignore what they say. Arenia is marching to attack with a large force, and we must prepare to defend Greche." He called their attention to the maps. "They tell me that there are two valleys where an army of this size could pass safely into the kingdom. Other routes would be difficult and slow, giving us time to respond. The Arenians travel quickly and do not know yet that we have been warned. They will come through one of these two passes. How quickly can we prepare to march?"

"How many are coming?" asked one of the captains, a young man named Fordic.

"From the report of these men the Arenians are bringing an army numbering in the thousands."

"To raise a force like that will require weeks," said Captain Fordic. We could not hold a force of that size with what we can put in the field now. We need to delay them."

"It would take a brave man to stand before a force of that size, or a fool," said Woldemar.

"My lancers can be ready to ride in the morning," said Fordic. "If you can give me some archers as well, only men who can ride, we may be able to get to the valleys in time to hold them until you arrive with the army."

Woldemar looked at his young captain. "Are you a brave man or a fool, I wonder?"

"Neither. I am a soldier who believes in the courage of his men, but I think there may not be a need to fight. If I can position the archers on the high ground over the valley and place a line of lancers across the valley, we may be able to make King Leopold believe we have more troops in reserve. If he holds while he tries to determine our strength, we will have given you the time you need to bring the army. If he attacks, we will do everything we can to make our deaths take as long as possible and to keep him in the valleys."

There were no better ideas put forward so the king agreed to send Fordic's lancers ahead, along with fifty archers. "I will also give you six Haafi. They have good minds for fighting and their advice will be useful, but I send them to offer protection should Leopold try to send spies into your camp." The Haafi were King Woldemar's personal assassination squad, very quiet and very efficient. Fordic was both surprised by and grateful for the inclusion of the Haafi in the advance force. Although very skilled and dangerous the Haafi had never before been sent into battle.

"We will follow with the army as soon as we are ready to travel. I hope that we are in time. Go well, Captain."

CHAPTER 17

Pouliquen told Camille and the other women the story behind the prophesies of Afi. "It was at the battle of the beach where the auchs won their freedom from the humans. It is odd that the auchs remember it well as there are no memories of the battle among the humans of today. Either the humans who fought did not survive or they have moved to a place I do not know. The human losses were terrible that day."

"But what about the prophesies?" pressed Camille.

"I am coming to that." He took a breath. "It started when the humans tried to stop the wraith from leaving. A fight broke out between the group and their guards and while this was happening more guards moved to stop the auchs joining in. One of the wraith, Darkward, died trying to protect the auchs and Ngai. With his death, Ngai called for his people to rise and fight. The auch losses were light, but there are casualties in all battles. They give thanks to Ngai and Darkward that the auchs are free today, or even that they survived, because the humans would not have been lenient if they had won the day. During the heat of the battle a human got behind Ngai when he was occupied fighting two others and Afi stepped between as the sword fell towards Ngai's back. He killed the man but in doing so he received a severe wound to his side. For four days he lay while others tried to save him, but his wound began to rot and his fever was terrible. As it consumed him, Afi raved and rambled with the pain, but occasionally he became lucid and spoke of things yet to occur as if they had already come to pass." Pouliquen paused to refresh himself with a glass of water before continuing. "Over the next weeks the first of the stories came true with such accuracy that the remaining tales were committed to memory before they were lost. It now falls to the elders that these are never forgotten. These are now known as the prophesies of Afi."

"Have more of these come true?" asked Marie.

"All of Afi's prophesies have proven most accurate to date. Only the final five remain."

"And you believe that the next prophesy is upon us?" Camille asked.

"Yes. The signs all point to the next two prophesies, told at different times but of the same event. With what has been foretold I believe it's time is upon us. Knowing the accuracy of what has gone before, I fear that the coming times may be very difficult for all."

Alayna asked, "Can you tell us what these next two have to say?"

"I will try to recall the next prophesy of Afi, as I heard it." He closed his eyes as he sank back into memories and began to recite, "This fourteenth vision Afi the prophet. Heed these words. Many years auchs live in peace. But peace grow out of fear. Humans find auchs again, watchers die. Dark shadow spread over land, time of peace broken. Elders forget lesson of Ngai, forget honor of Darkward. Elders wait. But one does not wait. One remember Ngai, Darkward stand and die for auchs. One prepare for war." Pouliquen shook his head as if waking from a deep sleep. "That is the next prophesy as told by Afi," he said.

They sat silently, each savoring the words that Pouliquen had fed them until Alayna asked, "And do you think Bhata and the children are the watchers who were murdered?"

"Yes. There is much concern in the words for the auchs but I fear that the elders will not wish to hear of it. There is the talk that they must prepare for war but, if I read the words correctly, the elders will not listen because of the words of the next prophesy."

"And what is that?" asked Camille.

"The last four prophesies of Afi came in the hour before his disappearance and are not easily understood. He speaks of the defender and a weapon that will save the war. It is only when I saw this group sitting before the Torkeen that it started to make some sense to me."

Pouliquen closed his eyes again to recall the words. "This the fifteenth vision Afi the prophet. Heed words. King of auchs gather people to war. Battles fight over all land. Many fight, many die. Auch people tested, tested again, elders lose hope. Time of great need come, defender step forward. Defender use weapon not of trees and earth but of power born of power. Weapon both destroy and save. Defender break world. People must die so they can live."

Alayna was the first to speak when he had finished. "Strange words! Together they tell a dire story. There is much in these prophesies that the auchs must fear, but there is also hope. I can understand the concerns of the elders. Who is this king of the auchs, and who is the defender? The elders must fear them because it means the loss of their power. Or are they the same person? One thing is certain. There is going to be a war and if the auchs are to survive, then they must fight and they must use a weapon never before seen in this world. And they must find this defender and their king. How do they find them or the weapon?"

"We cannot influence the auchs in any of this," he said. Lysandra and Yvonne asked why. "It may be that Aiyu is the one they seek but if we are wrong, and the auchs follow him, it may lead to an even greater disaster. No, the prophesies must be allowed to develop as they were intended. All we can do is stand ready to assist as best we can."

Alayna nodded her agreement as Marie asked, "From the words of the fifteenth prophesy it seems that we are headed into a war that we cannot imagine. You wanted to speak with us. Do you think it will fall to us to find or make the weapon?"

"I don't think there is a need for us to find it," said Alayna.

"But Afi speaks only of things that have been, and it may be that we must assist or these predictions will not occur. By not acting, we may change history," Camille said.

"No," explained Pouliquen. "The weapon will be ready when it is required, and the prophesies tell us it will be the defender who must use it, and so it must be his to find."

"Then what are we to do?" asked Alayna.

"Nothing, I just needed to clarify my thoughts, and talking with you has helped. I will go to the elders and tell them that I think the next prophesies of Afi are upon us. We must allow the elders time to consider their next course of action. All we can do is declare our support for the defender when he calls for it," he said.

"We can do more than that," said Camille. "The elders have their Torkeen to discuss the needs of the nation and to make their decisions. We know that witches have fled the lowlands and are living in other cities as the elders have told us. We can send messengers and call together representatives for these women in order to see what skills we have available and how we can best use them to support the auchs. It may be written that the auchs delay but that does not need apply to us. We also need to know who will not fight against humans in support of the auchs."

"An excellent suggestion," said Alayna. "You can get started."

"But you are the obvious leader of our group," Camille said to Alayna. "I think you should be the one to gather the women."

"I agree," said Pouliquen. "Alayna should be the one to do this. Now I must go and speak with the elders but I will talk with you later, Alayna, to help if I can." With that he rose and made his farewells as he walked to the door.

"Wait." Pouliquen stopped at Lysandra's call. "What happened to Afi? Did he die of his wounds?"

"It is strange. Although his injuries were severe, the others woke one morning to find Afi gone. They searched the surrounds, but no sign of his passing was ever found. This only helped to add to the mystery of his predictions."

After he had gone Alayna turned on Camille. "A nice girl you are. You come up with ideas and then pass the work off." Then she smiled. "But it is a good idea. I will speak with Obiri as soon as he is available and ask him to organize 0the messengers."

CHAPTER 18

The army dragged itself south through the low hills of Arenia with Leopold riding proudly at the head of the mass of armor, swords, arrows and spears. He was still concerned that one of Woldemar's spies had seen the move and ridden to give warning, but his scouts had insisted that their ruse had been successful. They had ridden out of the hills onto the open plains and from that point there had been no cover to hide his army. Southern Arenia was open grasslands extending from the hills around Whitebridge to the low steep ridge that formed the border between Arenia and Greche. There was no way to avoid the open approach across the vast expanses of Arravale that continued well to the west of their route. With his army crawling across the plains, it would be easy for Woldemar to see them and be prepared for their approach if he had a man watching. He hoped the King of Greche had not thought it necessary to place lookouts. He had to reach the border first. That was the key to defending Arenia, because only then could he implement the plan they hoped would defeat Greche without too many losses to his forces. If Woldemar reached the border first then he would be forced to fight a very costly war. That evening, when the army stopped for a meal and rest, Leopold rode among his men and implored them to hurry.

"Greche dares to invade Arenia," he told them. "We are in a race to the border and the first to arrive gains control of the battle. If King Woldemar wins this race, it will mean many of us will die trying to stop him. But if we are first to the hills, we can lay a trap that will destroy his army and drive him back with his tail between his legs." Cheers erupted from around the camp. Leopold heard calls of "We'll get there first," and "They won't beat us." King Leopold smiled as he raised his sword. "Let's get a good night's sleep, men, so we can march quickly tomorrow and beat Woldemar to the hills. Then we can show him how Arenians treat invaders and give him a good kick where he sits." He rode back to his tent listening to the laughs and taunts behind him as his men tried to outdo each other with what they would do to King Woldemar. The race for the border had become a challenge, as he hoped it would. Arenians loved a good challenge.

#

King Leopold's army approached the twin valleys with no sign of the armies of Greche. He prepared to split his force into two equal parts as planned. The narrow ridge between the valleys provided an ideal location for his archers to close the trap and he sent them with soldiers for protection and instructions to remain hidden until the signal was given. His lancers would block the valleys while the remainder of the forces would be held behind the lancer lines. The army of Greche would be allowed to enter the valley and, once inside the confining hills, the archers would be able to reduce their numbers before the lancers charged. The soldiers in the hills could then drop down to attack any pockets of resistance while the remaining forces prevented any attempt to break for the open country of Arenia. A simple trap, but one that should work well.

"Something is wrong," he said to Lachlan. "If Greche has been waiting for word of our move north, their army would have been ready to march and should have been here before now. Could we have made a mistake about Woldemar, or is he coming another way?"

"Our logic was sound," Lachlan assured him. "Our ruse has worked very well and he believes he has plenty of time. He is in no hurry, but we should expect him soon. I will send some scouts forward to warn of their approach."

They continued to walk around the camp checking that all was in readiness. Very few archers remained in the camp checking bow strings and arrows. Most sat in small hollows or among the rocks up in the hills waiting for their chance to deliver their deadly rain upon the soldiers of Greche. Everybody was ready and keen for the battle to begin, but by now, the third day, Lachlan could see signs of distraction throughout the army. The soldiers no longer checked their swords as often and weapons lay idle against tents. Worse, he could occasionally see movement in the hills as archers left their cover to wander about and talk to friends. If any scouts from Greche saw the movement the ambush would be exposed. He was about to call a messenger to send a warning up to the archers when one of the scouts was seen riding hard down the valley, which could mean only one thing - the forces of Greche were coming. He called two soldiers to him and told them to get up to the archers fast and tell them to take cover. Another soldier was sent to warn the lancers to deploy before he ran to where the scout approached.

King Leopold had also seen the scout and the three met at the edge of the camp.

"Greche's soldiers camp near a small village not far from the valleys," he said. "It is only a small force and all on horseback. I did not see any sign of foot soldiers, but they could be here within hours."

"The foot soldiers will be close behind them," said Lachlan.

Leopold looked back and forth between the scout and Lachlan before commanding, "In my tent, and send word that I want all commanders to join us." Once they had gathered, the King told them all of the approaching force. "The question is simple. Why such a small force and why are there no foot soldiers?"

"It could be a diversion, to gather our forces while their army comes through elsewhere," suggested one commander.

"Possibly," said Lachlan, "but I doubt it. If they were to come through elsewhere, it would be to circle us and attack from our rear or to move on to Whitebridge while we are occupied here. There are no other valleys nearby that would allow an army to get around us. To ride north would leave them in a position where we could attack their rear or their flanks. I will send some scouts back to make sure we are not being taken by surprise."

Another commander spoke up. "Then this is an advance squad."

"Why?" asked Lachlan. "They are ready to invade, so why send a small squad ahead? If they know we are here they would be sending them to certain death and if they don't know about us, what are they doing?"

Leopold suggested the answer. "They don't know we are here. They have no reason to suspect we know their plans so their aim is to take southern Arenia and hold it. If I were in Woldemar's position I would send a fast and efficient force ahead to take and secure the valleys and as much land as possible in the first days so the army could follow in safety. So what should we do?"

"We must destroy this advance force. I doubt that we will be able to stop word getting back to Woldemar so we must send him a warning that he should think again before setting out to invade Arenia. Our plan is still good - in fact this helps us. We will allow this force to enter the valley and then we will spring our trap. This will send the strongest message to Greche. You all have your orders. Go and put them into action.".

CHAPTER 19

Captain Fordic recognized that this was going to be his opportunity to prove himself. He was old enough to understand the intricacies of battle while still being young enough to think that nothing could happen to him. He rode at the head of his men, wearing his full dress livery of blue and red tabard over chain mail. Beside him was the archer, Martin. He led his men not by appointment or rank but by the strength of character and Fordic respected the man for this. In contrast, the leader of the small squad of Haafi had no need to earn respect. He was respected, and indeed feared, simply for who he was. The Haafi did as the king ordered without question and when Woldemar placed T'Anassah in charge of the group, his men obeyed. The Haafi wore black like it grew on them; boots, trousers, shirt and cowl were all black. The only exception was the blood-red stone set into the black metal bracelet each wore on their left wrist, the symbol of their calling. Fordic had heard that these bracelets were a gift of magic that gave the Haafi their ability, that if one looked into the stone, it appeared alive, twisting and turning with glowing worms. Though thought of wearing such a thing gave Fordic a momentary shiver of fear, he sometimes fantasized what it would be like to possess such power. He had heard the tales told around fireplaces that on each man's left arm were tattooed crosses, one for each man he had killed in the king's name. The Haafi did not observe rank in any other areas of the army, but the king had placed him in command of this action and told them to obey.

The column passed out of the city and Fordic led them in a steady canter. He would alternate the pace between this and walking in an effort to balance the speed and the strength of his men. For the first few days they made very good ground. They had left the farmlands around Winesprings on the second day and now travelled along the road through low rolling countryside covered with wildflowers. At times the land was a sea of green sprinkled with stars of yellow waving in the breeze and at others it was covered with the grey-leafed bushes adorned with the sweet-smelling mauve flowers that the women loved so much. But his favorite time was when the world was awash with poppum flowers, the inspiration for the lancers livery, with their bold red and blue petals.

The rain that hit them on the fourth day was inconvenient as it soaked their clothing and forced them to keep to a walk. Then it became troublesome as the breeze lifted and the chill began to bite. Fordic worried as their progress slowed dramatically, the road turning to mud beneath the horse's hooves, the wagons bogging down behind them. Considering it unlikely that the Arenian army could be this far south without a word reaching him, he decided to stop the column and allow the wagons to lead where the ground had not been cut up by the lancers. There was nothing else he could do. They had to stay on the road because taking to the fields would be worse. It needed another day after the rain stopped before the road became firm enough to move the wagons back, and still another before they could again travel at full speed. In quiet moments he hoped the weather had not allowed King Leopold to lead his men into Greche. Without the confined spaces of the valleys, he had no chance of stopping them with his small force. He pushed his men as hard as he dared until the small town of Three Oaks came into view.

The road led them into a beautiful little town where the houses were all timber clad and whitewashed, with the small windows and doors dressed in red wood. The dirt streets were well maintained, and light wisps of smoke rose from the many chimneys. As they rode along the main street people flowed from the houses to greet them. A large well-dressed man stepped from the growing crowd in front of them.

"Welcome to Three Oaks. I am Albert Fagg, Mayor of Three Oaks."

Fordic smiled. This man obviously thought he was very important. He gave the man a slight bow from his saddle.

"Thank you, Mayor Fagg. We were told that you were threatened by the army of Arenia. Where are they?"

"They reached the hills and stopped. I don't know what they wait for."

"I would guess that they rest their men and horses before they begin their push into Greche. What do you know of them?"

"They occupy both valleys to the north and there are too many to count."

"Is there anyone here who could show us these valleys and give us their local knowledge?"

A man stepped from the mass of people. "I am Rarbin. I own a farm near the valleys, and it is my warning that was sent to the King. I will ride with you and assist as best I can. I only ask one favor."

A frown spread across Fordic's face. "And what would that be?" he asked.

"I brought my wife here from the farm, away from the fighting. If things go wrong, will you see that she is kept safe? Her name is Emma."

"That I can do," Fordic promised. "Now tell me how you came to discover the Arenian army."

Rarbin related the story of the hunt and the ride to Three Oaks in order to get a warning to the king. By the time he had finished they were approaching the rest of the squad waiting on the outskirts of the town and Fordic ordered that they make camp for the night. He asked Rarbin and T'Anassah to join him in private. The three stood studying the map spread out on the table. "From what Rarbin has told me, King Leopold must be holding at the head of these two valleys. I am surprised he has not already come through. T'Anassah, can your men go out tonight and see what is keeping them without being seen yourselves?" T'Anassah gave him a deadly glare. "Good. When we know what they are planning, we can set up our defenses."

CHAPTER 20

Aiyu squatted on a rock overlooking Konungssonur, thinking of many things. The loss of his family still dominated his mind, but he was embarrassed that he had allowed his sorrow to consume him to the point of revenge. From the time of an auch's birth they were taught to preserve their solitude and to obey the elders. Strictly speaking, he had not disobeyed but only because he had not waited for the elder's decision, knowing that it would not be what he wanted to hear. In doing so, he had put the lives of all auchs at risk. He was grateful to Hirith for the gentle way he chose to show him his error and to Bhata whose voice still echoed in his head. Obiri knew what he had wanted to do, so the time had come to go home and face whatever the elders had in mind for him. However they wished to punish him, he would ask to be allowed to go and visit with Bhata's family first.

Aiyu rose with forced determination and set out for the city, marching across fields of broadfruit plants, beans and spikeapples, up the ramp to the galleries. At Obiri's door it was an effort to stand straight and raise his hand to knock. Before his fist struck the thick timber, he heard someone call his name. Battok was walking towards him.

"Good see you again," said Battok. "If you want see Obiri, he in meeting hall. I go watch. Walk with me, talk on way." He took Aiyu's arm and swung him around so that he had no choice. Battok chattered away, never allowing Aiyu the opportunity to speak or answer any of the questions interspersed throughout the spiel. He did not stop until they stepped through the large double doors into the hall. Obiri sat on the stage with the other elders in front of a hall filled to capacity. The five witches sat in the front row and another human sat on the stage, concealed mostly by a cowl and cloak.

Obiri broke the silence that followed. "Aiyu, son of Yent, son of Avgar, you allow grief to consume you. You seek revenge, No consider decision of elders or people. You prepare risk all that auchs believe, risk lives of our people for revenge." He paused, giving Aiyu the opportunity to defend himself, but Aiyu stood silent. "You no alone in that desire, but you find wisdom. Concern for our people overcome your desire for revenge. Elders grateful and proud. Even elders no too old understand love. We know strength needed do right when inside tell you do other. Welcome home Aiyu. Find seat. We continue."

"Elders hear words of friend Pouliquen. Wizard give much to think about. We consider options. Our decision is attack on our people no from desire of lowlanders to start war. If want war there be other attacks. Watchers see no movement below Edge. This is reason we decide to keep ways to lowlands but permanent guard be set. Any attempt lowlanders return to our land we stop by any means. This include destroy all passages. Watchers stay but must not use ways for any reason. This our decision, no more talk. Torkeen over." He walked out of the hall with the other elders. The auchs began to file out and Aiyu was happy to join the crowd. Only Pouliquen and the witches remained.

"This is wrong," said Camille. "A war is coming and the auchs must prepare to defend themselves."

Pouliquen contradicted her. "No, this is right. This is exactly as Afi predicted."

#

Aiyu put the final items in his bag in preparation for the trip to Ptoraki. It would be good to see Bhata's family again, but he was not looking forward to their first meeting and their grief. He looked once more at the room that had been their home before hoisting the bag over his shoulder. As he opened the door, he was surprised to see Battok standing outside with his fist raised, caught in the act of knocking.

"Sorry," he said. "I know you go away. Obiri send me. Ask you come speak with him before you leave. He say it important."

"Obiri tell what he want?"

"No. He speak many hours with other elders and wizard. Elders leave, go back to homes, he sit in room until he call. Tell me bring you message. Sorry Aiyu. I no guess his thoughts."

"I know soon. I see him, then go."

As Aiyu walked, he looked around. He had grown up running around these galleries and the city was familiar to him. Now he saw it through Bhata's eyes, the first time she came here to live. The complex patterns of the galleries and buildings were similar to the roads of Ptoraki and they held a structured beauty like that of a bee's honeycomb but with a more intricate shape. He also saw it as Camille first saw it, with patterns too complex to grasp, a mass of shapes fallen over each other, and he understood her wonder when she first saw the patterns. It was a hard place to live and an even harder place to leave, believing that he would never see it again. His mind was not in this city any more. He yearned to be away from the memories but knew he must wait a little longer.

Obiri's door rattled with the unintended force of his knocking, and he heard the call to enter. Obiri sat in his chair looking older than Aiyu remembered. His skin seemed to hang more loosely and showed even less color than normal while his good eye lacked its usual intensity. The old auch seemed to be gathering his thoughts, or his strength and Aiyu became concerned for the elder. After what seemed like an eternity Obiri pulled himself up and spoke to Aiyu. "You leave now?" he asked.

"Yes, I go see Bhata family. Tell them of Agort and Paulk. Help them know what grandchildren were like, how happy they were here."

"When you return?" asked Obiri.

"I not know," Aiyu told him. "When time is right."

Obiri took a moment before going on. "I must tell something before go." He waited a little longer, collecting his thoughts. "Elders plan told at Torkeen. What is said no always what we talk about. Pouliquen say dangerous time come. We wait, hope peace hold. But no mean we must ignore prophesies. Deny omens, auchs could end in disaster."

"What you talk about?" Aiyu asked.

"Pouliquen tell he believe auchs face war with lowlanders. Elders want avoid war. Deny words. But can no deny prophesies. Must make preparations but no can alarm people. People afraid of war sometimes do something they no do at other time. Maybe make war come."

Aiyu nodded. "Like go to lowlands seek revenge," he said.

"Yes, but I tell Torkeen you see wisdom, just slow. You put nation ahead of own wishes in end."

"What you want me do?" asked Aiyu.

"I want you go Ptoraki, see Bhata family, talk to them. But I want to send message to elders of north cities. I want you take my message to elder Buit while there." He paused a moment before finishing, "I want you return as soon as can. Trouble come to auchs, we need watchers. Can you do this?"

Aiyu thought about Obiri's request. He had not intended to return. How could he explain to the old man that there was nothing here for him without Bhata to share it? He decided to limit his reply. "I take message. What do I say?"

"Tell her about Bhata and children. Tell her that omens point to words of Afi. She will know what I mean. Tell her I want her make preparations help, tell her to pass word throughout Konungssonur and other Sysla. War come, we must be ready. We must remember lessons of Ngai the Great. He tell we must sometimes fight for freedom and peace."

Another knock on the door interrupted them. Before he could tell the elder that he would not be returning, Camille entered. "I am sorry but I must speak with you both. The elders promised me the freedom of the north and I have a request. I know that Aiyu is preparing to leave for Ptoraki and I come to beg permission to travel with him."

Aiyu sat silent. Obiri told her that he thought Aiyu was about to tell him that he was not coming back.

Camille turned on her friend. "But you must come back. Everyone will miss you if you don't."

"Nothing here for me. Just memories I need be away from."

"There are all your friends."

"They will understand."

"Then take me with you."

"I not take you."

The words had come out of Camille's mouth before she had even thought them, but now they were out there, she knew this is what she must do. Something deep inside told her she must protect Aiyu. "If you are not here then there is nothing here for me. I would rather be in the mountains, knowing you are with me."

Aiyu sat thinking and his two friends waited patiently for his answer. "I return," he told them finally. "We travel together. When ready we come home Konungssonur but not know when."

"I hope see both when you come back," Obiri told them.

#

Aiyu and Camille set out the following morning for Ptoraki. The moist cool air sat on Camille's skin reminding her of the climb over the mountains. This time she was more prepared, with warm clothing supplied by the other women and animal skins from the auchs. Aiyu had promised her that they would take a more comfortable route and not climb down any more cliffs. For the first day they travelled quickly up the valley, leaving the farms far behind, and when evening came they set up camp among a small cluster of rocks for protection from the wind. The next two days continued as the first and by the close of the third day they were hiking across a vast ice field on top of the mountains. Everything was white and the setting sun threw rays of light up from the broken surfaces of the ground.

During a simple evening meal of dried fruits Aiyu spoke of Bhata's family. Her father, while not an elder, was very well respected and was often sought to give advice on problems while her mother's skill as a spirit talker was known throughout the land. She had a brother as well and Aiyu thought him to be intelligent but a little too wild. "I considered be wild auch," he told her, "but respect desire of elders. Went to seek revenge on Bhata death before elders say no. Return because I know elders no want, Bhata no want too. Dniat would no return."

Next morning as they set out across the ice, the wind had risen and slivers of frozen air cut into Camille. She trudged along behind Aiyu, breathing hard as the temperature dropped and snow began to fall, adding its chill to the air. The wind picked up and the skies darkened as rolling clouds blocked out the sun. By midday Camille was finding it difficult to see Aiyu walking six feet ahead of her and despite the extra clothing she began to shiver. She dropped her head to protect her eyes from the cutting air and walked blindly along in the hollows left by Aiyu's feet. Her mind shut down and instinct took hold as she dragged the fur closer around her shaking body and strained to see through the frozen air.

Suddenly there were no prints to follow. The wind had picked them up and thrown them away in its fit of rage. She looked up and realized that she could no longer see Aiyu in the whiteness. The wind-blown snow had turned her world white. Panic overtook her and she called out but the wind ate her words. Standing alone on the mountains she didn't know what to do. If Aiyu didn't realize she was no longer with him, she knew she would die here in the emptiness. Wandering off into the white would also surely mean her death from cold or by falling off one of the many cliffs she remembered so well. The world around her was as dangerous as if she were at the bottom of the lake. She was about to accept that this was where her life would end when a shadow moved in the white, the familiar blue shape of Aiyu. She grabbed him and cried into his chest.

After her sobs had settled Aiyu took her hand and led her forward to a depression in the ice where he placed his pack on the ground. They huddled down, using what little protection it provided to wait out the storm. Camille rolled herself into a ball and even tried to use Aiyu to shield her but nothing refused the hunting wind. It bent its way past the bag and cut into her flesh. Even the vast size of Aiyu could not protect her from its wrath. The snow was beginning to build around their bodies as they lay prone on the frozen ground. She closed her eyes and wished that they could find some way to be out of the wind. It wouldn't be as bad if the wind would just leave them alone. She could hear its roar in her ears as it charged across the ice, declaring its dominance over its domain. Aiyu moved beside her. She felt him move away and held herself in anticipation of the bite as the wind was sure to find new places on her body - but it did not come. The wind seemed to have stopped, but that was not true. She could still hear it. She rolled over to look at Aiyu who sat beside her with his head turned toward the storm. The snow did not hit him and he looked confused.

"What happen?" To Camille's surprise, she heard him clearly. Moving slowly, she crawled to her knees and looked into the storm that still attacked with all the force it could muster, but something denied it. An invisible bubble sat over the two travelers holding the storm at bay. The wind-blown snow was turned aside, blowing over or around them before closing in behind. "How you do that?"

Camille was shocked. "Me?" she asked. At that moment the bubble collapsed, and the storm pounced with the viciousness of a wolf, biting into them once again. Aiyu dropped to the ground, dragging Camille down with him. Camille lay in the cold again trying to understand what she had done, what she had been thinking when the wind stopped. She had been cold beyond belief and was wishing that the wind would stop or just leave them alone. She remembered asking herself, why can't the wind just blow past? That must have been when the bubble formed, but why? Her abilities had shown her to be skilled in healing and as a forestal. Could she also have influence over the air? Her thoughts went to the dress her mother had given her and the shield with six colored bars. If she was also an elemental with power over the air it would explain the bubble, but then the dress must mean that she possesses all six abilities in some way. Her body shivered with cold, and the dress and shield left her mind. The time would have to come later to solve that problem. She focused on the wind, and in her mind imagined a bubble of protection. The wind stopped. This time her mind held onto the bubble and the storm was stilled again.

They sat out the rest of the day in the depression protected by the little piece of calm that Camille had created, the trapped air growing warmer. By nightfall the snow stopped falling and the storm began to calm. At some time during the night the clouds cleared, and the sky became a brilliant field of sparkling stars. Camille still held the bubble in place around them, but she was tired and knew she could not continue to do so much longer. She signaled Aiyu to be ready and released the air from her grasp before falling face first into the snow. The next thing she knew, the wind was gone and the sun had risen, providing its meagre warmth. She was sitting on the ground against Aiyu's great bulk. He was watching her with concern.

"I'm all right," she assured him, "just a bit tired."

"What you do?" he asked.

"I don't really know. I need to think about it."

"We need move. Can you walk?"

Camille tried to stand but her legs would not hold her. She slumped to her knees. "Not yet," she said.

Aiyu's face turned serious. "Must move. Know you no like but I must carry." She did not offer any objection. He gently lifted Camille and placed her in the sleeping fur from his pack before hanging it over his shoulders. With Camille cradled in the warmth and softly bouncing against Aiyu's back they set out again. Soon she was dozing, knowing that rest was the only way she was going to recover from her exertions.

Aiyu set a fast pace across the ice and snow, much faster than they could have travelled if she had been walking. When night again wrapped itself around them, Aiyu carefully lifted the sling from his shoulders and placed her on the ground. Her strength had returned during the day and she was able to stand comfortably. She asked, "Are you tired? Do you need to sit?" Aiyu assured her that, although he was happy to take a break from walking, he was fine. Even so, Camille quickly scanned her friend to satisfy herself that he was telling her the truth.

"That was a good idea with the fur," she told him. "It was very comfortable and gave me the time to recover."

"This how auchs carry their young," he explained, and Camille was a little embarrassed to find that she had been treated like a baby.

Next morning a small argument broke out when Aiyu wanted to carry her again. Camille declared that she would not be a burden to him, but Aiyu explained that they would be off the ice and into more comfortable lands much sooner if he carried her.

"But when we are out of the ice I will walk," she told him.

"If that what you wish. If you worry too much, when we leave ice, you walk, carry Aiyu." He broke into peals of grumbling laughter.

During the following days over the frozen landscape, Camille had to admit that it made sense to ride on Aiyu's back. The trip was much faster and more comfortable although she still felt embarrassed at the nature of the ride. As she hung in her fur hammock, bouncing gently against Aiyu's back, she could not see ahead and had to be content with watching the frozen world disappear behind them. Eventually the ice gave way to rock and the rock gave way to patches of hard earth where a few hardy plants fought for survival in the bleak landscape. The afternoon light was dying as he set her gently on the ground. "Tomorrow leave mountains. Soon be area Bhata family," he said. The ground now sloped down from where they stood, out onto a broad plain. The change between where they had travelled and what lay ahead left her stunned - the land was as flat as polished stone. There were a few trees at the bottom of the slope, and only a few rocks and pockets of scrub to mark the smooth expanse of grassland. In the distance she could make out a line of low hills shining blue and pink in the fading light.

"How is this possible?" she asked. "It is as if some giant hand has smoothed the ground and pushed the unwanted soil and rock to the side to make the hills and mountains."

"Might be true. Spirits do many things we no understand."

"At least the walking will be easier now."

"Easier, but must take care. Ground appear firm but on plain no believe what you see. Sometimes ground only thin, below mud pull you down, hold you."

"Mud?" Camille asked.

"After longnights snow melt, water fill Sometimes Lake. Create great water, take many weeks before go. Then this land beautiful, full of birds and flowers. It is the time spirits create new life. Even fish fill lake. When water goes new life spread over world, fish find way back sea. Nothing left except rocks until grass return."

"But how do you know where it is safe to walk?"

"Walk where grass grow strong. Grass no grow strong if not good ground. Grass weak, take care. No grass, danger."

Camille sat and looked over the plain as the last of the light left the sky. Tomorrow she would walk beside Aiyu out onto that flat ground. Although she had been told of its dangers, she felt relieved to be away from the steep rocky terrain for a while. As the sun crawled above the horizon the next morning, they prepared to fight their way through the line of trees at the bottom of the slope. Camille had not seen anything like them before. They stood close together, their branches twisted and knotted worse than a tangled ball of wool. She felt their pain as she stood before them and something drove her to place her hand against one particularly gnarled trunk. The struggle for survival overwhelmed her senses as she now knew the anguish of searching for water, only to find it frozen and unattainable beneath their feet and then receive so much of the precious fluid that they struggled to avoid drowning in it. She thanked the tree for allowing her to pass and was mildly surprised by a feeling of warm gratitude that came back to her.

Aiyu kept them moving north as far as she could tell. It took them three days to cross the open flood plain and enter the low hills on the northern edge of Sometimes Lake. The landscape reminded Camille of the area around Thistledowne, with its low hills and wide grasslands, but she had never known a land that felt so healthy. The groves of trees seemed content and the animals she felt did not cower in fear. Eventually the city of Ptoraki showed itself on the horizon and they found themselves walking through the now familiar mix of fruit and vegetable fields. As they walked, she asked why the fields were so far from the city. "Ptoraki much larger than Konungssonur. More people need more food," he explained. As they grew closer the scale of Ptoraki amazed her. This city made Konungssonur look like a village. Ptoraki lay over the land like a blanket, too big to be considered beautiful like Konungssonur, she thought as they approached the outskirts of the city. Unlike Konungssonur, this city was built on the ground, but it had the similar appearance of jumbled wooden structures. Camille stopped. Something Aiyu had told her had surfaced in her thoughts.

"Aiyu, you told me that Ptoraki was on the edge of the world and that you and Bhata liked to watch the water, but I see no water."

"It is as I say. Ptoraki rests on edge of world. But I also say city is large. Sea still about twenty miles away."

Camille was stunned. She could not imagine a city being twenty miles wide. She noticed something else. A crowd was gathering in the streets before them and the grumble of conversation spread further into the streets. A tall auch, slightly thinner than her companion, separated himself from the crowd and approached. He introduced himself as Glong, one of the respected auchs of this area of the city.

"I Aiyu, this Camille. We come from Konungssonur, bring news for elder Buit. I also see family of Bhata, my mate, while here."

"I take you to elder Buit," he said, then to Camille, "Sorry if make you uncomfortable. We no see lowlander in Ptoraki before."

The word had spread of the lowlander and the streets were lined with people trying to see for themselves. Those who had the time fell in behind and soon they led a procession through the streets of Ptoraki. Camille stayed close to Aiyu. She had not been intimidated by the size of the auchs before but now there were so many she found it difficult to see anything other than walls of blue pressing in on her.

"All right?" Aiyu asked her as she pushed against his leg.

"I will be fine. It is just that there are so many people. The last time I saw a crowd was the night my mother died."

Aiyu reached down and lifted her in one motion, setting her on his shoulder. "Now you see over people," he said. "They see you more easy so no push so much." She reached her arm around and gave his head a soft hug in thanks. And so she entered Ptoraki sitting high on the shoulders of her friend.

CHAPTER 21

Early morning light drifted lazily over the camp as the small Grechan force dragged itself to life. Captain Fordic anxiously awaited the return of the Haafi. Those close to him kept their distance for fear that he would take his nervousness out on them. The army had almost completed its morning meal when T'Anassah and his men rode into camp and made their way to the command tent. Fordic rose as soon as they came into sight and sent word for Martin and Rarbin to join them. By the time T'Anassah entered, the others were gathered around the small table looking at the map of the valleys.

"The Arenians have settled in at the end of the valleys, here and here," said T'Anassah. "King Leopold camps here with his captains and most of his men. A force in the other valley is led by one of his captains. It appears they have been here for days and have no intention of moving soon. King Leopold has positioned his archers along this ridgeline where they can cover both valleys. It is a very defensive position."

"If it is their intention to invade Greche, why are they holding a defensive position?" mused Fordic.

"Perhaps they saw you coming," said Rarbin.

"Maybe, but I doubt it. There must be something wrong. Maybe there is disease in their camp or maybe they wait for more troops. It does not matter;

we only need to see that they stay where they are until King Woldemar arrives with the rest of our army."

"If they wait, then our job is easier," said Martin. "Our orders are only to hold them at the border."

Captain Fordic looked at the map and asked, "Do we hold back out of sight, or do we make our presence known? If we remain here, King Leopold can continue to prepare and invade at his leisure but if we move forward, he will need to keep us in mind. The downfall is that we may force him into moving into Greche. Fordic asked Rarbin to stay when the others left. "This is your land. You know these valleys better than any other man here. How strong is King Leopold's position?"

"I am not a soldier and do not know the science of war but, as a hunter, I see his archers hold the ridge between the two valleys. That ground is very rocky and provides good cover, whether you are hunting goats or men. From there his archers will be able to fire upon anyone who tries to pass. His soldiers will only have to fight those who survive the charge. Even when King Woldemar arrives with the full army, he will find it difficult to win this battle as long as Leopold can keep his archers supplied with arrows. The terrain will make it almost impossible to mount a charge on the ridge without the loss of many men. I think you need to take the ridge either now or when the king arrives but you will need luck to succeed."

"You know more about the science of war than you think, and I believe I may have brought my luck with me." Fordic pulled up a chair to study the map.

The group gathered again at noon. "Gentlemen, it is obvious that whoever controls this ridge controls the valleys. Currently the Arenians have the dominant position. We will only get one chance to change that. It is time to be bold. If we can take the ridge from them, we must use the advantage before they discover the loss. Martin, if T'Anassah and his men lead your archers onto the ridge during the night, can you take the ridge quietly?"

"We can try, but it will only take one man to call out and destroy the advantage you seek," said Martin.

"The Haafi can take the ridge for you if you order it and then the archers can move in," said T'Anassah.

"Good. You will move tonight. I want our archers in position before first light. If you are successful, you will report back to me and the lancers will move to the valley in the morning. Martin's men will also gain a supply of Arenian arrows. Now go, prepare your men and with luck we will strike a blow for Greche tomorrow. Strictly speaking, he had been told to hold Arenia at the pass, but if he could strike against them as he hoped, it would not only hold the valley but would be a very good position for King Woldemar to attack when he arrived. And it would not hurt his prospects for promotion either.

That night under the cover of darkness the Haafi and the archers rode north, escorted by six lancers whose job it was to bring the horses back. They were still half a mile from the mouth of the valleys when T'Anassah stopped and ordered them to dismount. From here they would travel on foot so as not to alert the enemy. Although they stood among them Martin found it difficult to see the Haafi in the darkness. That, along with their fighting skills, was what made them so dangerous.

They walked the remaining distance to the end of the ridge. Martin's men settled in to wait while the assassins moved on. Martin watched them go. They didn't walk or run, they silently blended into the darkness. King Leopold's archers were spread along the ridge, making it easy for T'Anassah and his Haafi. The first group of four sat talking amongst the rocks. They had no idea anything was wrong until their throats were sliced open. The attack was so quick and precise that all four men fell dead at the same time. The Haafi wiped their blades clean and moved on. Not one man was given the opportunity of raising an alarm. In a short time, the only living people on the ridge were the six assassins looking down into the valleys below. Not long after that, T'Anassah appeared among the startled archers and told Martin it was safe for his men to move into position. Greche's archers began to spread onto the ridge and the Haafi disappeared into the night. By morning Martin and his men had removed the bodies and positioned themselves to cover the valley.

#

"It is done." The voice startled Fordic and he looked around the tent. Only then did he realize it was not empty. T'Anassah was standing just inside the opening. "How did you get in here?" The stupidity of the question struck him as the words left his lips. T'Anassah smiled while he watched surprise become understanding. It was the first time he had seen the man smile.

"Do we hold the ridge?"

"The Arenians are no more. Your archers hold the ridge without loss."

"Are your men all right?"

T'Anassah swayed as he answered. "They have completed their duty."

Fordic was trying to make sense of the strange answer when the Haafi dropped to his knees. He jumped forward to catch the man by the shoulders before he fell further.

"Are you wounded?"

"I have reported our success. I have done my duty. Now it is my time."

One of the guards poked his head into the tent having heard the voices inside. "Go, get help," Fordic yelled at him, easing the Haafi to the floor to check him for injuries.

"Do not concern yourself," said T'Anassah. "I am tired and my duty is done. I go without regrets."

Fordic tried to make the man comfortable. He fetched a cushion for the man's head and laid his hands across his chest. As he did so, T'Anassah's sleeve fell back, revealing the man's bracelet. The once-writhing red stone was now the dull dead black of emptiness.

"What is wrong?"

"The magic is gone, and I go with it."

The man appeared to be aging, his face becoming hollow and his skin blotched and fading. "I have lived too long." Fordic held him as his body shook with a series of wracking coughs. When he regained his breath, he went on. "I have lived for more than a thousand years and served more than seventy kings. None of them were foolish enough to send the Haafi into battle. Now six have completed their duty and only six remain."

Another fit of coughing shook his body and his eyes closed. The guard entered with one of the men who had some experience with battle wounds. Fordic held up his hand for them to wait. With his eyes still closed T'anassah began to speak again. His voice was dry and rasping.

"In the days when magic was strong in the world, the king of Greche pledged himself and his family to the protection of the witches for all eternity." His breathing was becoming more difficult, and he seemed to fight for the air to tell his story. "In return the witches gave him the Haafi. We twelve were the inner guard and we were given the bracelets." His body lay limp on the floor as his flesh wasted away from his bones. With one last effort he finished. "The bracelets gave us eternal life along with the ability to hide in plain sight. We were bound to serve and obey the kings of Greche through the generations. Only one thing could break the magic that bound us to this life - we could never be ordered to fight against another king. The witches imposed this restriction so that Greche could not use us to gain control of the world. When King Woldemar ordered us here under your command, he thought it would only be in defense of Greche, and the magic would not be broken." He gasped for air and shook with tremors. "I suggested you send us to attack the ridge in the hope of breaking the hold of the bracelet and it worked. I thank you for releasing me and my men from the bonds that held us. With the death of the last Arenian on the ridge the duty of my men was complete and their spirits rest there in peace. I wish you good luck with your duty now." Peace settled over the face of the wasted skeleton.

#

Captain Fordic rode at the head of his lancers as they approached the valley. He gave silent thanks to King Woldemar for giving him the use of the Haafi and to T'Anassah for giving him control of the ridge though it meant the loss of six loyal men. In one night, they had eliminated well over one hundred Arenian archers and soldiers and handed him a major advantage. T'Anassah had tricked him into giving them their deaths but in doing so he had saved the lives of many men. He only hoped King Woldemar saw it the same way.

Fordic walked his horse forward with his lancers fanned out in a shallow 'V' formation. He did not want to give his lack of numbers away easily, so they rode in two lines knee to knee. His lancers held the front line, lances aloft, while in the second line rode the men of Three Oaks. For as long as possible he wanted to hide the fact that he had no soldiers behind to back up any charge that the lancers would make. It was a bluff he hoped would work, when he was forced to implement it. He would stop the lines at the mouth of the valley and wait as long as he dared before he attempted it, because then there would be no turning back. He would be committed to fighting a battle with an army more than six times the size of his.

CHAPTER 22

Xavier sat at a heavy wood desk in a small dark office hidden deep in the tunnels beneath the city, surrounded by shelves and cupboards, lit only by the flickering of the few candles placed around the otherwise stuffy room. Before and around him were the stores and files that were once the secret property of Lord Lipstadt. They contained details of the active squads of The Society and their leaders with comments on the abilities and achievements of each. It had been interesting to read what his previous leader had thought of him and his men. He had learned that there were twenty-two active squads, each containing between twelve and twenty men, three hundred and fifty fighting men in all. He had command of an army. It was true that it was a small army and that they were spread out all over but no one but a few trusted members knew they existed. The armies of some of the kingdoms were not much larger, he told himself and relied on the estates to fill their numbers. But he also had reserves. There were large numbers of people throughout Arenia who had once been squad members but had aged, and there were the untrained members who could be rallied. Their contribution to an army would be small but they would swell the numbers, making the army of The Society appear a very powerful force. He had much work to do, however, if he was to familiarize himself with each squad. This knowledge could prove the difference between success and failure, knowing which leader he could trust with any particular mission.

But still he felt trapped here. There were too many king's guards in the city above and they all knew to keep their eyes open for him. It could be months before he would be able to show his face in Whitebridge again, and even then he would always be looking over his shoulder. Beth entered the tiny room without knocking and took a pile of papers off one of the chairs before sitting down.

"Good morning, Councilor Xavier," she greeted with a smile.

"Is it? I wouldn't know. I don't like hiding in this hole like a rabbit frightened of the hounds."

Beth laughed. "It's not forever and you have work to do. This way there are no distractions."

"Well, not many," he agreed with a grin spreading across his face. He had grown closer to the girl over the last weeks and looked forward to her visits. Beth had explained her role as head of the spies and the two had formed an immediate bond. "What else have you brought me?" he asked, seeing the package in her hands.

She bowed low and held the parcel reverently before her on outstretched arms. "I bring you a present. Every councilor has a copy and this is yours. It must not be lost or misplaced because this is our history, the history of The Society. It used to belong to Lord Lipstadt and now it is yours to care for." He undid the tie and carefully unwrapped the cloth covering to find an old book. Its cover was patterned in scrolls and swirls around a four-pointed star, carefully carved in the ancient leather bindings and secured with a tarnished brass clasp. At the center of the star a yellow stone had been set in the leather. "This book holds copies of the original Charter of The Society and the journal of Tam. Read it and you will learn how the auchs came to be and how they plotted to bring destruction upon us, forcing our people into hiding.

The Council guides The Society, but this book guides the Council. Study it and you will understand what it is to be a councilor."

Xavier carefully opened the tome to reveal the yellowed parchment pages within, secured with a frayed black ribbon. He opened to a page at random and read: Today, The Society leaves the isolation of this island to return to the world of man. The members are excited by the prospect of war with the dwarves, but I fear Kees' control of the Council. His words have corrupted the teachings of the forefathers, and I worry that the auchs are a two-edged sword.

Xavier closed the tome and held it reverently. Tam was one of the greatest leaders in history. Stories were told among the members of how he single-handedly rescued The Society from annihilation when they were attacked many years ago and of how he led The Society to freedom to hide them among the people of the seven kingdoms. But those few words on old pages were enough to throw doubt on all that the members had been told.

Beth's voice broke through his thoughts. "Now, what were you doing when I came in?"

"I was just trying to understand the squads, their strengths and weaknesses, and wondering what is happening in the world of men."

The smile left Beth's face. "I have heard rumor that Leopold has not taken his army to fight the auchs. For some reason he has circled the city and moved south towards Greche."

"What is he doing?" Xavier thought aloud. He went over recent events in his mind and tried to look at them from the king's point of view. "There is no reason for him to go south. Is your source reliable?"

"It is only rumor but when I hear the same rumor from three different agents I am inclined to listen."

"I will ride and check." Then more meekly, "I mean, I will send Jaimz and his squad to check the true location of the army." Beth smiled at his correction. Xavier quickly scratched out a note and called for a messenger. He instructed the lad to take it as fast as he could to Nate's farm and hurried him on his way.

Beth sat silently while he wrote and sent the note. Then she asked, "Now is there anything else I can do to distract you from your life as a rabbit?"

CHAPTER 23

After Aiyu and Camille had left Konungssonur, Obiri sat alone in his room wondering if he would ever see them again. He did not doubt Aiyu's word that he would return but he knew that his time in this world was coming to an end. His mind was still keen, though it fought its own battles, but his body ached with years and failing strength. He had lived a long life and knew he held the respect of all the Sysla, but the world was changing, and he was not confident he could change with it. The time was fast approaching when Kallu would take charge. He did not wish for death, but he had no desire to live through the war that Pouliquen believed was coming. He was forced to admit that he saw the approaching war, and in his heart he knew it heralded the end of the control of the elders. This is how it must be, because it is as Afi said. All he could do, he told himself, was make it possible for the auchs to survive the coming years. He sat in his chair and allowed his memories to consume him. After so many years his childhood was lost to him, but he remembered the day he was chosen to become an elder as if it were yesterday. In fact, that day was clearer in his mind than yesterday. He had felt proud and honored to be chosen, even though it meant he could never be selected for a mate because his life from that point in time was given to the Sysla. He had applied himself fully to his training and now he was ready to pass on the responsibility. Almost ready, he corrected himself. There was still work to be done. He picked up the heavy cane he now used for walking and knocked it on the floor. The door opened immediately, and he smiled. They never left him alone these days in case he needed something. A young auch waited at the door. Obiri was embarrassed that he could not remember her name. To hide his embarrassment, he grumbled roughly, "Get Hirith and Ethru." He was sorry for how he said it but the girl was gone before he could apologize. The door opened again, and he stopped the girl before she disappeared. "Forgive old man who hate himself. He hate age and infirmity, take frustration out those around who young and strong as he would like be." The girl smiled and closed the door, leaving Hirith and Ethru standing before him.

"Well, no just stand there. Come sit," he grumbled. When they had done as he asked, Obiri went on. "You know Aiyu leave and travel Ptoraki. Camille go too." Hirith nodded. "This leave me need someone watch Edge near Aiyu farm." Ethru's eyes widened. "Need more than watcher. There trouble in lowlands. Wizard Pouliquen believe auchs must have war with humans. Lowlanders will come to farm. Lowlanders know they get past Edge there." The couple sat silent, waiting, but concern was evident on their faces. "Need more than someone I trust go watch. Need someone take charge if trouble come. There no be time wait decision from city. Elders decide auchs no attack but no say no defend if lowlanders come. Hirith, need you take charge of watchers. They auch first defense. If trouble come you must do what necessary. Humans can never come again to auch land. War maybe come soon, I think not time yet, but must protect auch nation. I no want start war but hiding time over. Will you do this?"

Hirith sat stunned by the request. He understood how Aiyu and Bhata chose to live away from the city, but they were very different people. He had never considered the idea for himself or Ethru and the thought scared him.

The idea was still spinning in his head when he heard Ethru answer. "If that is Obiri wish then Hirith be honored obey. Hirith go to Edge. I go too."

He turned to look at his mate as he heard Obiri reply, "Good. That settled. Leave as soon as ready, there much to be done."

Hirith opened his mouth to object, but Ethru spoke again. "You ask large task. I sure Hirith appreciate help. Suggest Battok and Zon go too. All know they enjoy good joke. Their pranks be useful if humans attack."

"Take with you. I ask much but auchs need this. Go now. Time for me to rest."

Ethru ushered Hirith out of the room and back along the galleries not allowing him the time to say anything. Finally he stopped and refused to be pushed any further. "What you do?" he asked.

"Obiri need you."

"But I no watcher."

"He know, still he ask you." Hirith thought about what she was telling him. "You are leader. When you ask something be done, people enjoy do it for you. This what Obiri need. You lead, I help."

"Yes you help. Get me in this. Understand only time I be out Konungssonur when father bring meet you, and days go bury Bhata. You give more trouble, Battok and Zon. Why we need them?"

"You lead watchers but what you do if lowlanders come? They be playing pranks on people all lives."

"How do pranks win battles?"

"It not pranks you need. You need ideas. Pranks come from ideas, they have best ideas. Think what they do with all auch nation to do their work. Together they stop lowlanders. Make lowlanders run like dog after sit on fire. They make ideas, Hirith make happen."

"Maybe Obiri no need Hirith. He need Ethru because she always win. If Hirith leader then first order is Ethru ask Battok and Zon come with us, but

I think I go and jump off Edge now."

"Why?"

"Because just think about what those two do to lowlanders see me die laughter."

#

"No," said Battok. "I no die to fight lowlanders. Too many jokes left. Even if not die, I no able to live out there."

"Battok, you friend. I follow you, help you many jokes when children. Now need you help. Elders very wise but their decisions take much time. Pouliquen believe auchs go war with lowlanders. Obiri need auchs who make pranks. He need auchs think quick. He know elders no able do this. Obiri want me organize watchers. Can do this but if anything happen I need someone understand what they see, think of prank to defend against attack. You and Zon ones for this. You not only think of best ideas but understand how make work."

"We no can live outside city," protested Zon.

"Pouliquen think all auchs soon need leave cities, fight for freedom."

The discussion went on for hours. Ethru remained silent for most of the time but when the stalemate brought about an extended silence she spoke. ""Zon, we good friends since day we first meet. We see mate's support each other in all they do. Hirith need you and Battok support now. This much more than prank. Mean survival of our people. We go our rooms now, prepare leave at sunrise. Both want you come too. Come now, Hirith, we must get ready. If we no see you again I say goodbye now."

They returned along the galleries to their rooms in silence until at the door Hirith said, "I think we need come up with own ideas."

"Why?"

"Battok strong, no change mind, now there only two of us."

"They be there. Zon no allow Battok let us go alone when need his support. She just need time to show she support mate, talk to him until Battok know it his idea to go with us."

Hirith stopped and looked again at his mate. "Is that what you do me?"

She raised her hand and gently caressed his cheek. "You too smart for me get away with anything like that."

#

The next morning Hirith and Ethru waited until the sun was well clear of the horizon before they picked up their packs and made their way along the galleries. Ethru wondered if she had misread Zon or if Battok was more strong-willed than she thought. Either way she was concerned for Hirith. He would need people he could trust, people who were smart enough to offer suggestions and wise enough to know when not to. She blamed herself for making them leave without Battok's word that he would join them. To make matters worse, Hirith had not said a word since the sun first began to rise. She could not tell if he was angry because she had said they would leave the city or if he was more concerned now that she had given him false hope. They reached the edge of the city and turned to walk down the ramp when Hirith stopped in front of her. She was taken by surprise and walked into his back but he didn't seem to notice.

"You late. We begin to think must sit here all day." The voice came from the ground and Ethru looked around Hirith to see Battok and Zon sitting on their packs at the bottom of the ramp. The smiles on their faces told her that making her worry was another of their little jokes. It didn't matter. She could see the appreciation on Hirith's face.

She pushed past him and strode down the ramp with a stern look on her face and fists on her hips. They stood in front of her, their faces twisting with the effort of holding in the laughter. Then she laughed too. "Good joke," she told them.

The four friends set out for The Edge. As they walked through the farmlands Hirith explained, "First two problems. How we know when and where lowlanders come, how we get news to watchers quick. Watchers spread out along Edge, that concern me. If I no able pass message or news quick I no be able send help where it needed."

Battok suddenly stopped and told them that he and Zon needed to return to the city. "Go ahead. We follow later. First there something we must do." He and Zon headed back. Without another word Hirith walked on, trusting his friend. They arrived at the farm without incident to find two auchs preparing to return to the pass. After they learned that their names were Teek and Kuir, Hirith asked if there had been any sightings of the lowlanders. Kuir told them that no humans had tried to gain access since they had been there. Together the four left the farm and made their way to the pass where two others stood watch. When they were all together Hirith informed them of Obiri's request and asked how many times anyone had gone to the cliff to see if there was any movement below. Kuir, obviously in charge, answered for them. "Kuir told to guard pass, no allow lowlanders back to high country. It our duty stay here. No one go to cliff."

"You do duty well but I like to see someone go walk Edge each day. If they see lowlanders approach, we no be caught by surprise. Lowlanders no like dark so build fire when sun gone. These easy see." Kuir huffed his disapproval at the suggestion that he could have performed his duty better. "I know Kuir pride himself on duty," said Hirith, "and this why I ask you do first walk along Edge. I trust you no allow anything go unnoticed. It be good for others to see importance of this task. It require someone of your dedication see it completed properly."

Kuir looked at the other guards who were watching the exchange with interest before nodding and turning to walk to the Edge. "You right. This job be done properly. I do it."

Later that day Hirith and Ethru sat talking to the remaining guards when

Kuir returned to report that he could find no sign of the lowlanders. Hirith thanked him before asking, "How you think we should organise tasks? How often you think someone should walk Edge?"

After making a show of thinking about the question Kuir replied, "I think each day one auch is enough to guard pass and one go to watch at Edge and check again after sun go to look for fire."

"That good. Can you see that guards understand importance this duty?" Kuir puffed out his chest and assured Hirith that his guards would do their duty well.

Early next morning Ethru came out onto the veranda of the cottage and saw three auchs approaching. She decided not to wake her mate and sat in the low chair to wait. They had not come much closer before she heard Hirith grumbling and banging his way around inside. He joined her and followed her gaze. He waited until Battok stepped onto the veranda.

"Look, Zon, they worry we no come. They sit watch for us."

"Never doubt you come. Zon too good person no keep your word," said Hirith. "I know you be thinking how big joke you can make if all auchs help. But I admit I no think you able talk someone else come."

Zon chuckled and stepped forward. "Hirith, Ethru, I ask Tuuki come. She spirit talker of great ability. She agree come and help with problem." Hirith clearly did not understand the offer. "You tell us you want Battok come because he able to think of ideas. Battok think brilliant plan and that why he go back city." Hirith shook his head still not understanding. "He need discuss plan with Obiri and ask him give what you need. That why Tuuki agree come. Battok tell Obiri Hirith ask for strongest spirit talkers join watchers all along Edge. Obiri send word other cities do same. Spirit talkers ask birds and animals if they see lowlanders. Watchers know quick if lowlanders come. Ask birds pass along message so you hear word quickly. But Tuuki no sure if she able explain this to spirits or if spirits agree."

A broad smile split his face and he began to laugh. "That why I need you."

#

The sun spread its warmth thinly over the land next morning as Hirith stood at The Edge looking over the forest below. Battok had joined him as he took some time to think about the task Obiri had given him. The air was clear, and they could see far out into the lowlands. Nothing moved to indicate the forest hid anything other than the animals that lived there. "What does great leader do now?" laughed Battok.

"That why you here. What joke you suggest we prepare for humans stop them coming up here again?"

"You no object if they get hurt?"

Hirith grew solemn. "I see what they do Aiyu family. I think I like see lowlanders hurt, no worry how bad."

"Then prank so simple even you think of it. Collect rocks. Store near Edge over entrance. Auch no like get hit on head by rock fall from here. I no think lowlander be very happy if happen to them."

Hirith smiled at the thought of humans dancing over the rough ground below as rocks fell on their heads. He looked around. "No enough rocks here be serious threat. Lowlanders will send many men."

"Plenty rocks down there," said Battok pointing down to the base of the cliff.

Hirith looked to the rocky ground below before setting out in search of Kuir. When he found the guard he told him, "Need rope, enough reach bottom of Edge and good furs carry rocks. Need auchs collect rocks at base, others lift them to top." Kuir gave him a questioning look. "We prepare big joke for humans if they attack again. I wonder how hard their heads are."

Kuir caught on quickly and grinned at the thought. "I send someone bring workers from city. While wait we prepare for them get here."

"Good. When he go to city ask Obiri send groups to other watchers do same." Kuir went to carry out the order and with nothing more they could do at the moment Hirith and Battok went back to the Edge to watch and wait.

CHAPTER 24

The tunnels beneath Whitebridge were busier than Xavier had ever seen them. Messengers hurried back and forth, taking news around the city. He would have preferred the tunnels to be empty, as they were so often, as he walked beside Beth sharing light-hearted banter, making their way to the meeting room. The Council was gathering for what promised to be a lively discussion following Jaimz' return yesterday with confirmation of the king's movements. He and Beth had considered the various options throughout the night but his mind still tumbled over the possible outcomes of this day. By the time they reached the meeting room he was feeling ill with tension. He had come up with a plan and, though Beth supported him, it would test his political abilities to see it accepted. He took a deep breath before following her into the room filled with the low babble of voices. The full Council is here, Xavier thought with some relief, for he needed their agreement if his plan was to succeed.

Arwen wasted no time in bringing the meeting to order. "We have all heard the news. Has anyone any further information to add to this discussion?" He waited as the story came together like the pieces of a children's puzzle, revealing a picture, but still incomplete. "We know what happened, but we need to understand why if we hope to salvage the situation and turn Leopold's eyes back to the north, and the auchs."

All had come to the same conclusion - Leopold had decided that he faced a danger from Greche. One by one they fell silent in thought and Xavier took the moment to speak up. "I have only been in the council for a few days but I have thought hard on this. Lord Lipstadt was arrested and I was hunted by the guards following our news of the attacks by the auchs. Even the proof of our story that we delivered to the king was not enough to convince him. Then the king takes the army and marches south, away from the threat. This all leads me to only one conclusion. King Leopold knew about the auchs and trusted that they would not attack. He must have some secret treaty with them."

"A treaty with the auchs," exclaimed Arwen. "Why would anyone do such a thing? How does this help us?"

"I don't know yet, but if I were Leopold and I had such a treaty, my first thought would be that the auchs had broken it. But I am not Leopold, and I do not know how strong his treaty is. It must be very strong for him to refuse accepting that it would be broken." He relaxed, seeing that he had the full attention of the other councilors. "If this is the case he would look elsewhere for understanding. Suspicion would naturally fall upon the man bringing the news and request for aid. No matter how perfect my story, it could not overcome his belief in this treaty. When Lord Lipstadt supported me he must have said something that the king knew to be untrue. It was probably said in the king's private chambers, so we cannot know what it was, but it resulted in Lord Lipstadt's arrest and the guards looking for me."

"So, you are saying that you are the cause of our recent setbacks?"

"No, I am saying King Leopold had information that contradicted our story, and he trusted that source more."

"How does that relate to the army's movements?"

"We plotted to encourage him to attack the auchs, but he rejected the story we gave him. I don't believe he knows about The Society, because he would have stayed in Whitebridge and searched us out, so he must suspect a threat to his kingdom from another direction. I believe that he deduced that threat came from Greche and so now he marches south to face it."

"But why march north and then circle the city?"

"If he suspects a plot from Greche, then he believes we were part of it to open the way for invasion. He would believe us to be spies and assumes there are others. He started out north to fool these spies so they would not race ahead to warn any approaching army of his movements."

"We must stop him and divert his attention back to the north," said Grarm. "We need more evidence that the auchs are the real danger and that they are beginning to attack. Xavier must send some squads to the north to draw out the auchs and make them move into Arenia. If we can do this in time, Leopold will have to turn his army around and face them."

"Xavier's reasoning makes sense," said Beth. "Leopold must believe he faces invasion from Greche. But it is not the role of The Society to stop him. It is the natural urge of man to prove his superiority over others and wars will be fought. The Society must follow the charter and the teachings of Tam and protect all humans from the dangers of the lesser beings."

"Are you saying we should let Arenia go to war with Greche and do nothing?" asked Arwen.

"We are saying that there is another choice," Xavier told the room. "I have been reading the charter and Tam's journal, and our answer lies in the words they hold. The forefathers founded The Society to ensure that only the strong survive. Mankind is that strength, and the strength of man is The Society for it is the vision of the Council that allows us to live in the knowledge of our superiority." He opened the book he carried. "If you will allow me I will read some words from Tam's journal, though I am sure you are all familiar with these words. The Society must be true to all men and teach them all to be vigilant if we are to remain the masters of the world. Its members must spread throughout the kingdoms and teach all men our message. Our duty is clear. We are to be the guides to a future where all creatures bow down to man." He closed the book carefully and his eyes took in the councilors. "And what better way to guide them than as rulers of the kingdom."

"What are you suggesting?" asked Jozef.

"The king has left the city, taken his army and personal guard with him and has left that fool Darveed in charge. We would not need many people to take the city, and the man who rules Whitebridge rules Arenia. Even Leopold's army could not successfully lay siege to this city, particularly when we have the tunnels to move supplies and troops in and out in secret."

The words brought silence to the room as each councilor sat considering the possibilities of having one of their own people crowned as king. It would certainly help their cause if they were the ones making the decisions.

Arwen provided the first words of doubt. "But Tam also saw how Kees almost destroyed The Society and was forced to put in place the guidelines preventing any one person ruling The Society again. Placing one of our own on the throne of Arenia would go against Tam's warnings by giving too much power to one man. The Society may once again be threatened."

"But this only serves to strengthen Tam's words. The Society will still be ruled by the Council while the King rules Arenia. By having a king who is loyal to The Society we allow the ideals to be spread openly without endangering the Council because all actions would be attributed to the king."

"I like the idea," said Grarm.

Jozef agreed, but added, "It is a big step. We have survived for all these generations by working from the shadows. To seize the city we must declare ourselves to the world and be prepared for anything that follows."

"Both plans show merit. It would be advantageous to rule the people openly but our goal must be to the charter. It is our responsibility to see the other races either subjugated or destroyed, beginning with the auchs," said Arwen. "But who would you see as king?"

Beth cut in before Xavier could respond. "You are the senior counsellor. It is obvious you would be our choice for king."

Arwen looked around the room and all eyes looked back at him. "I think we could achieve both plans with enough men and a little planning. We would only need a few in the palace to take control and keep it and we only need enough in the north to draw out the auchs. Leopold will be split three ways, facing his perceived threat from Greche in the south and the real threat from the auchs in the north while we hold his city and his nation. If he chooses to try and take back Whitebridge, he will lose his lands but while he fights to save Arenia we will have time to secure the capital. When he finishes in the fields he must lay siege to his own city with our troops at his back. I like this plan. Are there any objections?"

No one dared to offer any objection and Xavier held up his goblet. "All hail King Arwen of Arenia," and the councilors toasted their new king with him.

#

Later Beth sat with Xavier in his room discussing their plan to take control of the kingdom." Arwen is a fool to take on Leopold and the auchs at the same time," said Xavier. "He risks everything for his own glory."

"But we cannot deny that both operations are in the interests of The Society," Beth replied. Xavier scowled at her comment and Beth said, "Don't look at me that way. This may all work in our favor in the long term. If we can take control of Whitebridge, we will see The Society in a position more powerful than it has ever been in history, and if Jaimz is able to follow your plan we will rule while Leopold is forced to do our bidding."

"And when we have finished, we will have replaced one fool king with another."

"Most kings are fools but who is king is not important. It is the decisions he makes that will guide the world. The Society and the council will guide Arwen. He is too loyal to the cause to do otherwise."

Xavier sat sulking in his chair, refusing to talk any further on the subject until Beth turned to leave. He looked up and called her back. "I need to go up to the city. Living under the ground has made me as intolerant as a badger," he said. "Will you come with me to the White Star Inn for an ale or two?" Beth hesitated then agreed, thinking the risk worth taking, if only to break him from his moods. He rose and the two friends walked casually through the tunnels until they reached the ladder up to the inn's wine cellar where Marcus stood waiting.

"Welcome, my friend. It is good to see you looking so well. Don't worry, all is safe. The guards no longer sit all day in the tavern although they do keep a regular watch on the street and business is returning. Come, the back booth is free, and my man watches at the door to give warning if danger approaches." He led them into the tavern before going to the barrels and returning with three foaming ales. "The best I have," he told them.

As they sat in the shadows at the back of the room, Xavier felt some of the tension flow from his body. The sun shone through the windows, lighting the front of the tavern and raising his spirits. "Business looks slow," he said.

"It has been worse," Marcus told him. "After the guards took everyone out that night and took up residence at the front tables, people were afraid to enter. Now they have gone, my regular customers are starting to return and if the guards don't make any more trouble things may return to normal in a few weeks."

"Never fear, my friend," said Xavier. "I have a feeling that things will get better soon."

CHAPTER 25

Jaimz checked up and down the street. Nothing raised any alarm, so he dismounted, tied his horse to a hitching post, took one more look and slipped into the tavern room. The Whitestar Inn was quieter than he remembered. Marcus stood at the serving table with one big hand holding three tankards while the other operated the tap on the keg before him. He looked up as Jaimz entered and signaled him into the hallway at the back of the room where he joined him. Marcus told him to go to the top of the stairs and wait inside the first room until he was called. As a soldier, he understood the stress of waiting but he was nervous about the situation he had been thrust into and fidgeted as he followed the innkeeper. Something was happening and he was being swept along like a twig on a swollen river. He smiled to himself, knowing the twig would at least stay afloat.

He sat beside his bag and contemplated recent events. Xavier had left him and the squad at the farm and returned to the city alone. They had heard nothing until the note arrived, instructing him to discover the true direction King Leopold had taken. The lack of news continued, and he had begun to wonder if Xavier still lived. Then the messenger arrived with instructions to come alone to the inn. He sensed the twig was approaching something big and hoped it was a quiet lake and not a waterfall. His anxiety was now fueled by the silence as he was forced to wait three days without further contact. Late on the third night, when the tavern had emptied, there came a knock on his door. He picked up his sword, only to find a young serving girl standing outside. She told him he was to go down to the tavern room. Well, little twig, he thought, it seems we have arrived. He strapped on his sword belt and headed for the stairs. A candle burned on a table and heavy sheets had been hung over the windows, confirming his growing suspicions that no one was to know of this meeting. Feeling the approaching waterfall, Jaimz walked to the table and only then did he see the two people standing in the dark.

"It's good to see you again, Jaimz. I'm glad you could make it."

"I didn't think I had a choice," he replied as he took a seat. Jaimz wanted to question Xavier about his long silence but could see his friend was not yet ready to give him any answers.

"The others should be here shortly and then we will tell you all you need to know," said Xavier. Jaimz looked at the girl and recognized her as one of the serving girls from their earlier visit. She and Xavier took the chairs opposite and leaned back to wait. The girl reached across to firmly grip Xavier's hand. Now he knew some of what his friend had been doing. Before long they were joined by four other men, though Jaimz could see that none knew each other.

"I am sorry for the lateness of this meeting, but no one must know that we meet or of the instructions I am about to give you," Xavier told them.

"Who are you to give us instructions?" asked one man. He was older than the others, slightly overweight with a bald head and a small but prominent scar on his chin.

Xavier looked the man in the eye. "You must be Harold." The man nodded in response as Xavier continued. "You see, I know you quite well, though we haven't met before. You are all squad leaders and have proven yourselves in the field." Jaimz's sharp look did not go unnoticed. "Yes, Jaimz, you are leader of my squad now." The candle flickered low and flared again as if anticipating what was to come. "Harold here has been doing the work of The Society in the northern lands of Greche and has been so successful that no word of his exploits has made its way to the leaders of the kingdom. He has shown the truth to the people and guided them in the elimination of over thirty of the half-breed witches." Seeing the looks on the faces around the table he explained further. "Yes, I too did not understand until it was explained to me that the council has determined that the witches cannot be pure humans and must have interbred with the elves sometime in the past. That is why we show the people they cannot be trusted." He waited, giving his words time to settle. "We also have Gregory who has done good work in the south-west of Arenia, and Samuel and Ronald who have been in the north-west. Jaimz now leads my old squad and has worked in the north-east. All of you are proven leaders and have earned the right to be at this table."

Harold looked around the table but directed his question at Xavier. "You still haven't answered me. Who are you?"

Beth answered for him. "He is Xavier. He replaces Lipstadt as leader of the operations of The Society. He is responsible for all squads in the field, not only the ones represented by you gentlemen. He has also been named the newest member of the Council. I am Councilor Beth."

Jaimz looked at Xavier, wondering even more what had been happening in Whitebridge in recent weeks.

"What happened to Lipstadt?" asked Harold.

"Lipstadt was arrested by King Leopold on a charge of treason. His death left a vacancy in the Council, and we have chosen Xavier to take his place."

"From this time on you will receive your orders from me," Xavier told them.

"So we have a new commander," said Samuel who seemed unimpressed with the changes announced. He was a tall man, young and fit with a body and face that ensured he had the admiration of all the women he met. "Now, do we go back and continue our work or have you other plans for us?"

"There are to be changes in your orders. I think you all will enjoy what you are about to hear and will look forward to your promising futures." He called into the darkness and Marcus appeared, bearing a tray holding eight goblets of wine. One was placed before each person and when all were served, Marcus pulled up a chair and joined them. "I hope you don't mind but I have asked our host to join us to hear the news first-hand. This way he will not need to employ his more subtle methods of discovering what is happening." Marcus gave him a hurt look. "Since the time of Tam, The Society has worked from the shadows. It has taken many generations, but we now find ourselves in a very unusual position and we cannot afford to allow this chance to pass. I have news that only the Council and a few others yet know - the auchs still live in the mountains to the north!" An explosion of questions erupted around the table, but Xavier held up his hand to quiet them. "Not only do we have proof but a way into the mountains has been discovered. There is a cave and passage that leads to the high country above the cliff. The barrier that has barred humans for so many years is gone." He waited for the importance of the news to register with the group. "The Society tried to guide King Leopold in an attack on the creatures, but circumstances were against us and resulted in the loss of Lipstadt. It appears that the king had determined from all that occurred that he faced invasion from Greche and has taken his army to stand against King Woldemar. Unfortunately, good King Woldemar will not be there to fight him unless he hears of Leopold's march. Now you all know briefly where we stand, and this is where your lives become interesting." The room remained silent.

"The Council has decided that the time has come when The Society no longer needs to work from the shadows. We are declaring ourselves to the world," said Beth. "Xavier is reorganizing the squads into a regular army that will become known as the Fist of Man."

"You gentlemen will command the five fingers of the Fist," said Xavier. "The other squads have been assigned to each of you in a way that will distribute our strengths well. At the end of this meeting Beth will give each of you a list of the squads that will join you, along with information on their achievements. Study these. Each squad leader will be given the rank of sergeant, each of you will hold the rank of Field Captain. You will each select one man from your squad to be given the rank of sergeant in your place. Now if you are to be an army you must look like one." He rose and disappeared out of the sphere of candlelight to return carrying a bundle that he let drop open. In his hands he held a black cape with a white star on the back. "The uniform of the Fist," he announced. "It is like the one worn by the army of Tam as best we can determine. There are enough for every man in your command. To the Fist of Man and its new Field Captains," he said as he raised his goblet. Everyone joined him in the toast.

"Now for your orders," he said. "The Council has decided to take two actions besides the formation of the army. The first is to draw the auchs out into Arenia where they will be left for the army to turn and face. We don't know how many exist, but their numbers cannot be large. The mountains could not support more than a few hundred at the most, but it will be enough to occupy Leopold. Ronald, Samuel, Gregory and Jaimz will take the bulk of our army north to engage them and lead them to the king. Even he is not so incompetent as to lose the little battle we will give him. Because he knows the area and has been to the high country, Jaimz will lead this part of the operation. He is new to his role, and I am sure he will listen to your advice, but trust in his ability."

"Where will I be going?" asked Harold.

"That is the greatest news of all. You will be going nowhere. Your finger has been chosen to ensure the other task of the Council is brought to a successful conclusion. Your squads will be arriving over the coming days and will wait outside the city until they are called. We will guide them into the city in secret, where they will then take Whitebridge from Leopold. We intend to rule Arenia with members of The Society filling all vital positions, from the king down." A stunned silence followed. Xavier raised his goblet again. This time a broad smile crossed his face as he toasted "To the future king of Arenia and The Society, rulers of the people."

"To the king and The Society, future rulers of Arenia."

CHAPTER 26

The tunnels beneath Whitebridge were crowded with five squads under the command of Field Captain Harold. Eighty-two soldiers stood ready to take the city that all of Arenia and the world considered impregnable. Beth had made a number of her people available as guides around the underground maze. They stood grouped to one side waiting for the operation to begin. Xavier watched as the men received their final orders, becoming impatient for the day to begin and his soldiers to disperse. He wished he could join them; the work of a councilor was important, but he liked to be part of the action. He consoled himself with the fact that he was now a more important leader than he had hoped to be at this point in his life. Beside him, Beth must have sensed his impatience and mistook it for concern, because she leaned close and whispered, "Don't worry. These men can take Darveed and the palace. Soon we will be the rulers of all Arenia."

Harold waited as the guides led his men away in small groups. Many of them would be taken to the barracks where most of the city guards slept. Others would be taken to locations around the city where guards patrolled the streets above. All of the city's guards would be given the chance to lay down their weapons, surrender and join the new army of Arenia. There was no advantage in killing good men. Having seen most of his men disappear into the tunnels Harold indicated to his guide that she should lead them on their way. She was a small girl with plaited, long dark hair tied and a young face. Although she looked no more than a child, she was competent enough to be chosen to lead his squad. They were soon passing between solid stone walls that he assumed formed the foundations to the palace. The girl indicated that they should be quiet while she carefully opened a small panel to check all was clear before unclipping and opening a hidden door in the wall of the tunnel. The gap was narrow, but he slipped through sideways and waited for his men to join him one by one. Once they were all through, the door slid shut, leaving their guide in the tunnels. From this point on Harold and his men were on their own.

Beth had given him a map of the palace layout. He looked around to confirm that he was in the kitchen pantry, as he was told they would be. They made their way quietly out through the vacant kitchen to the narrow servant's stairs at the back of the room. Two floors up the stairs opened out onto a wide hallway with a blue tiled floor. Windows along one side overlooked the courtyard, and doors shared the other wall with carved busts on fluted columns. Harold looked out from the shadows of the stairway to see the two guards about halfway along. He had been warned they would be there and had come prepared. Two of his men dressed as chambermaids left the shadows to walk along the hall, nattering to each other and ignoring the guards as if they had not seen them. When they drew near, one guard stepped in front and stopped them. His face carried a leering grin until suddenly he found the hilt of a dagger protruding from his chest. The other guard's throat was opened before he had the chance to draw his sword or call a warning. Both guards were caught preventing the sound of their falling bodies alerting anyone inside as Harold and the rest of the squad arrived.

Beth had told them that behind the door was a sitting room with a desk and chair on one side, and a table and chairs for meals on the other. Behind this room was the lord's bedchamber. Harold gave the prearranged signal and his men spread out, covering each door and the head of the stairs at each end of the hall. With his sword drawn he opened the door and entered the apartment beyond with a small group of men. The room was empty. He moved quickly to the other door and listened. Sounds of snoring came from within. They entered and surrounded the large soft bed. Lord Darveed woke to find a sword tip nudging at his throat.

"Be quiet, my lord," warned Harold. Keeping his sword ready, he allowed Darveed to sit up. "Lord Darveed, I must inform you that Leopold no longer rules Arenia. I represent the Fist of Man, the new army of Arenia, and my men now have control of Whitebridge where Arwen will soon be ordained as the new King." He waited, allowing his words time to sink into the sleep-clogged mind of Lord Darveed. "My lord, you are being offered the honor of being the first to swear fealty to King Arwen. If you do, you may live the next five years of your life in the dungeons before your release. The choice is yours."

"While King Leopold lives, he is King of Arenia, and I have sworn to him."

"Your loyalty is touching but it will be of little value to you or Leopold." Harold thrusted so quickly the sword pierced Lord Darveed's neck from front to back. The stricken lord tried to call a warning, but only soft gurgling sounds came from his torn throat as he fell back onto the bed. Moments later he was dead, and Harold took his men to round up the occupants of the other rooms.

#

Willian lay asleep in his bed. Since King Leopold had led the army out of Whitebridge, he had been forced to find tasks to occupy himself while he listened for any hint of an uprising. He had taken to spending some of each day in the stables helping Ben. He found he enjoyed being around the horses, but the work was tiring. His days consisted of checking with Lord Darveed after breakfast to see if he was needed, then going to help Ben with the stable work, after which they would sit and talk for hours before he wandered around the palace, listening at keyholes. He had told his new friend of his life on his father's estate, how he had been included in all his father's decisions from a very young age, and how his father had explained that he needed to listen to people and understand them if he was ever to be a good leader. In return, Ben told of how he had grown up on his parent's farm with many brothers and sisters, where life was difficult with so many mouths to feed, and how his father had been forced to indenture him to the king to learn the skills of horse and saddle care.

His sleep was broken abruptly when a large fist shook his shoulder and dragged him from his bed. Two men stood over him dressed in black capes. They growled at him to hurry and pulled him from the room into a crowd of palace staff gathered in the hall where they were watched by other men in black. The sleepy staff looked terrified as men herded them through the corridors of the palace towards the throne room. Willian concluded that these men must be soldiers because they wore a uniform and spoke and acted like trained men but, searching his mind through all the information his father had given him, he could not recall any army that wore these colours. He needed to learn more. Shuffling his way through the growing mass of people, he walked near a few of their captors.

"Who are you and where is Lord Darveed?" he asked in his best, scared child, voice.

"Don't worry. You are not going to be harmed, and you'll soon know who we are," said one man.

"Lord Darveed won't be joining you," said another. "He has been a little clumsy and had an accident. He tripped and fell, unfortunately landing on our Captain's sword." They all chuckled at their friend's humor.

They entered the throne room where they forced them to kneel with their faces to the floor. Willian took the opportunity to look about the room while their captors were occupied. It appeared that everyone in the palace had been gathered here. He could see Ben crouching not far from him. When Ben smiled at him, some of the nerves that tightened his stomach began to settle.

A small group stood on the dais at the front of the room. They were dressed in black capes similar to the soldiers but theirs were trimmed in pale green running around their necks and down the front. Willian's eyes locked on one man in the group. Recognition flashed through his mind as the man stepped forward, his long red locks bouncing on the sides of his head. He remembered the man's name and the story he had given to the king. They thought he had escaped Whitebridge long ago but here he stood in the King's throne room.

Xavier spoke; he listened closely. He knew that when the little show was finished, he would somehow have to get word to the king. They had been fooled. Everything that had happened had been well planned so these people might take control of the city.

"My lords and ladies," Xavier said, "you have been gathered here to witness the beginning of a new era for Arenia. Leopold was a good king, and we admired him, as you do. As king he ruled his people fairly for most of his reign. We were satisfied to sit quietly and accept his wisdom. Like you, we were happy - that is until we discovered the truth about Leopold, a truth so terrible that we have been forced to act, though we hated doing so. Leopold plots behind your backs for the downfall of Arenia. Your king has formed an unholy treaty with our enemies and at this moment takes his army against his allies in Greche. He does this for personal gain. We cannot allow him to continue. We care for the men and women of Arenia far too much to stand by and allow one man to destroy them."

"Evidence was placed before Leopold that the auchs are real and living in the mountains that border the north of our country. These creatures have attacked our people, burning villages and killing men and women of Arenia. I have seen the destruction, and it is I who brought word to the King. And does Leopold ride to protect his people? No. He rides to attack Greche in support of the auchs. That is why we have been forced to say that Leopold is no longer fit to rule Arenia. This country needs a king who is not only fair and just in his decisions but who is ready to face the enemies of man. Arenia needs a king who not only cares for his people's present needs but fights for their future. Leopold has proven he is not the right king for Arenia so we must have a new king. My lords and ladies, I give you King Arwen."

Arwen stepped out of the King's private chambers and made his way to the throne. He looked resplendent in his new purple velvet robe trimmed in gold. In his hand he carried the king's staff, its shining black capped in gold. He stopped for a moment in front of the throne before sitting.

"Bow to your new king," called Xavier. "All hail King Arwen."

CHAPTER 27

Aiyu stood before the large wooden door, afraid to knock. Camille waited patiently. They had passed on Obiri's message to Buit and had learned that news of Bhata's death had reached the city, so Aiyu was spared the task of breaking her parents' hearts. Still, he was anxious about the meeting.

"You must do this," said Camille. "They deserve to know the story of what happened, and it will do you good to tell them of it."

"I no able do this. Bhata family must hate me. I responsible take her away to hard life. I responsible leave her be killed by lowlanders."

He was about to turn away when the door swung open and a large auch rolled out to engulf him in her massive arms. The woman held Aiyu in her embrace while tears flowed freely down her round face. Camille saw that Aiyu too was crying.

When they finally separated, the woman saw Camille for the first time. She stepped back and composed herself as Aiyu introduced them. "I am very sorry," said Camille. "I only knew Bhata for a short time, but she was good to me and I liked her."

Mizq ushered them inside and sat them at the large table before preparing cool drinks and food for her guests. By the time she sat down with them the table was laden with plates of sliced fruit, a bowl of warm vegetable broth, biscuits and even a vegetable tart. Unable to think of anything else to distract herself, she asked, "How you be?"

Before Aiyu could offer a reply, the door swung open to reveal Runag, Bhata's father. "So, news correct," he said. "No expect you come here."

"I must come. I need tell how Bhata happy, love children. It what Bhata want."

Runag stood in the open doorway for a few moments more, then ignoring Aiyu he spoke with his mate. "I have things do." He turned and left, closing the door behind him.

Aiyu sat watching the closed door while Mizq encouraged him to have a piece of tart.

"Or maybe you like some fruit?"

"We leave now," Aiyu answered, still watching the door.

"Bear-dung. Runag no blame you. He just need time understand. You stay this house while you in Ptoraki. Help him accept wishes of spirits."

Aiyu looked Bhata's mother in the eye. "I no think Runag ever forgive me for take Bhata away to die. I know I no forgive in his position. I also no understand how you be so welcoming."

"You come here tell us about Bhata children. I know you do this because you love them. I know she happy in that love. Nothing to forgive. I no happy after hear news Bhata die. I now happy that you come and show us she happy. Tell me how she die."

Aiyu explained how he had found Camille and how Holdbori had spoken with Bhata and told him to take her to Konungssonur. "When I return, I find lowlanders come and kill Bhata and children. They leave bodies near farm and return to lowlands."

Mizq turned to Camille and asked, "Why you so important that my daughter her children must die keep you safe?"

"I am very sorry. If I had known what was going to happen I would not have come to the mountains. I liked Bhata and her children taught me to play slapstick. If there was any way I could bring them back I would leave now and go back to face your daughter's murderers."

"It no your choice. Holdbori bring you to Konungssonur. Holdbori choose price. I wonder what you must do that spirits ask so great price see you protected."

"I tell Camille you powerful spirit talker," said Aiyu. "She spirit talker too. She begin learn powers. I see she very strong."

"Who teach you?" Mizq asked.

"No one teaches me. Alayna and the others say that if they instruct me it will limit my ability to their expectations. They tell me I will only reach my full strength if I am not bound by others ideas and must develop my ability from within."

"Bear-dung. What rubbish this? How can anyone learn if no one teach them?"

Camille saw an opportunity and jumped at it. "Maybe that is why the spirits have brought me here. Could it be that I was meant to come to Ptoraki to be trained by you? Do you think that is possible?" Mizq ignored the question and Camille decided not to press the issue.

Instead, Mizq asked Aiyu to tell her more about her grandchildren. They spoke for hours. Camille could see how much it helped her friend - his face came to life when he spoke of his family - but when the story came to his finding them hanging from the tree he stopped talking and sat back in the chair, not wanting to tell Mizq such details. The room was quiet as they gave him time to collect himself until Mizq said, "Prepare place for you sleep while in Ptoraki."

Aiyu's head snapped up. "No. Runag no allow."

"Runag allow because I tell him he allow."

"He blame me, no bear be here with me now. And Camille lowlander.

We no force ourselves on him. It no right. We find somewhere else stay. We see you again if you wish but give Bhata father no more pain."

Hearing the determination in Aiyu's voice Mizq conceded. "I take you to the home of Zazuk then. She friend, live near. She take care you if I ask. Camille find her interesting too."

"We go now. You send word Runag we no longer in his home."

Mizq led them only a short distance from the house before she knocked on another door. The auch that opened it was Zazuk. The old woman's cheeks hung at the side of her face, framing a mouth full of broken teeth. She welcomed them inside with a voice that rattled her entire body. Zazuk waited till Mizq had left before offering her condolences to Aiyu and asking why he came to Ptoraki.

"I not know," he admitted. "Seem like something Bhata want me do. I think ittle these last weeks. Now think need be on my own." With that he rose and left, closing the door behind him.

Camille was on the point of following him when Zuzak raised a hand to stop her. "Let him be. Need time clear head for what he must do."

"And what is that?"

"Must learn live again. Man without woman like world without trees, empty, lifeless." Camille looked at the closed door, accepting the old woman's wisdom. "Why you come Ptoraki?" Zazuk asked.

Camille thought about the question for the first time and was forced to admit she didn't know. "I was concerned for Aiyu and when I heard he was coming here, I felt I had to follow. I don't know why."

"When spirits speak you must listen, follow. But never follow a man. If you want to follow same path it sometimes wise let him think he lead you. Make man feel good."

As they spoke for hours, Camille wondered if this is what it was like to have a grandmother. She quickly warmed to the woman. Zazuk was one of the few elementals born to the auchs and, while others helped with her training where they could, she had been left to learn mostly from her own experiences. There was sadness in her voice as she told Camille that without proper training, she had never been able to learn the skills she believed were within her. Camille asked her why there were so few elementals among the auchs.

"I not know this for true but it what I believe. Many auchs born to serve spirits. How we raised as children guide us to understand what we capable of. Humans and auchs agree there six abilities, but difference between knowing and understanding." Zazuk fell silent but Camille hoped that she would continue. Eventually she spoke again. "I was terrible child, very strong-willed and questioned everything. Parents very frustrated when I no blindly follow tradition. Many childhood friends carry scars my over-zealous play. But think this free my abilities, allow me control air. Control of elements different kind of speaking with spirits. Auchs taught from childhood, obey without question. I think this destroy ability inside us. So elders prevent those with ability grow but they do this without knowing, they do with good intent. This what I believe, why many think Zazuk mad."

"But these other abilities, how are they different?"

"Spirit talkers must be able listen. Mizq very good with this. Those who heal must learn, see what others not see. Ones who talk to world must understand ways of elements."

"What of the sixth ability?"

"No one help with that. Once was great magic, six abilities but no for auchs. In time magic go, ability go. When auchs come this world, hear dwarves very strong sixth ability, but dwarves go too. Now no one remember."

#

Next morning Mizq left the house early. Over the years she had learned it was easier to think as she walked and occasionally the spirits would talk to her as she wound her way through the streets. With some luck, today would be one of those days. Sleep had not come to her the previous night as she wrestled with the conflicting emotions that had arisen when Aiyu appeared outside her home. She was certain of his love for Bhata, but Bhata had been killed by lowlanders and now he had brought one of them to her home. Aiyu obviously looked fondly on her so she knew she would try to make the girl welcome, but she didn't have to like her. How could Aiyu think so kindly of someone who was a natural enemy? Even if she were not an enemy, how could she be a friend? A night of thoughts turning circles in her head had left her no closer to an answer and now she walked the streets in the vain hope of thinking through her dilemma. Without looking where she was walking, she suddenly found herself at the edge of the city overlooking the end of the world. Something had brought her to a place that her daughter loved, where Bhata and Aiyu had come often in their mating year.

Standing on the last road of the city, Mizq wondered what force had brought her to this place and accepted it simply as the will of the spirits. "If this where spirits want me be, this where I look for answers." Short grasses grew along the side of the road with an occasional tree providing shade. Mizq found a large tree with a twisted trunk and leaves spreading above like green beet biscuits standing to cool after coming out of the oven. She sat on the grass with her back to the tree and watched the small waves quietly crash onto the yellow sand. Each wave tumbled toward the shore in a thin line of white foam before retreating to the safety of the deeper water. As it withdrew it left behind an intricate pattern of white foam on the narrow film of still water until the next wave wiped the water clean to write its own message on the shore. Mizq looked up into the distance, far beyond the patterns of the waves to where the sky met the sea. This was why her daughter had loved this place, to look at the end of the world and wonder what was beyond. She could never understand how anyone could think that there was anything out there but Bhata had always insisted that the stories of Ngai the Brave told of how they had walked across the sea from a place beyond the world to come to this land. Logic told her that her daughter was wrong, maybe this is what the spirits brought her here to understand.

Her eyes dropped again to the waves and the patterns of foam along the shore. Watching the constantly changing shapes of white, it occurred to Mizq that the spirits might be writing their message on the water. She watched, waiting for something to appear but the sun and last night's lack of sleep conspired against her. Her eyes closed as she drifted into sleep. The next thing she knew was the voices calling her name. Listening with all of her being, she could not make out the message the spirits were trying to give her. She opened her eyes to see Aiyu and Camille watching her with concern.

"We worried. We try wake you," Aiyu told her.

Mizq understood that the voices she had heard were theirs and not the spirits trying to give her direction. She looked again at the sea and sand, and out again to the end of the world. There were no messages for her to hear.

"What you do here?" she asked.

"I bring Camille see place where Bhata and I come talk, the place where she become part of me."

Mizq looked at Camille trying to see why Aiyu was so captivated with the little lowlander, but she could not understand it. "I must return," she said. "Runag be worried." She took one last look at the waves before turning to leave. But she didn't go. Instead, she looked up into the tree where Holdbori stood on a branch looking down at them. No one moved for the next few minutes. Holdbori and Mizq stood locked in each other's gaze while Camille watched them, trying to capture the feeling of what the bird wished. Aiyu watched all three without understanding what was happening but knowing he was witnessing an important moment. Holdbori broke the spell when he dropped off the branch and spread his black wings to soar out over the beach. Then with three powerful beats he lifted himself into the air to disappear back over the city. Standing under the tree Mizq tried to make sense of what had just occurred. Camille stood before her and she studied the little lowlander.

"Holdbori want me train you," she said simply.

"I didn't hear anything."

"Message no meant for you hear."

Camille didn't know how to reply so she just thanked the older woman.

"No thank me. Holdbori tell me all that occur necessary, that it important you learn skills quick so he bring you to me. I no see how lowlander so important to auch people but I do as Holdbori ask. We begin here tomorrow morning. Not keep me waiting."

CHAPTER 28

This man is a fool, thought Willian. When word reaches King Leopold of this night's events, he will be furious and the people behind this plot will feel his wrath. But where had they come from? He had seen no sign of plotting within the palace. The guards had been searching for Xavier for weeks. Where had he been hiding?

Following the meeting, the nobles were led away. Willian assumed they were being taken to the dungeons, until they posed no threat or were executed but why bring them here and explain if they were to be killed? Each member of the palace staff was forced to bow before the new king before they were allowed to leave and go about their normal duties. When his turn came Willian stepped up to the throne and gave a fumbling bow that allowed him to deny failing his king in his own mind.

"What is your name, boy?" asked King Arwen.

"Willian," he said quietly.

"What are your duties?"

"I'm a pageboy."

"If you wish to continue as my pageboy, you had better find someone who can teach you how to bow and how to address your king," Arwen scolded.

Willian hurriedly withdrew, inwardly pleased with himself that he had not really done or said anything to acknowledge him as king. When he was clear of the throne room he made his way to the stables. He didn't have to wait long before Ben stormed in and marched towards him, his head turning back and forth to see that they were alone.

"There is no one here," Willian assured him.

With the freedom to speak Ben let his feelings be known as he grabbed a shoeing stool and threw it across the room.

"Who, in the name of putrid magic, are these people to think they can throw the King out of Whitebridge? Leopold is a good man and would not do the things they say."

"He didn't. It was a trap set by these people to draw him and the army out of the city. What has made their challenge so much easier is that they have taken a little truth and twisted it to their advantage. King Leopold did know about the auchs and a treaty has existed between them and Arenia for many generations. He told me this when we were preparing to arrest Xavier and Lord Lipstadt. But they lie when they say the auchs have attacked our people. From what the King has told me, the auchs are afraid of us and take great care to keep their existence secret from the world."

"That don't matter. Leopold is the true king, and I follow him. That man inside was the one he had me watch. From what I saw, I would not trust him if he told me the sun would come up in the morning."

"Lord Darveed is dead, and the others may join him soon. Do you know who they are?" When Ben could provide no further information, he continued. "They are well organized and from what I heard they now hold the city as well as the palace."

"What does that mean?"

"If they were able to take the city guard, there are more of them than we can imagine. With them in control of the city walls it will not be easy for

King Leopold to return."

"Can we do something to defeat them?"

"Not that I can think of. There are too many and they must have the support of many more people to be able to do this. They were able to hide Xavier from the guards for a long time. All I can do is take word to the king."

"But he is at war with Greche."

"I'm not sure about that. Xavier's story of the auchs was intended to get the army out of Whitebridge. It served their purpose. I don't think there was ever any threat from King Woldemar."

"So what do we do?"

"You can provide me with the horse to ride to the king, and I need a way to get out of the city."

Ben thought for a minute. "A wagon is sent out each morning to the farms to bring in supplies for the day." He selected two good horses and hitched them to an old wagon. "This old cart has proven useful in the past," he said as he hid two saddles in a secret space beneath the floor. "Their soldiers aren't the only ones who know how to sneak in and out of the city."

"Will the guards look there?" Willian asked.

"The secret is to distract them," Ben answered before collecting a cover and piling it suggestively in the back. Satisfied with his work he went to the back of the stables and returned with a pile of rags. "Put these on," he said. "We can't have you looking important, can we? We'll leave by the stable gate. It will take us out of the palace into the city. They won't think to check that for a while."

Willian did as Ben instructed and by the time the sun spread the first hint of light in the eastern sky they were sitting on the wagon approaching the south gate. Ben had timed the ride perfectly, arriving just as the gate was being opened for the day. The city guards went about their duties, but they were unarmed and being watched by two black-clad soldiers. Ben slowed the horses and whispered, "Don't speak, and look stupid."

The guards stopped them as he had expected and told them, "No one passes today without proper business. Go back to your home."

"The name's Ben and we go to collect the supplies."

"Where's the normal man?" One of the soldiers approached, listening to the interchange.

"My father's ill and I'm helpin' him out."

"Who is that with you?"

"This is my brother. He's only small and a bit slow but maybe a bit of work can fill him out."

The soldier looked behind them and drew his sword. "Watch them while I see what they hide," he said.

"There's nothing there," said Ben but the soldier ignored him. Using the tip of his sword he flicked back the cover but was disappointed to find nothing beneath. He dropped back to the ground and waved them on, but warned, "You have three hours. Report back to me when you return. And lay the cover flat in the future."

Ben assured the guard that he would do as they asked as he urged the horses out of the city, past the docks and through the ploughed fields. Once they had passed the outer limits he pulled the wagon to the side of the road.

"That was easy," said Ben.

"Too easy. Once they realize I have gone they will know we ride to warn King Leopold and will come after us. We need to get moving."

CHAPTER 29

The members of the Council sat in the living room of King Arwen's new apartment as he presided over their meeting. They had been monitoring the coup and were surprised that they had won out with so little blood spilled. Xavier took the opportunity to watch the reactions of the members as each new piece of news was brought in. This night had made one thing clear in his mind, though he had suspected the truth since he became a member five years ago. The Council of The Society had no real direction and were only capable of reacting to events that unfolded around them. Of them all, only Beth showed that she was capable of looking to the future, and have the strength to do what was necessary. Only she could see the possibilities of having a Society king on the throne. But even she did not understand the extent of his ambition.

Capturing the palace had proven to be easier than they thought. With almost everyone asleep at the time, it had been simple to gather and inform them of the change in leadership. But they were more concerned with their success outside the palace gates because that was the key to holding Whitebridge when Leopold returned. They had listened to reports as Harold's men worked their way methodically through the city, capturing the guards walking casually through the streets unaware of the night's events in the palace. The few who dared to put up any challenge to the city's invaders were quickly dealt with, but most quickly changed allegiance when given the alternative. The remainder of the city guard woke to the sounds of yelling, to find they had been locked in with heavy timbers placed on the outside of the doors and windows. Convincing them to lay down their weapons was not as easy as their group captains were among those still locked up.

By sunrise The Society ruled the streets of Whitebridge. Harold's men marched in groups to make their presence known. By mid-morning they had full control of Whitebridge and had closed the city gates to prepare the people for the announcement of their new king. As the sun slowly climbed to its peak the guards remained locked away and the people wondered what was happening.

One of Harold's men reported that after searching the palace they had found no sign of the king's pageboy. "We sent word to the gates. A boy left on a cart this morning with his brother to collect vegetables. He was dressed in rags and did not speak. His brother said he was simple. They still had not returned when the gates were locked," the soldier told them.

"Send someone after them. They ride to warn Leopold," Arwen ordered.

"No," Xavier countered. "This is perfect. If they cannot reach Leopold and the army engages Greche, he will be trapped and unable to withdraw without suffering heavy casualties."

Gramm continued, "If they are in time Leopold will return and try to take Whitebridge. We are equipped to withstand his siege and when our army brings the auchs south he will be forced to defeat them for us. Either way, it leaves us in a stronger position."

The moment was rapidly approaching when a decision would have to be made as to whether Arwen or the Council had the power in Arenia. Xavier knew that Arwen did not have the character to force his will upon them. He saw Arwen's hesitation as he wondered if he should agree. Their argument was sound and this was not the issue Arwen needed to contest to assert his control. When his rule was accepted by the people, he would feel he was in a stronger position.

Discussions moved back to the guards in the barracks. Arwen did not want to be forced into killing so many good men who he was sure would serve his reign if given the facts and the opportunity. Xavier made a suggestion that was accepted and a message was sent for Field Captain Harold to join them. While they waited they prepared a list of prominent citizens who would have influence throughout the city. When Harold arrived, there were twenty-nine names on the paper before them. Xavier instructed his field captain to have the group rounded up and brought to the palace courtyard and to fill the yard with members of The Society.

King Arwen used the time to suggest that the apartment of the king was not the right place for their meetings. "We need a council room," he told them. "While this may be appropriate for friendly conversation it does not show the people that we rule as a body. We need a formal room with furniture suitable for a place of power and there must be a place for a scribe to document all our important decisions." They accepted the idea as if it was in their interests to do so. The king was pleased that it had been so easy to remove them from his quarters, allowing him to rule without their interference when the time came.

Early afternoon was upon them when Harold opened the barracks door and allowed the senior guards to exit, as long as they were unarmed. They were brought into the palace courtyard where they joined the large group of people from all over the city. Xavier stepped out onto the balcony and looked over the crowd gathered below, faces showing excitement and trepidation, expectation and determination. He gave his speech again, this time with the flourish of practice, the people carrying him onward with their calls of encouragement and support. Surely this would convince the guards and the selected citizens that the time to forget King Leopold was here. When it came time to introduce King Arwen he was intoxicated with the power of his own speech and could have continued for hours. They chanted for him and hung on his every word. It took a massive effort to stand back and give Arwen his moment. He moved in beside Beth and basked in the sounds of the crowd. She leaned towards him and whispered, "You may think yourself a soldier, but you were meant for this. Politics suit you." They waited while Arwen accepted the adoration of the people and spoke a few words before they all retired back into the palace.

In his new apartment Arwen again sat with his council. "That went very well. Now we wait to see if the guards accept the will of the people or hold to their old loyalties." They did not need to wait long before Harold entered to report that almost all the city guard were now loyal to King Arwen. "Two tried to rally some men against you but their words were no match for a sharp sword. The rest saw sense and now followed King Arwen and those who control the city."

#

Jorja lay in her bed wondering what had woken her. The night seemed quiet. All she could hear was the deep breathing of her brother asleep in the bed beside her. She lay her head back and shut her eyes but as she did, the voices came again, and she realized that this was what had woken her. She sat bolt upright when the door of her home broke in, jarring the silence. Boots thumped across the floor. Her mother screamed. Then the men were in her room, black capes barely visible in the dark. One man grabbed her nightdress and dragged her from her bed while another picked up her screaming brother and held him under one arm. The men quickly looked around the room before taking them into the kitchen where others stood over her mother and father as they crouched on the floor. She and her brother were thrown down and told to sit quietly. One guard who appeared to be the leader of the group walked over and kicked her father as he lay prone before grabbing her mother's hair and pulling her head back.

"You can thank your husband for this," he growled before throwing her back to the floor.

"What did he do?" her mother pleaded.

"He proclaims King Arwen to be an impostor and Leopold to be the true King. He should be more careful with what he says."

Her mother seemed about to say something more, but the soldiers grabbed her and her father, tied their hands behind their backs and gagged their mouths. She and her brother were similarly bound and all four were pushed out into the street. A covered wagon sat in the shadows. When they reached it, the guards tied their feet and threw them in, not caring how they fell. Two others already lay on the floor, an elderly man and woman, and when all were loaded the wagon moved on, quietly making its way through the city streets. From where she lay, Jorja could see the south gate as the wagon passed beyond the walls.

They had not gone far before the wagon rolled to a stop. The soldiers appeared again to drag them out onto the ground. The area was dark, but she could see they were at the south end of the docks beside the river. The guards pushed them to the river's edge where they were forced to kneel in a line in the shallow water. From one end of the line she watched as a guard drew his sword and stepped up behind the old man and swung, removing his head in one cut. With his boot the guard shoved the body out into the river before stepping behind the old woman. One by one he moved down the line and Jorja watched as first her father and then her mother died while her brother whimpered beside her. She saw how proud and strong the old couple and her parents had been and determined she too would be strong. Her brother's body was kicked out into the river and she straightened herself and held her head high ready for the strike.

#

The new council room had all the trimmings of a seat of power. The red upholstered chairs were well padded, and the room boasted an overly large oak table. The walls were decorated with fine paintings and above the door hung a large timber star painted white. There were no windows. King Arwen explained this was to avoid the possibility of having their meetings overheard, and to remind them of the days where they worked from the shadows.

"Things go well in the city," said Arwen. "I must admit I am surprised at how easily the people have come to accept me as their king."

"That is because the people only wish for fair and just leadership," said Beth.

"Has there been any talk of Leopold being the true king, or any signs of protest?"

"The people adore you and are happy. There have been no complaints or problems," Xavier assured him. "If there were any problems, people would be asking for an audience to air their grievances, and no one has asked."

"Then I am king by popular demand and, as such, the true king of Arenia."

"Of course you are the true king," Xavier assured him. "But I still advise caution. Until Leopold concedes the loss of Arenia or dies in the battle with the auchs or Greche, you will need to tread slowly. But after Leopold is finally gone, The Society will rule Arenia."

CHAPTER 30

Things had not changed much since he was last in Thistledowne. The land was still dry, and the farms still struggled to produce any usable crops. Jaimz led his men around the town onto the now abandoned farm of Merle Unwood. Nothing remained to show of the witch's occupation other than the ash-stained ground in the small clearing. The three other field captains rode with him followed by their men. "There's not enough room and we are too close to the town," said Gregory. "It may not have been wise to choose this place to build an army." Jaimz ignored the comment and dismounted, passing his reins to Thom before walking up the rise to look over the clearing, waiting for the other field captains to join him.

"We'll have the men clear that brush," he said waving his arm in a sweeping gesture behind him, "and we'll set up our command tent here." In short time, the soldiers were using their swords to clear the scrub while others carried the cut bush away. The rest of the men began to erect the tent city that would be home over the next weeks, as the rest of the army arrived.

Jaimz left the men to their work and rode into the Thistledowne to gauge the feelings of the townsfolk. On the pretext of having the blacksmith check his horse's shoes, he spoke with some of the people. It appeared that none remembered him. He asked if there were any witches about so he could obtain some herbs for a pained ankle, but no one mentioned the recent death of Merle Unwood. He received the impression that it was a topic that was not for discussion, maybe because they were too embarrassed about what they had done. When the smithy gave him the clearance for his horse, he thanked the man and paid him well for his assistance before riding back to the campsite. The people of Thistledowne would hear the rumor he had spread, that auchs had attacked other towns and they were sent by the king to guard them. He could foresee no problems with these people.

That night the new field captains of the Fist of Man relaxed over goblets of wine that Xavier had sent with them. They discussed the rise of The Society from obscurity and the opportunities it offered for strong military leaders. When he felt the time was right, Jaimz went to his saddle bags and brought out a note sealed with wax and the mark of a four-pointed star. Xavier had told him to open it with the others when they had gathered at Thistledowne. He broke the seal and read aloud.

Good evening, Gentlemen,

Welcome again to the army of The Society. As a soldier I wish I was with you at this time, for the coming years will see many of you write your names in the history books of the world. After uncountable generations, we have the chance to assert the dominance of man as never before. Together we will shape Arenia and the world. Men and women will look back and say, "They were great men of vision and courage".

I apologize for having deliberately misled you during our meeting at the inn. I could not allow any chance of your true orders being discovered by anyone in the city.

If we are to be successful, our army must be strong. You have all shown skill, but the work of the future will be more demanding than anything we have faced before. Each of you now has command of more men than you have ever imagined, and this will require you to stand back and allow your sergeants to do the work you would have done yourselves for these last years. You must now instruct and lead. It will take time to learn these skills as it will take time for your men to learn to be an army and work together. These coming times will test you further than anything that has gone before.

Unfortunately, you have only the next four weeks to train your men and yourselves. The land to the north of Thistledowne has varied terrains and is an ideal place for this training. As your other men arrive, they will need to be brought into the army quickly. Time runs short and we must be prepared. So, take this little time I give you and learn your craft again.

Gregory will lead your training because of his experience and my belief in his tactical mind. Jaimz will be responsible for discipline. He understands what I need. He holds further sealed orders, to be opened on the night of the first day of winter. Then you will see what plans The Society has for each of you.

Harold will lead the home guard as well as the king's personal guard. His role and the skills of his soldiers are different to those required of your men and will be learned here in Whitebridge.

For the sake of all mankind, I wish you good luck.

Xavier, Councilor of The Society.

The army of The Society was born.

The next few days proved to be difficult for the new field captains. Their problem was not that the men had always fought in small groups, they had a problem in accepting the chain of command. Each sergeant thought he knew better than those above him and many refused to follow the orders of the day. As a result, most days started badly and finished worse. Gregory vented his frustrations in the command tent after a particularly trying day and the other field captains agreed, having faced their own disciplinary problems.

"We have no choice," said Jaimz. "If we don't act now we will never have the army ready in time. Tomorrow when the men assemble, we will stand them down and call all sergeants and their seconds to a meeting. There is a place in a grove of trees just to the north that will give us the privacy we need. I will take Thom's squad and make preparations. Gregory's old squad can ride escort duty for you and the sergeants. I will see you in all the morning."

The next morning dawned fine and sunny. The soldiers of the Fist dragged themselves out of their tents to the sounds of the banging of pots and pans. They gathered in the clearing to hear the day's orders. Some looked to the cooking fires in the hope that the morning meal would soon be ready while others rubbed their eyes and wished they were still asleep. Some had not even bothered to dress. This was not true of all squads. The few sergeants who understood that discipline was the key bullied their men into line and had them organized and ready when the field captains appeared on the small rise.

Gregory stood and looked out at the sea of faces before him. "You all know there is much to do if we are to build an army, but it is obvious to us that you are tired of having us command you around the fields. That is why we have decided to give you the day off. Go back to your beds or do as you wish for one day but at this time tomorrow you will all be ready to ride. There will be no exceptions."

The men turned to leave, talking in small groups. "Stop." Gregory's voice rolled across the clearing and many faces turned to see what he wanted this time. "You have not been dismissed. Fall in until the order is given." Some ignored him and continued towards their tents, but Gregory had anticipated this response. The members of his old squad stood as a line between the soldiers and their beds with swords drawn. "If you want to leave here, you will form up ranks behind your sergeants. Second-in-command for each squad will join their sergeants at the front."

Other trusted squads appeared. The soldiers of the Fist found themselves surrounded by armed men. Amid protests and grumbling, the soldiers were pushed back into a semblance of order. When he was satisfied that he had their attention Gregory called, "The Society has changed in recent weeks, and it is the role of the army to ensure that The Society succeeds in this new path. This army will become the best disciplined army in all the kingdoms, because if it is not, none of us will live to fight a second battle. You may have this day but tomorrow we will work. Sergeants and their seconds will join us in a ride to the fields where we will discuss your training program. Sergeants and seconds, mount up. The rest of you are dismissed." This time the men broke up hesitantly and watched as their leaders were led away.

The ride north was tense. The sergeants and their seconds were kept in a tight group surrounded by armed men as they rode. At the grove more armed men waited. They were ordered to dismount and walk the remaining distance through the trees. Jaimz had chosen this place carefully. During the night his men had dragged rocks and logs into the clearing to give the sergeants a place to sit, with a large rock on one side forming a natural stage. As the men entered the clearing, they first saw Jaimz standing on the rock with the sun filtering through the trees behind him. A second look, as their eyes adjusted to the light, showed twenty nooses hanging from the branches either side. The armed soldiers took up positions on the boundary of the clearing.

"It seems we have a problem. The Council of The Society has chosen to build an army but our soldiers seem to think they know better than our leaders. We will soon be going into battle, and I want good fighting men at my side when we do. You all know our instructions come from Councilor Xavier and I will not disappoint him. When we return to camp you will all speak to your men and explain to them that you have decided to accept your duties as members and officers of The Fist. Tomorrow your men will be ready to ride at dawn. No one will be late, all weapons will be cleaned and ready, horses will be fed and saddled. If there is any sergeant here who feels he cannot have his men ready," he took a moment to glance meaningfully at the nooses behind him, "I am sure your seconds will gladly accept a promotion and do the work for you."

Jaimz drew his sword, rested its point on the rock and leaned on the hilt. "Tomorrow we will ride north where we will form up as Field Captain Gregory commands. Each squad will ride out in two lines led by their sergeant and second. There will be no excuses for tardiness." He looked around the group sitting in the small clearing, his eyes resting momentarily of those whom he believed could cause trouble. "Does anyone feel they cannot do this?" he asked, once again glancing at the nooses. When no objections arose, he ordered them back to camp. The field captains gathered.

"Do you really think that will work?" asked Ronald.

"No. But after one or two are replaced by their seconds tomorrow night I think we can expect to see an improvement. I hate having to hang good men, but we cannot afford to have the army defeated from within."

#

As the sun rose on the following day Jaimz looked down from the rise on the lines of soldiers dressed and ready to begin work. He gave the order for them to mount up and watched as they filed past. Gregory deliberately led them past the grove where yesterday's meeting had been held on their way to the open fields in the north. The small army spent their day forming up into lines and charging an invisible enemy before falling back into defensive positions as the enemy suddenly became an overwhelming force. Only one squad seeming to go out of its way to upset the operations by falling behind the charge or not dropping into its correct defensive position. Jaimz and Ronald watched from a hill as the day progressed.

"Who leads that squad?" Jaimz eventually asked.

"Marris. He has an excellent record of achievements, but his methods have often been brought into question. Many think he is interested only in causing pain and fear and if he cannot find an enemy, he is happy to target anyone close. Many wonder about his commitment to the cause."

"You have watched with me. He has demonstrated he is not suitable to lead part of this army." Ronald nodded in reply.

That night after everyone had been fed and were finding their way to their beds, a soldier appeared at the tent of Marris' second-in-command to tell him he was needed by the field captains. The man was led through the rows of tents past tired soldiers who paid them little attention. At the entrance of the command tent, the messenger stepped aside, allowing him to enter. Jaimz sat at a wooden travelling table with Samuel and Gregory.

"You are the second to Marris?" Jaimz asked. "What is your name?"

"Billington, sir."

"I am afraid I must inform you that Sergeant Marris has had an accident this evening. It seems he was riding in the dark through some trees and got his head caught in a rope that someone had inadvertently left there." He watched to see what expression would show on the man's face but Billington seemed unmoved. "As a result of this accident your squad finds itself without a sergeant. In the coming weeks we will be going into battle and our soldiers must be ready. Do you think your squad could learn to work as an efficient unit in that time or do we need to break them up and place the men with other sergeants?"

"The squad does not need to be dispersed. They are good men who believe in the cause. They followed Marris because they are soldiers, and he was their leader. There are a couple who may need some extra convincing because they liked Marris' methods, but that will need to be done whether they remain as a squad or are sent to other commands. I want to be part of this army and the men will follow my orders."

"Your belief in your men is commendable, we trust it is justified. We will leave your squad together for the time being, but they will need a strong leader to make them change their ways. I hope you are strong enough, Sergeant Billington. I expect your men to be ready tomorrow morning."

Over the next few days, the man proved himself to be a capable and promising leader. The squad showed itself to be able and willing to learn the skills of fighting in a larger army, though Jaimz did notice some soldiers wearing blackened eyes.

The field captains decided the time had come to reveal their next step in the building of an army. Another meeting was called with all sergeants and again, the grove in the north was chosen for their purposes. Jaimz stepped up on the makeshift stage with the others at his side, but this time no nooses hung from the branches.

"We have asked you here today to congratulate you on your work so far. You have come a long way in a short time. Already we can see the beginnings of a strong army that will lead The Society to a glorious future. With our strength, mankind will remain dominant in the world for years to come." Cheers broke out among the sergeants. "You are right to cheer. The Society is strong and through you it will become stronger. You have shown that you are capable of working together and supporting each other in defense and attack. All of us are still growing into our roles. We must remember that if we are to succeed, we must never stop learning. We must always strive for improvement. But no matter how much we improve, we will never defeat an organized army unless we are prepared to accept change."

"I ask that you take the time to consider our next step," said Gregory. The sergeants watched intently, concerned for their positions and their men. "All of you are skilled soldiers but within your squads and yourselves you have strengths and weaknesses. These changes will be a testament to those strengths. As of this day we have created a new rank to work between ourselves and the sergeants. Some of you will leave here with greater position and responsibility. With these promotions the army is taking the next step in its growth. Those of you who remain as sergeants will find their roles have also changed."

Jaimz spoke again. "All of your men know how to ride and use a sword or spear while some can use a bow to good effect. Having these skills dispersed among the squads was ideal for the work we did before but now it is not efficient. Five sergeants from each of our fingers will take the new rank of

Lenk. Each Lenk will be strong in different skills and will lead men with similar abilities. We will need archers to give our army long range capability and, of course, we will need swordsmen. Some of the men will become pikemen. I understand that this is a skill that will need to be learned but we have chosen sergeants who we think will be able to develop these skills. We have no lancers, or even the powerful horses for this work, but we do have good riders, and these men will become our light horse cavalry. The last role will be filled with skilled men who can infiltrate the enemy lines and work to achieve the greatest results with only small numbers. We have chosen to call these men the Shadow for they will be hidden in plain sight of the enemy. All of the men have been reassigned so that each sergeant will have eight to fifteen men in his command. You will receive a list of those men as you leave, and you will be placed under the command of one of the Lenk. Training will begin again tomorrow. Now I am sure you wish to hear who we have promoted. Field Captain Samuel, would you begin?"

Samuel said, "Sergeant Billington, you will be my Lenk-Shadow." The men waited as each field captain read out the list of promotions and the sergeants were given their assignments and the names of the men they now commanded. The meeting finished quietly with those present given the rest of the day to find their new squads and prepare for training.

The Fist began to train in earnest now that the structure of the army was established. The new Lenk-Archers were very pleased. They had been given all the skilled bowmen in the army and many proved to be excellent at hitting a moving target at fifty paces. They practiced with targets drawn behind horses, running and falling in to deliver a volley, as well as the art of camouflage. Meanwhile the cavalry, swordsmen and pikemen concentrated on working in formation along with their individual skills. More than anything else the sergeants emphasized the importance of discipline.

The field captains had done their job well when selecting the men for each squad. Faster than any of them could have imagined, the army became a reality. By the end of the four weeks the Fist worked as a single unit and, while there were still areas that could be improved, they were satisfied. Although the army was ready the field captains were anxious to hear their orders and urged Jaimz to break the seal. He carefully unfolded the paper before reading.

Greetings to my field captains and soldiers of The Society.

I am confident that, as you read this, the Fist is ready to stand before the world as the true defenders of mankind. The Council is proud of the work you have done. If all has gone to plan, the world has changed greatly during your time of preparation and The Society now rules all of Arenia, because if we do not, I am dead along with the others of the Council.

If we have failed you, I am sorry, and The Society must go back into the shadows to wait again for the opportunity of leading mankind in the struggle against the lesser beings. The Fist will need to disappear as if it had never existed. But we are strong, and I am confident that The Society will triumph and rule over Arenia. In time we will show the world the truth of the superiority of man. You must assume we have achieved victory.

Our tasks are now twofold. We must draw out the auchs so that they can finally be destroyed, and we must secure the throne of Arenia. Jaimz will take his finger north to seek out the auchs. He will draw them into open ground where they cannot hide in caves and holes and where he will determine their numbers and strengths. Having done this, he will return to Whitebridge and report. Gregory, Samuel and Ronald will return to Whitebridge immediately. Leopold will not accept the new order of things easily and is certain to make an attempt at taking back the city. It will fall to you to show him that his time has passed. Your advantage lies in the knowledge that he has no idea that your army exists. Use this. We rely on you to make secure the throne for The Society.

Good luck to you all.

Councilor Xavier, Military Leader of Arenia..

CHAPTER 31

There was very little furniture in the tent. A bed stood against one wall with a single blanket and a chest at its foot for his clothes. In the center of the room a chair and small table served as both a work and meals area. It was annoying having to put his work aside to eat. Sometimes he simply placed his plate on top of the river of papers that flowed across the table, as he had done this morning. When they had first arrived, Leopold had doubted himself as they had waited for the army of Greche to appear. Now the report of the lancers camped not far from the valleys and the news that no one in Thistledowne had seen any auchs, let alone been attacked by them, had given him back his confidence. Not only had his belief in the treaty been justified but the lies of Xavier and Lipstadt had been exposed and proven to him that Greche was the true threat to Arenia.

Lachlan rushed into the tent. His captain had to fight for the breath to give his message. "Greche approaches the valley," he gasped. The King pushed his meal away. In a small way he was satisfied that all their thoughts and plans were proving to be correct. He asked how many soldiers Woldemar had brought as he reached for his sword belt. "We can only see one battalion of lancers but there must be others somewhere. No one would go to a war and not bring foot soldiers."

Leopold ensured he was properly dressed and looking like a king before he stepped out of the tent and called for his horse. Lachlan's words reignited his recent doubts. Where were Woldemar's foot soldiers? Why could they only see one battalion? Was there still more to the tale of Xavier? Lachlan rode beside him as they moved forward to observe the approaching lancers. The enemy rode in line abreast, a formation meant for battle where they could charge unimpeded, but if that was their intent then they would have foot soldiers follow them and harass the survivors of the charge. His concerns grew as he searched for signs of the rest of Greche's army.

"This cannot be their entire force," said Lachlan, showing Leopold that he shared his doubts. Leopold looked back to see his lancers lined across the valley with the foot soldiers behind. That is what I expect to see, he thought. He looked again towards Greche where the line of lancers had stopped at the other end of the valley.

"This is an advance force," Leopold thought aloud. "They do not expect us to be here. Woldemar has sent then as a mobile force to enter Arenia and be in position to harass us when his army meets us further north so they must travel fast and have no need of foot soldiers. The full army must be a few days behind them."

Lachlan expanded the idea. "Then they will not attack. They will sit there and wait until reinforcements arrive. But if we could encourage them into the valley our archers would make short work of them. We could have the place cleared and Woldemar would not know we wait for him. The archers would have a second chance to do their work."

Leopold considered this. "Prepare to attack," he said. "We want to look as if we are going to charge, but our army is only bait. They must hold here."

Lachlan passed the orders and the lancers of Arenia looked down the valley at their counterparts from Greche. When all was in readiness, he raised his arm above his head and a line of lances rose like a sharpened forest suddenly grown from the earth. Leopold saw the enemy also prepare and smiled. Their trap was going to work - but nothing happened. Both forces stood ready and waited. It was like a jester entering the court, he thought, and raising his lute as he walked around the room, never playing.

"They need encouragement," he said. "Get our men to walk forward fifty paces and hold. Make it look like we are getting ready to charge."

Lachlan gave the signal to walk and, as one, the line of lancers moved out. The king watched as the line at the other end of the valley mimicked their movement.

"Let's give them something to think about. Bring your men up to a canter for a short distance."

The Arenian line sped up and the king watched, expecting to see the same from the lines of Greche.

"They've stopped. Something's wrong. Stop the line and hold them ready," yelled Leopold, but it was too late.

It started with just a few who let out their war cry and lowered their lancers as they kicked their horses into a gallop. Others joined, thinking the order had been given. Leopold and Lachlan watched helplessly as more than half his lancers galloped their mounts into the charge down the valley. Though the trap had not succeeded, he should still win the day, though his losses would be unnecessary. He was about to order the remaining lancers into the battle when a flight of arrows appeared in the sky, falling like steel-pointed rain on his troops. A second flight followed, then another. The charge was broken as men tried to turn their mounts and retreat, but the tight confines of the valley became their undoing. More arrows rained from the sky till, of all the men that rode into the valley, none returned. He looked to the ridge above the valley. Now we know where Greche's support soldiers are, he thought.

The lancers of Greche retreated out of the mouth of the valley and he gave the order to do the same. He had lost half his lancers in the charge, and almost all his archers. A very large portion of his army had been destroyed in one morning by a much smaller force and he had not taken one enemy life in return. He turned his horse and rode in sullen silence back towards his tent. Lachlan fell in at his side, but he was too stunned to speak. They had barely taken a dozen steps when the king reined his horse and looked back to the ridge. "Haafi!" he exclaimed. Lachlan stopped beside him, not understanding the King's meaning. "Woldemar has sent the Haafi into battle." His Captain still did not understand. "The Haafi have never been sent into battle before. Never in the history of Greche has any king used his personal assassins against another country. But it is the only explanation for how our archers were overcome so silently to turn our trap upon us."

"What does this mean?"

"If the Haafi are used in war then no one is safe. It is said that a person can sit in a locked room with his meal and a full circle of guards around him and one of them could slip in and cut his throat without being seen. I cannot begin to see what will happen now."

A soldier rode up and reined his horse. "Captain Lachlan, two men approach from the north riding fast." No sooner had they reached the camp than Willian and Ben rode up on horses panting and lathered in sweat.

CHAPTER 32

Lachlan settled into the saddle and took his lance from the soldier waiting beside him. Alone he rode into the valley, his lance riding comfortably in its pocket while the white banner hung limply from its tip. He rode slowly with the eyes of Greche and Arenia upon him, stopping a mere two hundred yards from the line of enemy lancers. The captain of the Grechan forces let him wait, knowing that his nerves would be building. He hoped that when they spoke, he would be more likely to give away useful information but Lachlan was experienced in dealing with soldiers and kings and sat patiently. The time he was left standing would tell him much about the man who led the opposing forces. A rider broke from the line to walk towards him. Lachlan admitted to himself that, in the same position, he would have left his enemy standing for a similar time. The gap between them closed until their horse's noses were so close that it seemed they would share the same air. The Grechan's horse was as well trained as his own, he thought as he waited for the man to speak.

"Why do you approach under a flag of truce? Are you here to surrender?"

"I bring a message for King Woldemar," Lachlan said.

"I speak for King Woldemar."

"Who would you be?"

"I am Captain Fordic of the Royal Lancers of the Kingdom of Greche. Whom do I speak with?"

"I am Captain Lachlan of the king's personal guard and commander of the army of Arenia."

"So your king sends others to do his work. Why does he not come and speak for himself?"

"Maybe for the same reason you are here. King Leopold would speak with Woldemar. Can this be arranged?"

Fordic did not wish to reveal that King Woldemar was still days away so he tried to find an answer that would satisfy this officer.

"King Woldemar may speak with your King if he feels it may help but it could be some time before he will be ready to do so. He still rages at Arenia's attempt to invade Greche."

"That is the issue our kings need to discuss. We came here only to defend Arenia from invasion by Greche. That is why we hold at the border."

Surprise showed briefly on Captain Fordic's face. This was not what he expected to hear. "I will relay your message to King Woldemar and tell him of your reasons for being here. If he believes that you speak the truth a message will be sent. If not, you will receive a different message." Lachlan wheeled his horse to turn his back on his enemy, but his curiosity overcame his desire to remain unmoved and he looked back to see the Grechan Captain rejoining his men. Leaving his horse to be cared for, he strode through the camp and was ushered in to report. "King Woldemar is not here," he answered to Leopold's first question. "We will need to wait for him to arrive, but I am sure that the Grechan Captain is sending word to him to hurry as we speak."

#

A Grechan rider approached the middle of the valley under a white flag. Lachlan rode out to join the man in the valley. Once again, he found himself face-to-face with Captain Fordic. "It has taken days, but I have finally convinced King Woldemar to meet with King Leopold and hear what he has to say."

Lachlan kept his face still as he replied. "So, your king has finally arrived. That is good."

Fordic returned the expressionless look for a moment before smiling. "Yes, he has arrived. Now how do we arrange for our kings to meet?"

#

The table was set at the middle of the valley below a canvas shade. The banner of Arenia flew on one corner opposite the banner of Greche. King Leopold rode out with Captain Lachlan at his side. Ten of the king's guard rode in line abreast behind them. At the other end of the valley the scene was mirrored with King Woldemar and Captain Fordic trailed by ten lancers. King Leopold wore his finest red silk shirt embroidered in silver thread under his purple velvet cape. His blue riding pants hugged his legs as they disappeared into his polished black knee-high boots. On his head sat the crown of Arenia, a thin gold band with three peaks, above his forehead. He dismounted and walked to the table with Lachlan at his side.

In contrast the man who sat opposite wore plain brown riding pants and shirt. He did not need to bother with cape or crown, his presence was more commanding. Age and confidence gave him dominance over the younger king. Captain Fordic sat very quietly and did not appear to be the confidant soldier that Lachlan had described. Then with sudden force Woldemar demanded, "Why do you invade Greche?" King Leopold shrank back, feeling like a small boy trying to explain the disappearance of a pie to the cook, while wiping crumbs from his chin. He related how he had been convinced of an invasion by Greche and how he had mobilized the army in defense of Arenia. A guard behind Woldemar roared that Leopold was trying to salvage the situation of his defeat with lies after his attempted invasion failed.

"Daniel," roared King Woldemar without turning his head. The man stopped as if he had been slapped though his hand still rested on the hilt of his sword. "My son leads the guards today and it seems he does not believe your tale."

"In his place I would not believe it either," Leopold admitted. "But I tell you in truth that when we came south it was only for the protection of Arenia. I know now that our assumptions were wrong. After the battle I received news that everything that had led us here was false, fabricated only to draw our army out of Whitebridge."

"What purpose could be served by having Arenia and Greche go to war?"

"I doubt the intention was war. We were probably meant to receive word before our armies faced each other."

"What word?"

"Whitebridge has been taken."

For the first time King Woldemar showed surprise. "I left Lord Darveed in charge of the city. He has been murdered, and foreign soldiers control the city. My pageboy and a stable hand escaped to bring me word that they plan to crown their own king in my place."

"Soldiers?" asked Woldemar. "Soldiers from where?"

"I don't know. There were no reports of large numbers of men entering through the gates yet they appeared within the city and the people of the city support them. I am told they wear all black emblazoned with a white star."

Woldemar sat quietly, assessing the truth of Leopold's claims. "Your tale is beyond belief but for that reason alone it may be true. There are many stories you could have told that would have been easily accepted but the fall of Whitebridge is not one of them. I will need more before I will take your word on this. Send one of your guards to bring the pageboy here where I may speak with him."

Willian dismounted and walked to them. King Woldemar sat studying the boy as he approached the table.

"Do I know you?" he asked.

"My father's estate is on the border, and he has spoken with you on occasion. He allowed me to sit and listen at those times so that I could learn the ways of leadership."

Woldemar questioned the boy and, after Willian had given his answers regarding the soldiers and the reasons for Arenia's march south, he said, "I thought my father had taught me all the uniforms of all the Kingdoms, but I do not recognize these soldiers."

"Do not think you have failed at your lessons," said Woldemar. "You learn more than my own sons and I am sure none of us know their uniform either. I wonder where they come from."

#

Light rain covered the camp on the following morning. All of the equipment and tents were heavy with moisture, as heavy as the army's spirits as they tried to pack and prepare for the march back north. King Leopold was keen to get back to Whitebridge and reclaim his city. Woldemar had been very understanding when finally believed that Arenia had no intentions of invading Greche and, because Woldemar had reported no casualties among the Grechan troops, he had agreed to walk away, with only monetary compensation to be paid after Leopold took back Arenia. The King looked down the valley to where the line of Grechan lancers sat their horses, obscured by the haze of moisture. Leopold encouraged his men to hurry and cursed the rain that seeped through his clothes to his undergarments and marked the polish of his boots. By noon they were ready, and he gave the order to mount and move out. As his army filed past Lachlan began to worry that half his force had been lost and yet he was going to attempt retaking the most heavily fortified city in all the kingdoms. He did not even have the long range ability of the archers. If an army could be said to have moods, then the mood of this one had changed. Coming south it had been a mixture of excitement and confidence but now the excitement had turned to despair. Even though Leopold had not told the men of the loss of Whitebridge, news like that was secret no more. The thought of laying siege to their own city further dampened the spirits of his men. The rain only lasted one day but the mood stayed with them as they re-crossed the plains and joined the King's Road.

CHAPTER 33

Excitement flowed through Camille's body like fire jumping along the ground when the grass burned. Finally, someone was going to help her in learning her abilities. She had woken before the sun and found her way back to the beach in time to see the first colors of pink and apricot light the eastern sky. The waves were a little larger than yesterday, but their muffled roar crashed unheard on her ears. Other than the waves, nothing moved. No birds drifted on the cool air, no fish broke the smooth surface of the water, no one walked on the road or the beach. The world was hers to enjoy. She sat under the tree, taking advantage of her time alone. When Mizq arrived, Camille thanked her for agreeing to share her knowledge.

"No thank me. It the will of Holdbori, only do as he ask. You ready begin training?"

Camille assured her that she was.

"Then we start. For first lesson, you sit here, listen. When I return, report all you hear." Without any further word Mizq disappeared back into the city.

Not understanding what she was listening for, she closed her eyes and concentrated. She was surprised when what had been so silent only moments before, now carried the sounds of the world. Besides the waves came the rumble of the waking city, people moving in their homes as they prepared for the day, and the occasional thud of feet as they moved along the roads. The distant squawk as a bird soared over the sea blended with the rustle of small animals as they scurried from shelter to shelter. The morning passed as she tried to identify all that she heard. Time rushed by as she relaxed in the cool air under the tree. Camille began to wonder how long she would be left to sit here. She was determined not to leave until she was released from her task. When the sun kissed the western horizon Mizq and Zazuk appeared beside her.

"What you hear?" Mizq asked simply and remained silent as Camille ran through her catalogue of sounds, fish jumping, birds feeding, a crab scuttling along the beach. When she was finished, confident that she had missed nothing, she fell silent and waited for her mentor's appreciation of her effort.

"You listen with ears," Mizq said. "Must listen with mind or you hear nothing. Listen not to sounds world makes but to what world tell you."

Confusion must have shown on Camille's face because Zazuk tried to explain. "It like listen to man. Words have no meaning because they full of noise. To listen to man, must listen to what he not say. Only then know what he think." Having no experience with men, or even boys, this didn't help.

"We try again tomorrow," said Mizq. "No keep me waiting."

Zazuk waited with Camille after Mizq left, so that she did not get lost finding her way home. When they were alone the old auch and the young girl strolled home through the streets of Ptoraki.

"I don't think Mizq likes me. The thought of having to talk to me is an effort and now the spirits tell her to teach me and she does not like it," Camille said.

"Even though she no see Bhata for years it pain her that she dead. But she loyal to spirits. If Holdbori want her train you she do it."

"Aiyu is afraid of her. He believes she hates him for taking her daughter away to die. He doesn't understand that the hate he feels comes from within and he cannot forgive himself."

"You have much wisdom for one so young. You right. Must learn he no blame. Men strange creatures. Think they understand all things. If that true why spirits choose speak only with women?"

"You seem to have great insight into men."

Zazuk creased her old face into a smile.

"Make it life work study them," she said.

The next day Mizq set Camille to listening again but by the end of the day she could offer no better answers to the question of what she heard. That night she sat and spoke with Zazuk about her failure. The old woman was unsympathetic.

"No complain what you no able do when you tell us otherwise. Spirits speak to us through plants and animals all time. All people hear voices, few know how listen. You one of few but your training should begin years ago. Now, go think of times when you truly listen. Tomorrow go show Mizq she no waste time." Camille had not expected Zazuk's chastisement but that only made her more determined.

#

The third day was yet to dawn when Camille sat on the beach waiting for Mizq to arrive. She leaned back and felt the gnarled trunk bite into her flesh. The previous two days had been tiring, and it felt good to simply relax and allow her mind to float.

"Wake up." Mizq stood over her with hands on hips and the sun lighting her stern expression.

Camille jumped to her feet, startled by the sound. "I am ready to learn," she said. "I wasn't asleep. There is a lizard in the grass beside the road and he has been afraid to come out for the last two days because I was here. I was telling him that there was no danger, and I would not harm him." As if in response to her words a horned lizard crept from the grass to lie in the sun, though it stayed close to the protection of the grass.

"So can listen," said Mizq.

"I didn't hear it. I let my mind search and felt he was there."

"You listen without ears. Now we begin. Show me again what you do." Camille let her mind search again for the lizard to give a message of peace and safety. This time, however, she felt a presence beside her, following her as she searched. When she drew back into her own body again, Mizq spoke. "You much potential but what you do clumsy. If you continue same way you never grow because you tire quick. First lesson, throw away all you achieve alone, learn conserve strength. This what happen when training ignored." Camille was not sure if the last was criticism of her, her abilities or lowlanders. "You find lizard again, listen what it say. Not tell him he safe, not tell him you not harm him, not tell him anything. Find him, listen what he tell you."

Camille cast her mind once more toward the lizard and the presence of Mizq followed. By the time the sun had reached its peak Camille lay on the grass recovering her strength. She had worked hard throughout the morning, hoping to impress her mentor, but the effort had been too much. Mizq waited for when she was able to stand without the dizziness threatening to tip her over. The older woman told her she had done enough and they would try again tomorrow but for the rest of the day she was to think on why she tired easily. Camille sat looking out to sea, allowing the calm beat of the waves to relax her before attempting to walk back to Zazuk's home. That night she sat talking with the old woman about her day.

"You no understand," said Zazuk. "All powers different, require different women use them. Why you think woman only have one man, most have only one ability? For a woman use more than one, must have skills adapt to each, same change for different man."

"What do you mean?"

"You train be spirit talker but use skills of elemental. All elemental abilities require women with strong will, be spirit talker, woman be passive and accepting. Must listen."

Camille was surprised. This was more than anyone had ever told her of her powers and she asked for more. "Elementals be strong of will. Even among these are differences. Some women quick to anger, dangerous be near at times. Find volatility and danger of fire suit them. Some have strength and patience, be prepared wait achieve their goals, like river take time to eat mountain, learn talk to water. Others strength in compassion, wish best for themselves, those around them. Ability lie in air that give life to all."

"If what you say is correct, how can any woman be skilled in more than just one ability? How can one person be both quick-tempered and patient? How can she be both strong-willed and accepting?"

"To live with man a woman not only learn all skills but also when each needed. Does not mother teach daughter this in lowlands?"

"I don't know about other mothers, but my mother never spoke as you have. Maybe she thought there was no need because no boy ever showed any interest in me. You have given me much to think about," said Camille. She thought of another question.

"Why is it only women who have these abilities?"

"Men only interested in food, prove how strong they are. Men no listen anyone, no even self. So how man listen to spirits? They no use minds so no can understand true abilities. Men like wind. Sometimes weak, sometimes strong, but rarely leave impression on world."

"But men can learn, can't they? There is Pouliquen the wizard."

"Any man learn not stand under tree if enough apples hit him on head," Zazuk said in a manner that appeared to leave a bitter taste in her mouth. The old woman obviously thought that matters of ability should be left to women. As the two talked late into the evening Camille knew that a strong friendship was developing between them, no matter how unlikely. She was a young human with little experience in people of any age, let alone boys, and here was an old auch woman who had devoted her life to understanding men.

The following morning Camille rose late and was forced to rush to the beach without taking time for food, arriving only moments before Mizq. She had lain in her bed thinking about Zazuk's words and was hoping to try something different before her mentor arrived, but now she would have to prove her idea while under scrutiny. Mizq sat on the grass beside her and looked out at the sea and waves. Camille followed her gaze. A low swell covered the water as if some being had pushed on the edge of the world and creased the previously smooth blue fabric. On the shore the swells pressed taller and fell upon themselves like a poorly hemmed seam coming apart.

"Storm come," Mizq said. Camille noticed that the normally smooth line where the sky met the sea had become blurred in grey while an occasional flash of lightning ripped at the seam. The elements of air, fire and water fought for supremacy and as the battle continued the thin line of dark cloud grew. But the voice of Mizq told her it was time to begin. The time had arrived to see if she understood what Zazuk had told her. Her mind drifted free as it had done on previous occasions and immediately the presence of her mentor was at her side. Previously she had pushed out, searching for others. She had used her will to drive her mind further and, if she understood Zazuk, this is where she went wrong. Today she didn't push. She allowed her mind to accept the images that came to her, listening for others to find her. Even the smile of her mentor did not distract her as she listened to the world. The lizard was the first to find her. She listened as he told her of the feeling of change in the air. Others joined in with their news. The world appeared to her as she had not seen it before. Her greatest feeling was soaring with the birds, carried by them rather than driving with them.

"Time return," Mizq called to her, still riding by her side even though she had forgotten she was there. Reluctantly she left the skies and opened her eyes. The sun was close to setting and the storm was almost upon them.

"What happened?"

"Easy lose yourself when speaking to spirits. You do well. In time you learn watch for signs of passing time."

"But I'm not even tired."

"Because you not push yourself on world. Much easier listen to others than force them listen you.".

CHAPTER 34

Fifty men crept along the bank of the silent river. It was hours before the sun would cast its light on the city ahead, but they moved carefully and kept clear of windows and doors. All was quiet on the docks. Two ships creaked as they moved against the wooden piers waiting for tomorrow's loading. On Captain Lachlan's signal, two teams broke away from the group, one heading towards each ship while the rest of the men followed Lachlan into the maze of buildings that lined the river's edge. They moved quietly but quickly from warehouse to office, from counting house to sleeping quarters, taking captive everyone they came across. Taking prisoners was easier than expected as Lachlan learned that not all the citizens of Whitebridge supported the new king and that those still loyal to Leopold were quick to point out those who followed Arwen. On board the ships the invaders moved to the stern to capture the two captains before any alarm could be raised. When the situation was explained to them with the tip of a sword at their throats, they were happy to offer their assistance.

The capture of the ships and docks had gone without incident and, as importantly, speedily. Lachlan moved back to the southern end of the buildings to wave the lantern he carried above his head. In the darkness he imagined the army riding over the low hill and spreading out to cover the western and northern walls of the city. Seventy-five heavily armed foot soldiers who had been waiting nearby jogged towards him under the weight of chainmail, swords and maces, along with four of the remaining archers, survivors of the battle with Greche. Lachlan directed them to the first ship where sailors roused from their bunks were preparing sails and releasing the ropes that bound them to the shore. While this was happening the captives were put to work loading the second ship with timbers, tables, boxes and anything else that could be found. By the time the first rays of daylight gently touched the walls of Whitebridge, the city was surrounded. Lancers and soldiers ringed the walls west of the Anura River while to the east the King's Road and the land on either side were blocked by the beginnings of an effective barricade. Any rider attempting to leave the city over the huge stone bridge would need to pass through the wall of refuse where they would be vulnerable to the few soldiers and archers that defended it. The siege of Whitebridge had begun.

Lachlan rode again beside his king as they moved among the men offering encouragement. Every man knew that Whitebridge had never fallen to a siege. King Leopold's great-grandfather had famously resisted the forces of Greche for three years and, although he had tried to learn the secret, Leopold had never discovered how his ancestor had kept his people fed and outfitted for such a long time. Some even said that his great-grandfather did not know how the supplies came into the city, only that when he required them the storehouses had sufficient for his needs.

Guards stood at their stations on the walls, but no one seemed to be concerned by the presence of his army waiting outside. They simply stood their watch and changed at regular intervals as if they could not see that they were being attacked. More likely, thought Lachlan, they have news of our failure and know that we can do nothing without siege engines or archers. Meanwhile the ships continued to move back and forth across the river and with each trip the barricade in the east grew. He only had a small number of men there, but they were well hidden and could hold off most attacks should the enemy break from the east gate. The river prevented his men being flanked just as effectively as it protected the city but the options open to him were limited. He could not break down the walls so he would need to draw his enemy out to where he could attack. The only sure way to achieve this was to cut off their supplies until he starved them out, which would take months or years, or to annoy them until frustration overcame sense. The second option was his only real choice.

That night, under the cover of darkness, his remaining archers moved forward to take up positions hidden in the maze of broken buildings that had once been the extended city. With the first light Lachlan ordered a drum to be sounded. At the signal the archers rose to their feet and fired at the guards on the wall. Lachlan saw one man fall with an arrow protruding from his neck before a line of bowmen appeared and returned fire. He watched as soldiers rose to cast burning torches down into the tightly packed rubble. The flames quickly took hold and began to engulf building after building as the sea of flames flooded the area. His archers hastily retreated while the hail of arrows fell from above. He had fallen into another trap, he realized, and he was lucky the men on the wall stopped firing or his remaining archers would have been destroyed. He watched helplessly as the extended community of Whitebridge burned to the ground.

King Leopold echoed his own thoughts. "We stand no chance without more archers. Gather a hundred soldiers who can learn and give them bows. Have the archers take them behind the lines and teach them to shoot without hitting our own men. We will likely be here for a while so they will have the time to learn. We may not have archers, but I will have soldiers who can use a bow."

CHAPTER 35

After three weeks the soldiers of both armies had settled into a routine. Those with King Leopold walked about casually, taking the time to chat with friends while staying just out of range of the bowmen on the walls, while those inside went about their daily duties and ignored the presence of those outside. The guards who walked the walls cast occasional glances towards the men surrounding the city but otherwise paid them little attention as long as they stayed their distance.

King Arwen sat on the throne and waited for the council members to arrive. He wore the new royal clothes he had ordered, made in purple with gold accents and trimmed with fur. He would have to retrieve the crown from Leopold, he thought, either that or have a new one made. A person could not be king without a crown. He was growing impatient with waiting. Too much time had passed since Leopold had surrounded the city and his soldiers had done nothing. Too much time had passed since he called for the Council to attend, and still he waited. The time was fast approaching when he would need to show them what it meant to serve their king. He fidgeted with the clasp of his cape and was about to order a guard to search for them when the door opened, and the members of the Council entered.

"I hope you haven't been waiting long," said Beth, sarcasm clear in a voice. "We were busy." She looked about the room. "You need some chairs in here. Where are we going to sit?"

Her manner was beyond disrespect. Arwen glared at the four people before him. They did not bow or kneel. They spoke before he gave them leave to speak and they showed no sign of respect for his title. "I am the king," he roared. "You will treat me as such."

"You are the king because we said you could be king," replied Grarm casually while checking his fingernails. Arwen spluttered in disbelief. "Don't allow it to go to your head. In public we will hail you as a King and give you the ceremony you desire but in private, we are equal. We are all Councilors of The Society and that supersedes any political position you may hold within Arenia." For a brief moment Arwen considered calling the guards and having them all thrown into the dungeons, but he quickly realized that Beth's connections would probably have her out in minutes. It would likely be the last order he ever gave. He needed to establish his position more before he could hope to do anything like that. In the meantime, he could only make the best of the situation.

"I understand my position only too well," he replied, supposedly defeated and pleading. "Within the council room or my apartments, I agree with you completely. But here, in this room, I feel that we are bound to respect the throne of Arenia. We do not know when someone may be watching and if we want the people to follow their king, we must be seen to respect the throne. And another thing, in this room there should be no mention of The Society."

The Councilors exchanged glances. "Agreed," said Grarm. "What you say is valid but don't allow these politics to come between you and the cause. Ours is the work of generations upon generations and has seen many leaders come and go. Even Tam's long reign was only a moment in our history."

The brief silence that followed screamed with veiled threats. Arwen knew at that moment that the only way he would really be king was for these people to die but Xavier controlled the army, and Beth had her own people. Xavier was new to the Council, so Arwen wondered if he could be encouraged to give his support against the others, but he rejected the idea immediately. He could see the hold Beth had on him. There was nothing he could do but secure his position and wait.

Bringing the conversation back to matters at hand, he asked, "What are we going to do about Leopold? We can't leave him sitting outside the city forever. The people may decide they want him back."

"You are right. This is not the place to discuss matters concerning your throne and our part in holding it for you. Would you recommend we move to the council room or your chambers?" said Xavier.

Arwen enjoyed his little victory, letting the Council see he gave them his full support. "This discussion should be taken to the council room." Arwen rose quickly and led the way to the door to ensure none of them had the audacity to lead their King.

In the privacy of the council room Arwen offered his opinions on ending the siege "Should we send Harold's men out through the tunnels to harass them from behind or send them out through the east gate to clear the King's Road? There is only a small force in the east and we have enough men to defeat them easily. Our only other choice is to sit here and that would be accepting defeat. None of us wish to see The Society defeated."

"The east road is controlled by Leopold. While it is only a small force, it is well hidden in that barricade. If we attack on horseback our men will be left stranded in front of the wall and if we attack on foot, we will need to cross too much open ground. In either case our soldiers will be cut down by the archers I have seen there. We could not win," said Xavier.

"Then we must move out through the tunnels and attack them from behind."

"Even if we were successful in our first attack, Leopold has more soldiers than we can put in the field and would easily win in the long term, weakened though he is. Here we are protected by the walls but out there we would be cut to pieces by his troops, and we cannot send the men out and leave the city unguarded. Your reign would finish abruptly if we did that."

"Then what do you suggest?" he asked, his voice heavy with challenge.

"We wait."

"We wait? We wait for what? Do you think if we sit here long enough, Leopold will walk away? Is he going to bore himself to death?"

"We wait for the Fist."

Arwen was confused. "But the Fist is in the north fighting the auchs. That is our prime objective, that is what I ordered. Why would they be coming here?"

"Because that is what I told them to do," explained Xavier. "You were wrong in your order and so I gave my own. One finger has gone north to draw out the auchs and then report back to me with details of their numbers and abilities. The prime objective is to destroy the auchs, but we cannot do that if Leopold wins back Arenia and we are all dead. We must secure the throne for The Society, or the work of generations will be for nothing."

Arwen was outraged. "But I ordered it."

"I was put on this council for my tactical ability and my duty is to the cause. This is the way it must be. Soon the Fist will arrive and Leopold will be forced to concede. Only then will The Society rule Arenia."

CHAPTER 36

Leopold's archers-in-training finished their breakfast and began making their way to the nearby field, hidden in a shallow gulley. The place was out of sight of the city to keep their training secret. Two instructors stood impatiently beside the newly-made racks of bows and cartloads of arrows. The men were in no hurry to start training. Most were resentful at being made to work while their companions sat around the campfires waiting in comfort. The instructors roared at them to hurry and fall in. They continued to bellow as the soldiers slowly dragged themselves into something that vaguely resembled lines. One instructor called for the first row to collect their weapons, only to be greeted with a suggestion as to where he could put his bow. The resulting wave of laughter was quickly cut short.

Fletchings appeared to grow out of the trainers' chests as a line of black-clad men rose from the grasses that covered the field. The men were given no time to react before the first volley of arrows ripped through their ranks. Those who survived the devastation of that first attack broke, with most running to collect weapons. A few less brave men ran for the safety of the army, but a second flight of well-timed arrows finished the job of the first. Very few of Leopold's new archers remained alive. These were captured; the wounded carried by their colleagues as they were marched off under guard around the hill to the hidden forces of the Fist.

#

King Leopold rode up to the small knot of soldiers sitting around the remains of the cooking fire. The men jumped to their feet, but he ordered them to relax while he asked them how things were going in the south. As with the men everywhere along the lines, the soldiers were becoming bored. "Where are my bowmen?" he asked.

"They are out in the field, learning not to hit each other when they fire."

"I suppose we wouldn't want the enemy to fall off the walls laughing," joked the King. His soldiers laughed dutifully at his humor. "But don't give them too much grief. There may come a time when their arrows may be needed to save your hairy hides."

Leopold rode on but after only a few steps he pulled his horse to a stop. A feeling emerged from deep within his being. Turning to one of the guards he said, "Ride out to the rise and check on the archers."

"Is anything wrong?" asked Lachlan, looking quickly around.

"Nothing that I can see or hear, but I feel something is not right."

They waited while the soldier rode towards the training ground, crested the rise and began down the other side. Leopold felt some of his tension leave as the man gave no sign of alarm. He was about to turn away when the soldier wheeled his horse and kicked it into a gallop. His body arched and slumped forward over the horse's neck before rolling to the side and falling to the ground. The King saw a figure dressed in black rise to stand on the hill and wave his arms above his head. Lachlan began shouting orders. Around him the camp had become chaos. Men ran to collect weapons that had long sat idle while lancers raced to have their horses readied, calling for armor as they ran.

The line of light cavalry rounded the hill, continuing to walk towards Leopold's army. Alarms rang out as Lachlan tried to pass the warning along their lines. Out in the fields the black-clad cavalry kicked their horses into a canter. There was no time for the defending lancers to dress in protective clothing. They called for horses and lances. All eyes were now on the approaching cavalry as they continued to close. King Leopold was not concerned by the small force approaching - he knew his forces could handle the attack - but he was intrigued by the black uniforms that he had heard about. "They must have slipped out of the city during the night," he said to his captain, but Lachlan was still yelling instructions. Foot soldiers began to form a protective circle around the king while he maneuvered his horse between Leopold and the approaching line.

About twenty lancers raced out of the camp, leaving the others to follow when they could. They rode to intercept the attack as Leopold watched the line of riders coming straight towards him. He drew his sword in readiness. The black army was only a hundred yards from Leopold, but it looked as if the lancers would be in time to break the charge as they rode to intercept from the king's right. But the line of riders surprised everyone. They wheeled to face the lancers without breaking stride or losing their formation, reining the horses and, as one, threw their spears. The lancers fell like dishes from an upset table.

The black-clad riders drew their swords and turned back to face the knot of men around Leopold. The deaths of the lancers had bought enough time. A second wave of lancers rode to meet the threat. This time, without spears and facing superior numbers, the black riders turned and fled back the way they had come, all semblance of order gone. The lancers didn't hesitate. They kicked their horses, charging across the open ground. The enemy's horses were built for speed, maintaining their lead over Leopold's lancers as they raced across the fields towards the hill. The lancers continued the pursuit until the riders ahead of them turned, suddenly armed again with spears and a wall of pikemen moved to close the gap where their quarry had passed only moments earlier. Behind the lancers more soldiers rushed to cut off any attempt at retreat while bowmen rose from the cover of the grasses with arrows trained on the trapped men. The king's soldiers could see the futility of fighting against the odds they now faced. With no officers willing or daring enough to order them to die for their king, the men laid their arms aside and surrendered. The black-clad soldiers moved in and took their prisoners away.

Leopold watched on, helpless and devastated. His army had fallen into a trap at the Grechan border where he had lost most of his archers and many of his lancers. Today he had lost his new archers. He was certain they were dead or captured, and he had just seen more of his lancers taken.

Lachlan didn't have time for regrets. He organized the remaining forces to protect the King. "Pikemen to the front, swords behind, prepare for battle. The king must be protected," he yelled. As the foot soldiers jockeyed into position, a call rang out, "For the king!"

Leopold and Lachlan waited in the middle of the clutch of foot soldiers for the black soldiers to make their next move.

In the city word had quickly spread of the battle taking place outside. The walls of Whitebridge were lined with soldiers and citizens, all keen to see firsthand how this day would end and they were not left to wait long. Everyone watched open-mouthed as an army dressed in black came into view and moved into position. Their numbers continued to grow and for the first time the king and his captain came to realize what they were up against. "Where did an army of this size come from?" Lachlan wondered aloud but the King had no answer. The black line of mounted soldiers spread across the land. As one, they kicked their horses into a walk.

As the enemy bore down on him Leopold could not help but admire the precision of their approach. They maintained their line regardless of grass or bush or stone. Like a black wave on a green sea, they approached with a single purpose. Lachlan yelled at Leopold to flee while they tried to hold off the attack, but he refused.

"No, we are at the moment when this war is won or lost. If we are to be victorious, I will stand with you. If we fail, I will not see nightfall. But I will have your promise that if I fall and all is lost, you will not throw your life away and that you will get Willian to safety. He holds the wisdom of a leader in his heart and he is loyal to Arenia. The two of you are the nearest thing I have to family."

The King insisted on his demands until his Captain grudgingly agreed. The remains of Arenia's army gathered closer around its king and prepared to fight as the black line came towards them. A call came. A second line of soldiers were approaching from the city. Lachlan urgently called for men to turn and protect the King from this new assault. He watched in frustration as the adjustments slowly took shape. It would be impossible to flee now, even if Leopold wanted to. He turned back to face the original attack and had to trust that his men would be ready in time to protect their rear. With less than fifty paces separating the combatant forces Lachlan was impressed by the precision of this attack, wondering again where they had come from. They rode with purpose. Just as he expected to see them drop their spears and charge they stopped. The second line of riders came between the men of the front line before they too halted. With a precision that matched their riding skills the bowmen drew and notched their arrows before firing on command. A second volley was notched and fired while the first was still in the air and as the initial volley bit into the soldiers around the king a third was leaving the bows of the enemy. With the third volley in the air the bowmen moved aside to allow the cavalry to move through and lower their spears to charge, still holding their formation while a further wave arrived and dismounted, preparing to eliminate any remaining pockets of resistance.

Lachlan glanced over his shoulder to see the second force still approaching, then back as the first flight of arrows cut into the soldiers around him, bringing down fully a third of their numbers. As the second flight hit, Leopold saw the arrow rip through Lachlan's flesh, stopped only by the bone of his shoulder. The impact threw him from his horse. He hit the ground, crying out in pain before losing consciousness. The arrows having done their deadly work, the spearmen were preparing to charge. Leopold yelled at some soldiers to get Lachlan to safety and two men sheathed their swords, lifted the unconscious captain and ran with the strength of fear and panic, hardly noticing the weight of Lachlan hanging between them.

The cavalry charged past and wheeled away. Leopold stood with his remaining forces and encouraged them to rally. His horse lay on the ground, kicking the last of its life away, a spear protruding from its panting chest. Leopold raised his sword and called, "Stand for Arenia". But only eighteen soldiers remained to hear his call. They ringed the king, ready to stand against the approaching might of the black army, knowing they were going to die without learning who they faced. Leopold stood swinging his sword as his men fell around him. A pike took him in the side, a sword entered his chest and he fell to his knees. Another sword swung to remove his head, but Leopold felt nothing. He was dead before the blow struck

CHAPTER 37

Inside the city, Xavier and Beth stood together and watched the battle unfold. Arwen came hurrying from his chambers to stand on the wall further down. Seeing the events taking place outside the city, the new King's elation was obvious, and Xavier smiled. The walls were already crowded but Arwen's guards soon made room for him.

When Xavier first received word of the arrival of the Fist, he had made some preparations of his own. He sent orders to the army before he called Harold and gave him his instructions, with a warning that no one else was to know what was to happen. He could take no chances. Although he couldn't see the training grounds of Leopold's archers, Beth's people had kept him well informed of their routine and progress. As the lone rider fell, he knew the attack had begun.

When the feint and subsequent capture of Leopold's lancers went exactly to plan, Xavier began to relax. He could see the end of Leopold and the capture of Arenia was assured. He hoped to achieve this with the loss of as few men as possible. He looked down inside the city to see Harold's men, mounted and armed, had appeared as if from nowhere.

From the top of the wall, he gave the order and the south gate swung open. All eyes were on the approaching army and Harold's men rode out and formed up without notice. Only when they rode to charge Leopold's lines were they seen, but as far as he could tell Leopold's army was not prepared for them.

With the death of Leopold, the excitement of the Fist flowed over the walls of the city. Xavier trusted the field captains would be able to control their men and remind them of the remaining soldiers still waiting around the city. "The time will come for celebrations," he thought aloud, "but not yet." The Fist retreated and regathered near the hill. One man rode back down to the field where the battle had begun. There he set a pike into the ground and placed the head of King Leopold on top for all to see, before riding casually back.

#

King Arwen was almost dancing with jubilation. Xavier despised the man for not seeing that the war was not over, that there were still many soldiers around the city whose loyalty to Leopold was uncertain. Arwen headed back towards the palace. Xavier needed to keep Arwen from ruining all he had achieved today with his enthusiasm. He took Beth by the arm and led her away from the crowds. As he approached the palace gate he saw Arwen ahead. The King was clearly looking to celebrate and called to them as they approached.

"A great day," he said as they reached him. His face glowed and his voice trembled with enthusiasm. "The Society can now show the world that we are truly the voice of mankind."

Xavier smiled. "Yes. The world has changed today."

"Join me," suggested Arwen in a moment of goodwill. "This day must be celebrated."

In his rooms Arwen fussed about. He was laughing as he poured the wine and almost skipped his way across the room as he brought the goblets to his guests. "Wasn't my army magnificent?" he gushed. "Did you see the way they separated Leopold's forces and isolated him. The attack on the King was perfect."

Xavier smiled again. It had been a very well executed operation, but it was not perfect. He had seen at least three men fail to hold a straight line on their approach and eagerness had caused the volleys of arrows to be mistimed as some of the men released early. "Now I am king," laughed Arwen. "You said so yourself. You said that I would only be king when Leopold was defeated. Well, he is gone, and his head stands outside the city for all to see. So, I am now the true King of Arenia."

Xavier raised his goblet. "Let us toast The Society, the guardians of mankind. May the years ahead be glorious for all. Also, Arenia, who now has a new king to lead her through these years."

Arwen laughed as all three raised their goblets and drank to the future.

"What will our new king do first?"

Arwen asked what he meant, and Xavier reminded him that the city was still besieged by the forces loyal to Leopold. While the numbers had improved, their army was still smaller and had now lost the element of surprise. He presented the possible negative outcomes of the day's actions and the possible consequences of Leopold's death on the soldiers and citizens of the city. Arwen's excitement became tempered with concern.

"What would you suggest?" asked the king.

"I would send a man out under a flag of truce to find who leads their forces now. I would give these men an offer to accept their men in the new army of Arenia. Their numbers would increase our strength. I see no reason for more men to die when we will need them to fight the auchs. As a gesture of your goodwill, I would allow the officers and anyone who wishes to remain loyal to Leopold to live on condition that they do so in exile and vow to never return."

"I don't know if it would be wise to allow them to live. They may rally the country against me."

"If they know they can live in exile they will be more accepting of a surrender of their troops, but if they are facing certain death, they will fight with all the force they can gather. In exile they will not be able to raise an army without you or I or Beth's spies hearing of it. It will show the world that you are a compassionate king as well as a great military leader who has won Arenia where all others have failed."

Arwen paced back and forth. He turned to Xavier. "Do you really think that I should allow them to live?"

Xavier looked Arwen in the eye. "It is wise."

The King still looked doubtful when the pain ripped through his chest. He looked down to see blood staining his shirt and Beth's hand still holding the hilt of the dagger against his body. The thin blade had bitten deep. When he tried to call for his guards only the sound of air gurgling through the blood in his lungs escaped his lips.

"I am sorry, my friend," she whispered. "You would have been a good king for Arenia, but The Society needs more. We need Arenia to have a great king. We must have a king who can think and guide both the army and the people. We need a man who is able to show the world his strength through words. You are not that man."

Arwen slumped to the floor as his last breath rattled in his throat.

#

Xavier stood on the palace balcony where he had introduced King Arwen to the people only weeks before. The courtyard was packed and more people stood outside the palace gates. Raising his arms he brought a hush over the crowd.

"People of Whitebridge," he began. "Some of you today witnessed the breaking of the siege that held our fine city in its grip. Our army won victory and the capital of Arenia continues its glorious history. We have never fallen to a siege and we never will." He paused for the cheers that rose from the courtyard. "I ask you all to remember this city for its glory. Arenia is strong and we will show the world that we are a proud people. All mankind will know that we do not surrender to adversity. We will not give in to our enemies and we will endure against all who wish to see us defeated." He waited again for the noise of the crowd to die down.

"But all victories come at a price," he told them, "and the cost to Arenia for this day is great. My good friend King Arwen joined his people on the wall to enjoy this wonderful victory. He was as excited as you were to see our army demonstrate its strength and skill. Tragically, a stray arrow came over the wall and took our king in the chest. We carried him back to his rooms to seek aid but his wound was serious and the king died today of his injuries. He was a good man and would have been a great king. I feel his loss with all my heart." Everyone was stunned by the news.

"Tomorrow will be a day to grieve the loss of our king. We will give thanks to King Arwen for his skill in ending the siege. We will drink to his memory and to all he may have done for Arenia if not for this terrible accident. With his dying breath he ordered me to make peace with the army outside the walls and offer them a place in our community. He did this because he was a compassionate man. I will see that his wishes are carried out."

Beth stepped forward and addressed the people. "I also counted King Arwen as a friend and his death cuts me deeply. The people of Arenia were robbed today of the chance to come to know him as I did. But, as Xavier has said, we are a strong people, and we will overcome even this great loss with time. But an army still stands at our gates, and we do not have the time to feel sorry for ourselves. Arenia must be strong today. To do this, she must have a new king. I was one of King Arwen's four close friends and guides. Xavier was another of those. It is he who leads our army, and it is he who advised the king on how to win this battle. Arenia needs a man who is fair and just, but she also needs a man with the skill to organize people. We need a man with the vision to see the future of Arenia and all the kingdoms of man. Xavier is such a man. As King of Arenia he would lead us into a life of peace and prosperity. I ask him to accept the throne and do his duty for his people."

Cheers of applause rose dutifully from the mass of people below. Beth stepped back and Xavier raised his hands for quiet. "Arwen was my friend and a good man," he told the crowd. "My respect for the king was great and it would be a challenge to follow him. To be a great king, a man must have the trust of his people. I do not make the assumption that I have your trust at this time. I cannot accept the throne without your support."

Beth stepped forward again. "It is this man's ability that gave King Arwen his victory today. Without Xavier's daring, this siege may have lasted for years. Although he was my friend, King Arwen did not understand military matters. Even great men have their limits. But Xavier saw the opportunity and took it, and you saw his victory. I know him well. This man is much more than a military man, he is a leader. He is the man Arenia needs to lead them in the coming years. He says he will not take the throne if he does not have your support. Does he have your support?"

Cheers erupted around the courtyard and beyond.

Xavier called for silence. "I do not wish to rule you, but I will lead you if that is your choice." The cheers that followed shook the ground. When the sound died down, he went on, "If that is your wish, I will accept the throne of Arenia. I hope to serve you well." Thunderous acclaim again echoed around them as Xavier stood to attention, held his arm straight with fist clenched, then snapped it back to his shoulder in salute. The soldiers and Society members in the crowd returned the gesture and many others copied them. A few of Beth's people placed in the crowd began to chant and the crowd happily joined in. "Arenia and Xavier. Arenia and Xavier."

Xavier felt the pride swell inside him as he stood on the balcony accepting the accolades of his adoring people.

ABOUT THE AUTHOR

Steve lives on the beautiful Central Coast of NSW, Australia, where the ocean and natural surroundings have always been a source of relaxation and inspiration. A former competition fisherman, Steve still enjoys casting a line whenever possible, finding peace in the rhythm of the tides.

Beyond fishing, a love for gardening keeps Steve connected to nature, while a passion for sport remains strong, even if he no longer plays.

Reading and writing fantasy are his favourite pastimes, with a particular focus on crafting rich, character-driven stories that bring unique worlds to life. Whether exploring new ideas or revisiting old ones, storytelling remains a cherished creative outlet.

www.ingramcontent.com/pod-product-compliance
Lightning Source LLC
Chambersburg PA
CBHW070925260626
47162CB00007B/2783